What people are saying about …

Scared

"Tom Davis weaves his heart for orphans onto every page. The journey of *Scared* might lead you on a journey of your own—helping the orphans among us."

Karen Kingsbury, New York Times best-selling author of *Every Now and Then* and *Take One*

"With unflinching detail, Tom Davis uncovers the atrocity of the African AIDS epidemic and God's impossible triumph in its midst. Both sweeping in scope and intimate in expression, *Scared* leaves the reader with one burning question: How can I help?"

Matt Bronleewe, author of *Illuminated* and *House of Wolves*

"Tom Davis's first novel, *Scared*, is a startling beauty-for-ashes tale that takes readers on a journey to Swaziland and introduces them to the least of these Jesus speaks about in Matthew 25. You can't help but be changed by this heartbreaking, hope-fueling, oh-so-real story."

Claudia Mair Burney, author of *Zora and Nicky: A Novel in Black and White*

"Evocative and intense, *Scared* cuts deep into your heart as you read along. Healing fills the pages, yet there are no easy answers given, and it shows how each day is a struggle for the people of Swaziland to even survive. That's why the orphans and the widows need people who care. I loved how *Scared* showed that many of the sick and dying were truly victims of AIDS through no wrongdoing of their own. I've rarely experienced this level of realism in a novel, especially in the CBA. It's so realistic, it's downright edgy. Like the Holocaust, there are some awful things that happen in this book. Unspeakable things. But it also shows how God holds those who suffer close to His heart. You see that in this book in a way that is rarely portrayed in Christian fiction. All of the ugly stuff is not smoothed over, nor is the God-given compassion. It's graphic and harsh in some places, but so worth reading. I highly recommend it."

Michelle Sutton, editor-in-chief of
Christian Fiction Online Magazine

Scared

Scared

A NOVEL ON THE EDGE OF THE WORLD

TOM DAVIS

David C Cook
transforming lives together

SCARED
Published by David C. Cook
4050 Lee Vance View
Colorado Springs, CO 80918 U.S.A.

David C. Cook Distribution Canada
55 Woodslee Avenue, Paris, Ontario, Canada N3L 3E5

David C. Cook U.K., Kingsway Communications
Eastbourne, East Sussex BN23 6NT, England

David C. Cook and the graphic circle C logo
are registered trademarks of Cook Communications Ministries.

This story is a work of fiction. All characters and events are the product of the author's
imagination. Any resemblance to any person, living or dead, is coincidental.

LCCN 2009902386
ISBN 978-1-58919-102-0
eISBN 978-1-4347-0033-9

© 2009 Tom Davis
Published in association with the literary agency of Alive Communications,
Inc., 7680 Goddard St., Suite 200, Colorado Springs, CO 80920

The Team: Andrea Christian, Steve Parolini, Amy Kiechlin,
Sarah Schultz, Jack Campbell, and Susan Vannaman
Cover Designer: Kirk DouPonce, DogEared Design
Cover Photos: iStockphoto (background; small photo);
Radu Sigheti/Reuters/Corbis (girl)

Printed in the United States of America
First Edition 2009

2 3 4 5 6 7 8 9 10

060409

A Note from the Publisher

Dear reader,

The story you are about to read is very much based upon real life. Some pages contain depictions of horror unimaginable to many of us but reality to some. It is a sad reminder that there is much darkness roaming the globe. First John 1:5 reminds us that God is light and there is no room in Him for darkness. In fact, one of the dear characters in *Scared*, Pastor Walter, will reference this verse when comforting a young Adanna who wonders if God is indeed present. Given the abuse, poverty, death, and destruction that afflict so many, one does wonder, "God, are You there?"

The answer to that question can be found in countless thousands of people who say in the affirmative, "Yes, He is here ... and He is light." Child advocate and speaker Tom Davis gives us a gripping portrayal of the hurt and pain that affects many in Africa. This story reminds us of our need to be engaged in being light in a very dark world.

Some scenes will grip and haunt you, some passages you will want to run away from—but this is real life. And real life requires true Christ followers to act justly and love mercy. May Adanna's story inspire and embolden you.

Thank you for reading,
Don Pape,
Publisher, David C. Cook

To Emily

My best friend these seventeen years

And to the Adannas of this world
who gave this book a voice

Prologue

The last thing I remember before going to sleep last night was the pain in my gut and the question of what I would wear to church this morning. These worries are for nothing, because I have no food and only rags to wear. Today is Easter Sunday. Pastor Walter calls it "Resurrection Sunday." A day of hope.

I think about what hope means for the people in my village. I try to imagine them rising up in glory, as Pastor says. But I only see twisted bodies, bones poking out of paper skin. They do not rise. They lie in mounds of yellow dirt. I think of my own body, wasting away because I haven't eaten for days.

Sometimes I wonder if the gods don't like me. Maybe it's because I am dirty and stained, like old rags. I've been told by Pastor and Momma, "Easter means new life." But our lives never change.

Stepping outside my home, a shimmering road unfolds in front of me. It is smooth, like a gift wrapped in gold.

Voices from ahead call out to me, and one foot hurries to catch the other. The sounds are beautiful, like a choir, their voices layered in perfect harmony.

I've never felt a road so smooth. It's like walking on cool water. The roads I know are brown and rocky.

A magical energy flows through every part of me from my feet to my head, refreshing my tired body. How can something so unfamiliar feel like home?

But this place is nothing like home. The horizon blazes beautiful, glowing colors—violet, blue, and amber dance like giddy fairies. The land is on fire with color.

I turn and see rows of trees taller than any I have ever seen. I could swing from their branches. I would write poems about their splendor. The leaves are leaping for joy. The apples hanging from the trees look like red balloons. One could feed me for a week.

Here, people do not pick up moon rocks and die.

My throat is parched, so I run to the banks of a river. The water is like crystal. It is so perfect I do not want to touch it, but I cannot help myself. I cup my hands and thrust them down to get a drink.

When I pull out my hands, they are no longer brittle and cracked. They appear soft, even glowing. My hands are new.

Thirst spreads from my mouth to every cell in my body.

I jump.

I glide through the water like the colorful fish around me, swimming free. Forgetting I am underwater, I suck in a breath. I expect to choke, but I do not. Taking another breath whisks me out of the water and onto the bank.

The jagged scar on my arm has disappeared. I feel new. Not hungry or sick. Even my scars on the inside seem to be gone.

In the distance a marvelous light pulsates, lustrous, pure, and white. What shines so warm and soft?

"Adanna."

The voice sounds like a thousand mighty rivers, a thundering boom. But I am not afraid.

"Who are you? And how do you know my name?"

"Adanna. Come closer."

I move toward an illuminated man. He is sitting in a golden chair. The music of many villages rises from where he sits. Love pours out, giving life to the grass, the trees, and I feel it growing roots in my heart.

"Are you the ruler of this world?"

"I am. This world and many others. I've waited a long time to be with you."

"I do not know who you are."

"I have known you, Adanna," he chuckles, "for a very long time. I have watched you grow. I have delighted in seeing you play, and I have rejoiced over how you have matured. My love has always surrounded you."

Maybe he is one of my ancestors.

"I'm not one on your ancestors, but you are one of mine."

How did he hear me?

"I do not think I have ever met you."

"Oh, but you have. Come closer, Adanna. I want to show you something."

Cautiously, I step forward. He is inviting me with his smile. He stretches out and opens his hand. On it there is writing.

"That is my name, but how did it get there?"

"I put it there."

"But why?"

"Because I have always loved you."

"But I am nothing special."

"Adanna, if you only knew the greatness inside you. You must trust me; I will draw out of you what the world needs to see. Here is your gift. Use it wisely. It will make the way clear for you, and it will save many of your people."

He extends a white scroll made of lamb's skin and hands it to me. I reach up and receive the scroll. "Thank you, sir. I am most grateful. May I ask who you are?"

"You will know, soon."

"Can I stay here?"

"Not now, but the time will come. Just remember this: No matter where you go, I will be there to help you."

"What is your name?"

"Whatever You Need. That is my name."

"I do not understand."

I take the parchment in my hands. I untie a silk ribbon and unroll it.

My eyes open, and the thatched roof of my hut shudders in the wind.

Chapter One

Democratic Republic of the Congo, Africa, 1998

Ten years ago I was a dead man.

It all began when Lou, my broker from Alpha Agency, said, "Stuart, how would you feel about heading to the Congo? *Time* is putting together a crew and needs a hot photographer."

He asked; I went. That's how I got paid then. It's how I get paid now.

My job was to cover a breaking story on a rebel uprising that would soon turn into genocide. Unfortunately, neither Lou nor any of us were privy to that valuable information at the time. We should have seen it coming. The frightening tribal patterns resembled the bloodbath between the Hutu and Tutsi in Rwanda in 1994. We knew what happened there had spilled over to the DRC—but we ignored it.

Our job was to focus on the story of the moment, whatever we might find. But this was more than a search for journalistic truth. It was an opportunity to win a round of a most dangerous game—the chase for a prizewinning picture.

The plane landed in the capital city of Kinshasa. A man in combat fatigues stood near a large black government car. Six armed guards toting fully automatic rifles flanked him.

"That must be the mayor and his six closest comrades," I said to our writer, Mike, as I swung my heavy neon orange bag over my shoulder. "Welcome to a world where you are not in control." This was Mike's first international assignment. I swear his knees buckled.

Our team consisted of me; Mike, shipped in from Holland (a lower executive from *Time* who was looking for a thrill and trying to escape his adulterous wife for a few weeks); and Tommy, the grip, whose job it was to carry our gear.

"Welcome to the Democratic Republic of Congo. I am Mayor Mobutu." We introduced ourselves, exchanging the traditional French niceties.

"Bonjour, monsieur."

"I must go and attend to some urgent matters, but there is a car waiting for you. These guards will take you out to Rutshuru, North Kivu."

He pointed to a Land Cruiser near the airport building. The mayor's face carried the scars of a rough life. His right cheek looked as if someone tried to carve a Z into it. His left eye was slightly lazy, giving you the feeling he was looking over your shoulder, even when you were face-to-face.

He turned to me. "You know how dangerous it is here. You are taking your life into your own hands, and we will not be responsible. We keep telling reporters this, but you never listen." He started to walk away but turned one more time and wagged his finger at each one us as if we were children. "Pay attention to what these guards tell you, and do not put yourself in the middle of conflict."

Nobody ever won a Pulitzer by standing at arm's length.

"Thank you for welcoming us, sir, and for your words," I said.

"We will keep them in mind." The guards nodded for us to and we made a solemn line into the Land Cruiser.

It was the rainy season, and on cue an afternoon storm whipped and lashed across the landscape like an angry mob. As we drove in silence, the hair on the back of my neck stood straight up. We arrived at the village that would serve as our headquarters. Amid the familiar routines of a small community that seemed oblivious to the dangers surrounding them, people who were displaced by violence congregated in huddles hoping for safety.

I snapped off pictures of the scene. Once the children noticed my camera, school was over. They surrounded me like ants on a Popsicle. I had come prepared. I handed out candy as fast as I could, then got back to the business of capturing images of this unsettling normalcy.

The sun hid behind the trees, and darkness enveloped the thatched huts and makeshift refugee camp, swallowing them whole. Our armed guards escorted us into a separate compound meant to keep us safe from any danger lurking in the nearby jungles.

We took a seat on concrete blocks to enjoy a traditional African meal of corn and beans, and we laughed about the monkeys we had seen on the road hurling bananas at our Land Cruiser. It was funnier than it ought to have been.

And then it happened.

The crisp pop of bullets battered our eardrums. The sounds ripped through the jungle night and into the village. Then the screams began. Screams that boiled the blood inside my ears.

I dropped, crawled on my belly to the window, and slid up along the front wall, craning my neck so I could see outside. A guard across the room mirrored my actions at another window. Everyone else was flat against the ground. As I peered through the rusty barred window, flashes of light pounded bright fists against the sky, the road, and the trees.

Buildings exploded with fire, and a woman cried out in terror. Shadows flickered, black phantoms haunting the night. I made out five or six soldiers beating a woman with their boots and the butts of their guns.

She quit screaming, quit moving, and then they ripped the clothes from her broken body. They began raping her. She came to and started to scream again, pleading for help, and they hit her until her screams choked on her blood.

She couldn't have been more than sixteen.

I turned my head.

The horror of this night was no act of God. No earthquake or tsunami. This was the act of men. Evil men. Demons in the guise of men.

The uncertainty of what might happen next hovered at the edge of an inhaled breath.

The armed guards screamed for us to lay prostrate on the dirt floor as bullets flew through the walls and widows, scattering plaster and glass. I wiped away salty sweat burning my eyes. But the sweat was thicker than it should have been. I tasted it.

Blood.

Fear strangled the air. Shallow breaths and rapid heartbeats echoed throughout the tiny room. I thought about my last conversation with Whitney.

My last conversation.

Was it my last?

Mike's hand slid up next to me. His whisper turned my head. "Ask not for whom the bell tolls, man."

Mike shoved his glasses back onto his oversized, pockmarked nose. "This happened to one of my closest friends in northern Uganda. The rebel militia mutilated everyone and everything in sight. No one made it out alive. No one. These monsters believe in a kind of Old Testament extermination of anything that moves."

"Thanks for the encouraging words."

"I always knew I'd die young."

He reached in his pocket and pulled out a string of wooden rosary beads.

"These were my mother's."

"I'm not Catholic."

"Neither was I. Until now ..."

"Shut up!" one of the guards hissed.

Rivers of sweat baptized our faces, our necks, our chests.

Death, real and suffocating, pressed in, driven by the wailing of dying babies, the yelps of slaughtered animals, the screams of women being beaten and raped.

My heart raced in rapid-fire panic.

I peered through a hole between a cinder block and a broken windowsill. Rebel troops swarmed like locusts, devouring every living thing in their path.

Mike elbowed me in the thigh. "Remember that story about an African militia group that raped a bunch of Americans? Men, women, children—they weren't choosy."

"You have to be quiet," whispered a guard. He got to one knee, steadying his gun. "Now shut up, or I'll kill you myself."

A rebel commander yelled something just outside the door. Another shot, and the guard who had just spoken fell dead right on top of me. His blood flowed over my neck and right arm, staining my Band of Brothers ring crimson. The screaming intensified; people ran, yelled, and died.

I scooted against the wall, huddled next to Mike as shots continued to shriek overhead. Plaster exploded and covered us. We tried to make ourselves invisible, curling into the fetal position, wrapping our arms over our heads.

A bullet whined by my ear, missing by centimeters. I crawled facedown to the other side of the room, trying to get out of the line of fire.

Then a sudden, deafening silence.

Nobody moved for what seemed like hours. Fear paralyzed me, and the silence thickened, punctuated by an occasional moan or a sob. We waited and waited, wondering when it would be safe to stand, wondering if it would ever be safe.

Finally, I gazed out the window, my eyes searching for rebel soldiers in the yellow-orange gloom of smoke. No figures or movement.

"I'm going out," I whispered to Mike.

He didn't respond

"Hey, listen. Let's go, man."

I elbowed him in the ribs.

"Mike!" I grabbed his jacket to turn him toward me. There was a pinpoint crimson stain on the front of his light blue shirt. His eyes stared through me.

I was frozen for a moment, not knowing what to do. Then I

pulled my camera out of my bag. I picked up Mike's gear and slung it around my neck.

Outside, the air burned of flesh. Some shadows moved in the distance, but the streets were barren. A few jerking and twitching heaps lined the road and quivered beside the buildings.

Oh, God. Oh, God.

I walked toward the flames. Everything was silent except for a sour ringing in my ears. Something compelled me to enter the destruction, to get closer.

Severed body parts lay before me in a display of such horror I began to heave. A young pregnant mother crumpled over, lying dead next to a burning haystack. She barely looked human. One leg lay at a right angle, an arm hung loosely from her shoulder, held there by a single, stringy tendon. Her stomach had been sliced wide open, the wormlike contents spilled in front of her, still moving.

There was nothing I could do to help her. Nothing.

I lifted the camera to my left eye. Snap. Snap. Snap. The lens clicked open and closed.

I stepped closer to capture the look on her face. Steam rose from her insides. More pictures. Through the blood and mucus by her midsection, I made out a face, a tiny face with eyes closed.

Voices rose over the roofs. Something was happening at the end of the village. Without thought, I raced through the corpses and debris toward the commotion.

The rebel troops had gathered the bodies of all the men they had slain. They were stacking them together in the shape of a pyramid.

As each body was thrown on top of the others, the rebels jeered, spit on the dead, and drank from a whiskey bottle, reveling in their triumph. They shot their guns into the air. Fire flashed around the perimeter. It was a scene from hell.

A man climbed on the roof above the bodies, unzipped his pants, and urinated all over the dead. The men slapped each other on the back and laughed.

Another rebel poured some liquid over the bodies.

I adjusted the camera settings and snapped a series of shots as fast as my fingers could click. The fire ignited, a pyramid pyre, and I continued to shoot. I snapped pictures of the dead—men I had seen earlier that day caring for their families—as their faces melted like candle wax. I snapped pictures of the rebels' ugly glee. And I felt like retching again.

I turned and walked, faster and faster, until I was running.

Each step I took pounded the question: Why? Why? Why?

I raced to the edge of the compound and saw Tommy hanging out the window of our car, frantically motioning me to come. We sped off, the remaining guard driving like a bat out of hell, for it was indeed hell we were escaping. As I turned to look out the back window, I saw Mike's body crumpled in the seat behind me. Like a rotted rubber band, something inside me snapped. My whole body shook. Sobs came without tears. I could muster only one coherent thought: If we get out of here alive, at least we can send Mike back to his family.

Back to his cheating wife.

Chapter Two

New York, 2007

As the cab rolls up to Madison Square Garden, my eyes immediately catch the large flashing electronic sign that says "Welcome, Guests of the International Press Association." I take a deep breath, step out of the cab, and force myself to walk in.

The doors slide open as smooth as silk, revealing three cloth-draped tables for guests to sign in and pick up their badges. Silver and black balloons decorate the expansive foyer. Waiters and waitresses swirl around the guests serving hors d'oeuvres and champagne. This is New York. Everyone's a professional.

A huge circle of flags on high golden posts lines the ceiling. I scan for the countries I've visited: China, Russia, Turkey, Jordan.... Then my eyes rest on the flag with the red strip down the middle with blue on each side and a yellow star in the top left. The Congo. My forehead breaks out in a cold sweat.

"Hello. You're Stuart Daniels, right?" I turn and see a tall blonde with short, smooth hair. She is wearing a tight black dress with a low-scooping neckline. It's hard to look at her face.

"It's so great to meet you. I'm Kristin. I'm a massive fan of your work. It's really powerful. Like, so moving."

"Thanks. I'm grateful."

Out of the corner of my eye I spot my friend Garrett heading toward me. He's a waddling, sweating orb. Not much to look at, but he's a great conversationalist—scary smart and a fantastic writer. He stays local, likes the political scene. I always wondered if he wasn't so big, maybe he could fit in an airplane seat and work internationally.

"Congratulations on your award," Kristen says. She moves in closer. "And if there's anything I can do for you tonight, here's my card." I notice the *Times* logo as I glance at the card.

Kristen takes my hand and bends a little lower, providing a clear view of a glimmering silver cross and a tattoo in the shape of a heart competing for my attention. Then I wonder if she really did pause on the word *anything*.

"Hey, Stuart." Garrett checks out Kristin as she walks away. "She's hot. Did I interrupt something?"

"Not at all. How are you?"

"How am I? How are you? Ready for the big speech?"

He's wearing a rented tuxedo with a black jacket and blue pants. I start to say something about his fashion sense, but common sense gets the better of me.

"As ready as I'll ever be." I pick up the seating card with my table number, and Whitney's.

"Where is the lovely Whitney tonight?"

"She's doing production for CBS *Live at Five* news. She should be here any minute."

"That's a great promotion for her. Man, she's the real thing. You need to hang on to her, dude. She's your salvation." His eyes shift to look beyond me. "And speak of the angel in blue ..."

I turn and see Whitney gliding toward us in a light blue strapless dress. She is wearing the necklace and earrings I picked up for her in Egypt last month. Whitney isn't flashy with clothes or makeup, but she does love exotic jewelry.

"And hello, Ms. Whitney. You're looking gorgeous tonight," Garrett says.

"Her face isn't down there, man."

"Listen, Stuart, I know a good thing when I see it."

Whitney can take it. She grew up with three brothers—and she's known Garrett as long as she's known me.

"Hello, Garrett, good to see you." She puts her arm around me and leans in to kiss me. She smells like orange and vanilla. The scent reminds me of better times. I inhale slowly, willing myself to relax.

"You look incredible." I mean it. The dress matches her eyes. The color of a winter sky.

"Whitney, I know this guy's won some kind of prestigious award, but if you want a real man to take you out after this, let me know, would ya?" Garrett's eyebrows jump up and down like two caterpillars in heat.

The thought of it makes us laugh. Garrett has always had a crush on her.

"I'm heading to the lav." Garrett points to the opposite side of the room. "See you at the table."

A voice to my right yells, "Congratulations, Stuart! The Horace Greeley Award for public-service journalism, what an honor!"

I recognize the face. Couldn't pull the name if my life depended on it though.

"Thanks." I hate these cocktail preludes. I turn to Whitney. "I need a drink."

"All this attention a bit much for you?"

"Thus, the drink. And you need one too." I put my arm around her narrow shoulders and we walk, trying to stay under the radar.

I get her a white wine, dry, and a Stoli and lime for myself. It doesn't even begin to touch my nerves.

"I'm proud of you, Stuart. This is a big night for you," Whitney says.

Now that we're out of the main foyer, I feel like I can let my guard down.

"You know, Whit, this all seems incredibly strange."

"What do you mean?"

"It just doesn't seem right that I should get an award for this. That day in the Congo wasn't an act of courage, more like desperation."

"Look, that picture did something. It changed people's lives. And it did something to change the world. Stuart, just try to enjoy this, okay?"

We've had this conversation before, and I can tell she is getting exasperated.

"Okay." She squeezes my hand and turns to talk to the woman sitting next to her. Whitney is patient with me, but only to a point. She's the kind of girl who cried over an A- in school, and she's climbed the broadcast-journalism ladder faster than most people her age. She's a Georgia country girl with little tolerance for weakness.

I order another drink.

I haven't been able to sleep since I found out about this award. The same nightmares I had after coming home have reemerged from some closet in my psyche. Dr. Brandon, my shrink, upped my meds and gave me something to help me sleep, but my nerves have been shot for weeks.

I unfold the paper in my pocket where I scratched out an acceptance speech on the way over tonight. Cab rides are good for something, I guess.

Chairs shuffle and squeak across the floor like dozens of metal monsters as people take their seats. A large man crosses the stage and raspily clears his throat. The emcee for the evening. Looks familiar. Ah yes, Charlie Swanson, CNN news anchor.

"Good evening, ladies and gentlemen, and welcome. We are glad you are able to be with us tonight on this very special occasion, one where we honor those among us who have gone above and beyond the call of duty and accomplished something truly worthwhile...."

As the night wears on and people are given awards they most certainly deserve, my mind wanders. I can't accept that some good came from this picture. It's a picture that I can't escape. But it's not just the picture of the dead men I see when I close my eyes. I also see the young woman I had spied through the window, the blows hitting her body, the heinous rape. I see the pregnant woman's broken body. And then I see the innocent eyes. I don't see them as they were. I see them open, alive, looking at me. They are pleading, and I can do nothing. I start to feel a wave of panic. I tug at my collar and wish I could run.

Whitney must sense this. She reaches over and squeezes my hand.

"I'm going to wait over there." I point to the side aisle. As I stand, someone sitting near the stage catches my eye. I see the African head wrap, and I know.

The emcee continues.

"Making the presentation of the Horace Greeley Award for

public-service journalism is a very special guest. We are honored she has accepted our invitation. This is a woman who has given her life in service to the poor and made our world a better place at great personal sacrifice. She is the recipient of the 2004 Nobel Peace Prize and the first African female to receive that award. Please welcome with me, Mrs. Wangari Maathai."

I fall back into my seat and my hand stops midair, sending the ice cubes in my nearly finished glass of water cascading onto the table. Stepping up onto the stage is my friend, a woman who bleeds African royalty. Wangari, in her vibrant dress and multicolored head wrap, walks gracefully to the podium and takes the microphone. A bead of sweat falls from my forehead onto my program. How fitting that a woman who was with me in the firefight all those years ago—though I didn't know it till we met months later—is the one sharing this moment with me now.

"Thank you, and good evening to everyone. Ladies and gentlemen, I am proud to be presenting our next award. As many of you know, this is one of the most prestigious awards anyone can receive in journalism. Men and women make many personal sacrifices and take great risks just to be considered. Past recipients have even lost their lives, but their sacrifices live on through this award."

The photo appears on the overhead screens: Pyramid of Death. I don't need to look at it to see it.

"Tonight, I am proud to present this award to a man I admire, one who will take his place among his colleagues in this hall of courage. Through his decade of work, he has become a champion for the poor and oppressed in many nations of the world. I am proud to call him a brother and a friend. The winner of this year's Horace Greeley Award for public-service journalism, Mr. Stuart Daniels!"

I'm not sure if it's the moment, the alcohol, or my state of shock, but I freeze. My butt won't move out of my chair. The clapping intensifies, louder and louder. Then, one by one, everyone begins to stand. Now I'm the only one sitting. A torrent of emotion rushes through my soul, emptying me. I stand. Everything is in slow motion now. I'm shaking, putting one foot in front of the other. Finally, I reach the platform.

"Thank you, everyone, for this great honor. I want you to know that I don't accept this award lightly. In fact, many sleepless nights have followed me since the night that picture was taken."

Looking back at the photo, I pause, caught by the immediacy of the image. Why did they have to blow it up so huge on the screen? A moment passes. Then another. I swallow hard.

"A friend, a writer, lost his life that day. The men in that picture, I talked to some of them that day. They had come to this place of refuge with their wives, their children. They were reconstructing life as best they could in a camp. And then the rebels came."

I've forgotten about the speech I wrote. I pull the paper out of my pocket and unfold it. The room is silent.

"All I can say, is …" I look at Wangari.

"This award isn't really my award. It belongs to the people who died for it. And to those who are changed for the better because of my work. And so, on their behalf, I'll accept it. And I thank you from the bottom of my heart."

Wangari hands me the award, a tall crystal trophy—so clean, so pristine. So unlike the image that won it for me. Then she embraces me and whispers in my ear, "You're a good man, Stuart. I've always known that about you. One day you'll believe it too." I try to pull away but she holds on.

My head weighs a hundred pounds and it falls onto her shoulder. I weep. It's all I know to do.

Chapter Three

The red clay from the ground sticks like gum to my bare, blistered feet. My stride is long and elegant like a giraffe. The water explodes as each foot lands in a muddy puddle. I'm running as fast as my feet will take me.

The sun is dipping down. The countryside radiates as far as my eye can see, and the sounds of life vibrate through the rocks. I love the silence and the appearance of twinkling stars. The cool night air smells different, like a freshly whittled stick. My breath slows, and I walk to the sound of crickets, their love songs rising into the night.

A few moons ago, I was walking in the night and I heard men's voices shouting in the distance. I followed the sound to the *kraal*. This is a place of meeting where important decisions are made. It is also where the spirits of our ancestors dwell. I was taught at school the importance of the kraal, how the spirits who live in the trees and the air give our leaders wisdom. I tiptoed through the grass and hunched down in the middle of the circle of brambly trees.

What I found was more valuable than gold: secrets! I felt like the most important girl in all of Africa. I heard about someone who was in trouble with the council. A man in our village had land taken

31

away because he stole a neighbor's cow. I discovered who would face trial by the council for neglecting members of their own family, and what sentence should be handed down to a man who was found guilty of killing a fellow villager because the villager stole five of his cows. In our culture, cows are everything.

My mother often calls me "the little spy."

"How do you know such things, Adanna?" she would ask and laugh. I would smile and shake my head. But I never gave away my secret.

Tonight, I am wandering outside alone with my thoughts, walking toward the kraal, and thinking about Momma, who is at home trying to get some rest. Precious and Abu are asleep, dreaming of candy, I am sure. It is better for them to sleep when there is no dinner. I can't help but think of the burnt corn we ate two nights ago. My mouth waters for more. When the food is cooked, some always burns. We scrape the kettle to save the char for days when there is nothing else to eat—but now that is gone too. I try not to think of the ache in my stomach, but it's almost impossible. I think the reason Momma rests all the time now is because of the ache in her stomach. Whenever there is food, she gives it to Abu first, then Precious, then me.

I can see every star in the universe. The sky is a deep blue bowl filled with magical, milky fairy dust. My mother told me that fairies live in the stars. The brightest ones are the most powerful. I dream one of those fairies will find me and give me three wishes.

I first would wish to see my real daddy again, the way he used to be, and have him home with us. The second would be lots of food so nobody in our village would ever get hungry. And the third would be wings, so I could fly away.… No, not wings. I don't need to fly. The third wish would be that no one in our village would ever get sick again.

My thoughts are interrupted by a familiar name. "Sipo." My uncle's name. Quietly, I wade through the dry, crackling grass near the kraal and lean forward to listen.

"We have to act. Something has to be done," says a deep voice.

"Would you have us remove all the sick to one building and just let them die alone, Bongani?"

"There are just too many of them. And now the sickness has attacked our elders and our children."

Something is moving on the other side of the kraal. I hear sticks snapping.

"Yes, it is a terrible thing that Sipo has fallen sick. It seems like yesterday he was fit as a lion."

What is that noise? I'm certain I hear the breathing of an animal. My face is burning hot, and I wonder if every creature on the plains can hear the pounding of my heart. I am as still as a snake under a bush.

"Now, Sipo has the look of the dead. No doubt he will soon join our ancestors and everyone else who have gotten the sickness. He will die."

"Listen to me, my brothers. Sipo and all who have died before him have made the ancestors angry and punishment is the result. This punishment will continue to fall on us until the ancestors are appeased. We must offer a blood sacrifice."

I can hardly concentrate; something is peering around the corner. It is no animal, but a person.

"Yes, then let's agree. A blood sacrifice on the first night of the next full moon."

I can see now. Cloaked in the shadows is my best friend, Tobile. My hand snaps to my lips to silence her.

"This must be kept secret," the same low voice says. "Bongani and I will seek the witch doctor."

"Then it is agreed." It is the voice of the chief. "We will seek witch doctor and follow her instructions."

Tobile scoots my direction and huddles by my side. We peek through the wood encircling the kraal. Shadows move about, flickering by torchlight. Shivering, we look at each other and know we are forbidden to whisper a word. The voices fade to a low hum, and everyone slips away. Once the elders have spoken and the chief makes a decision, there is no more talk.

My head is buried in my arm. I wish I could be invisible. Of all nights Tobile should not have come. This is a dark matter, and we both know it. We sit, stiff with fear.

After enough time passes, I tap Tobile's shoulder.

"Let's get out of here."

She nods, and we steal away like robbers into the night.

We run to my home. I can see a lonely candle flickering in the window. I remember the days when I would open the door to our house and find it filled with laughter and food. Uncle Sipo would come with his family, and we would play games. Our house was fun. But that was long ago.

Thinking about my uncle brings me to tears. I cannot imagine life without him. Tobile and I crouch down in front of our house where we cannot be seen.

"Adanna, what is happening? Why are the elders talking about blood?" Tobile asks.

"So many of our people are sick, and everyone is scared, Tobile."

"Why?"

"Our ancestors are angry because Uncle Sipo did not honor them. Someone said he made enemies with the witch doctors. I do not know what is happening, but the dead are filling the ground faster than the living can make graves for them."

I pull my legs in and hug my knees tighter. It is cold again tonight, and I will have to find more wood for us to stay warm.

"I wish I hadn't learned *this* secret."

Tobile kneels close beside me. "Adanna, why do you think Sipo is sick?"

"Something is happening to our village, Tobile." I can't stop the queasy feeling in my stomach.

"Why?"

"Someone was talking the other day about the moon rocks. They fell from the sky and landed next to the village. That's what they said. The moon rocks are making people sick. Maybe if we can bury the moon rocks, we can save our people."

"Maybe no one would have to spill their blood."

Suddenly the door opens. Momma peeks out.

"You two children running all over the country at night? Shame. Tobile, you get home right this minute, and, Adanna, get in this house, girl."

I whisper, "Tobile, we will look for the rocks first thing in the morning. The lives of our people depend on it."

Chapter Four

New York, 2008

The airport Starbucks is like heaven. Of course, the line's a mile long. At least I have some time before my flight.

"I'll take a grande drip of the day with a shot of espresso, please."

A young woman with a sizable lip ring takes my order. Blood still circles the steel of the recent piercing.

"Room for cream?"

"Nope."

I start to imagine blood dripping in my coffee, and then I stop myself. I'm far too hungover for that line of thought.

"Can I offer you one of our crème brûlée chocolate caramel fudge bars to go with that?"

I look at her dirty fingernails and hand littered with not-quite-faded *X* stamps from the clubs she hit the night before and shake my head.

"No, thanks. But I will take a tall caramel macchiato, half the syrup, with lots of whip." For Whitney. She called last night and asked if she could meet me at the airport. I'm sure she could tell from my response I wasn't too keen on the idea. I don't need yet another reminder of my growing list of failures.

I sit alone at a table for two. I can't believe I'm going back to Africa. I hate everything about it: the heat, the poverty, the corruption, the ignorance, the death that blows over the place like a dry western wind. Where's that Ebola virus when you need it? A breakout would give me a good reason to cancel.

At least I'm still good at leaving town. With a flick of my wrist and a twitch of my nose, things fall into place and I'm out the door. I can become someone else for a time. Or maybe I become myself—someone who cares just enough to get the work done but not enough to get sucked into the broken lives I'm capturing on film. All I need are some clothes, toiletries, books, a little Airborne, my computer, cameras, and prescription drugs. Too bad they don't give international awards to the fastest packer. At least winning that one wouldn't screw with my head.

I have to admit, though, that traveling isn't quite what it used to be. These crowds make me anxious. The best thing about 9-11 was that it cleared out the airports. I know it was a horrible tragedy, but something good comes from everything.

"Stuart, what are you thinking so intently about?"

Whitney is wearing her black jogging suit. Her cheeks are still flushed from her Saturday run in the park. Something we used to do together. If she wasn't so incredibly beautiful, maybe I could leave for good. And we could both just go on with our lives.

"Trying to get mentally prepared for my trip."

"Sorry I'm late. Traffic was a mess. Big surprise. I don't know why I don't move back to the country."

"Because you hate the country, and you would never become a network exec if you moved back to sticksville." I hand her the drink.

She gives me a look that straddles the line between "what's this for?" and "thank you." She takes a sip. Her expression settles on "thank you" but stops short of a smile.

"You know me too well."

"What are we doing, Whit? I mean ... what am I doing?"

"Only you can answer that." She doesn't look away. She seems to be searching for answers I don't think exist. "I know what I want you to do," she says, "but I can't force that."

"I know."

"I made a commitment to you, Stuart. I thought you made the same sort of commitment to me."

"I did. But ..."

"But what? But it's not working out like you planned? Look ... I'm sorry you're having a hard time with all this. I know this is tough on you. But it's tough on me, too. You seem to have forgotten there are two of us in this relationship."

"I haven't forgotten." But there were days when I wish I had. Not because I didn't love Whitney, but because I didn't think I deserved her. Not anymore. Not since I had become a failure, unable to get out of bed, bowing out or flaking out on assignments other photographers would kill for. Then the assignments stopped coming altogether. Until this one. One I didn't want.

"Stuart, I wanted to meet with you before you leave because—" She starts to cry. She's never been a crier. I can't help but think she's about to give me the final hatchet. God knows I deserve it.

"I love you. I still love you. But you've been so far away, Stuart. I want you back. I need you to come back to me. I need the Stuart I married."

She reaches over to grab my hands.

"I don't know that man anymore." It is the truth.

For a moment, she looks ready to give up on me. Her words speak of love, but her eyes are filled with pain and frustration.

"Stuart ... I've been praying for you—for us."

"You've been praying? I thought you swore off the God of the South."

"I did, but I've since realized the God who shames and demands isn't the real God, Stuart."

"When did this change happen?"

She grinds her teeth, grips my hands tighter. "Stuart ... it's been happening for a while. You just haven't been listening."

There's the understatement of the year.

"I'm sorry," I say. "You're right. I've been somewhere else for weeks."

"Months," she corrects.

"But I just don't see how God figures into any of this."

She softens.

"I'm not sure I understand either, Stuart. But I know He does. Somehow I know that. And ..."

"I am so tired of my thoughts, Whit. I feel like a character in a Shakespearean play who went on stage, acted their one great scene, and died."

"... and I think this trip is really important for you. For us."

What?

"You think this trip is a *good* idea? I thought you hated it."

"I *do* hate it. I hate that you don't get all the great assignments that you deserve. I hate it that this feels like a last-ditch effort to save your career. And I truly hate it that it takes you away from me when we're in such an uncertain place."

"But somehow, you think it's important for me to go?"

"Yes." She lets go of my hands and takes a long sip of her drink. "I can't explain it. It's just something I feel. I *know*."

"I wish *I* knew it."

"You're still very much alive, Stuart. You just need to remember who you are."

I think of Wangari's words, *Someday, you will realize who you are*.

"I don't know what to say." I glance at my watch. "I've gotta go."

Our chairs squeak back, and she comes to me with her eyes squinting and her forehead wrinkled. She holds me tight, "Find the answer, Stuart. Please."

She turns to leave, then stops and looks back.

I try to smile but manage what probably looks more like a sneer. She turns quickly and walks away.

Does she know I still have thirty minutes till boarding? I walk toward the gate. I need some time to think. Or maybe time to think of nothing at all.

A few splits of wine and an Ambien will help with the latter.

Chapter Five

◆◇■ Adanna ■◇◆

My name means "father's daughter." But memories of my father are
few. My mother tells me he was an important man. I do not know if
that is true, but I do know he was gone all the time. Sometimes that
made me sad. Other times I was glad.

My strongest memory of him was when we had our last family
brii. Every brii before that one, Daddy and Uncle Sipo and all the
men would fish from the river while Momma and Auntie got the
food and fire ready at home. But on that last brii, Daddy took me
fishing with him too.

Daddy wanted his firstborn to be a boy. Instead he got me. Since
I was the oldest and Abu just a baby, he sometimes treated me like a
boy. I did not mind.

Early that morning, my father and I walked five kilometers to
the river. Trees and flowers bloomed in every direction. Explosions of
color ignited the landscape. The bugs were everywhere that morning
too, and they were eating me alive. When we got to the river, the
grass all around was thick and green. Those weeds made a perfect
place to play hide and seek.

Back then, the river was so clean you could drink out of it. The
river settled me and gave me a feeling of peace.

"Adanna, come here and help me put a worm on this hook."

"Oh, Daddy, must I?" I hated the slimy feeling of those worms. And I could not stand to see their guts squish out all over the place.

As much as I wanted to show my father I was as good as any son, these kinds of things I didn't like. Our village celebrated special occasions and funerals by slaughtering an animal. The whole town would gather and people would crane their necks to see as if they were watching the South African soccer team play in a world-championship match. Everyone watched with anticipation as the glimmering knife came down and slit the poor creature's throat. I kept my eyes closed the entire time.

"If you were a boy ..."

I had heard this speech a hundred times. If I were a boy, I could catch the fish while father was preparing the brii. If I were a boy, I could make money to help support the family. I didn't mind the speech because when it was over, he would look at me with a huge smile and say, "But, Adanna, I wouldn't trade you for every boy in Africa!" In these moments, my father was a wonderful man, better than any man in the world.

"Now, Adanna, what kind of meal is there with nothing to eat? Go on, put the worm on the hook."

Gingerly, I pressed the worm onto the hook, its string of guts squishing out on each side.

We caught fish by the dozens that day. Their bellies were painted with the colors of the rainbow. My father and I laughed together until my stomach hurt as he told me jokes and as I tried to get the slimy, icky fish off the hooks and into the bag. We wrestled together in the tall grass until my back itched like a million bugs were scratching me.

When we arrived back home, I held the bag of fish high above my head and skipped to the front yard. Momma and Auntie clapped wildly for me like I had just scored the winning goal in a soccer game. It felt good to contribute to the family by working and catching the fish.

That night, Dad shared stories about his trips to the big cities like Durban, Cape Town, and Johannesburg. He was a truck driver and saw all of Africa on his journeys. He promised he would take me with him one day. I can still see his face, like Abu's. Same chin, same jawline. As he animated his stories with wild gestures, his face seemed to glow next to the fire. Every few minutes, he would have to stop as a cough overtook him. That's the last image I have of him, coughing by the fire, sweat dripping down his brow. He was going away the next day on a long trip to make lots of money. He was going to bring back exotic foods and candies from all over Africa. He said after this trip, he would have so much money he would never have to leave again.

But I never saw him again. I was only ten years old.

O■◊◆●————●◆◊■O

"Adanna, let's run to the river and play in the trees!"

"Okay, Tobile, I'll race you there!"

We don't mention the moon rocks. Maybe our secret games will make me feel better. The river was our source of life. Crystal clear and pure, filled with fish, it was a peaceful place of refuge.

After my daddy left, everything changed. More and more people became sick, hiding in their homes, never to be seen again. The next thing I knew, we were burying them in the ground.

Now, instead of green grass and trees, the ground is covered with thorns and trash—glass, garbage bags, and tin cans. The river smells like an outhouse. And when you run close to the banks, you have to watch so you don't step on something and cut your foot.

Momma and Auntie tell us all the time, "Do not drink that water, not even a sip, or you will get sick and die!" Everyone used to drink it all the time. But now the river's edge is dotted with small mounds where people have been put in the ground. I've heard the elders in the kraal say the river is poisoned.

There is not so much water now. The river is more like a creek. But I still like to come here to think or be alone. Today I am thinking of Uncle Sipo. This morning I went to visit my auntie Zoda. She stood outside in the wind and the dust refusing to let me inside. She didn't want me to see him.

"I don't know if he will make it through the night," she said.

It used to be the elders did not talk to children about serious matters.

Tobile and I grew up playing with each other before we could even walk. Our mothers carried us on their backs in a knapsack called a *kanga*. When they were close, we would grab and hug each other as they talked and cooked. Our bond is one only sisters share.

To cook, a woman stands over a hot iron pot forever. I know because this is my job when Momma is tired. We only eat a few times a week. There is not enough food for more than that.

Mostly we eat *pap*, a yellow corn mixture with a few beans, if we are lucky. We build a fire from branches that are becoming harder to find. Then the kettle sits on top until everything is ready. Pap is not delicious, but sometimes I can trick my mouth into thinking it is beef and fresh vegetables.

At times, we eat rotten food. Eat rotten food or starve—that is the choice. Rotten cabbages, rotten potatoes, maize with bugs and worms squirming in an old, rotting bag.

I put my finger to my lips. They are cracked and my mouth is parched and bleeds. The pains of hunger are deep. My insides burn. They growl and demand what I cannot give.

Yesterday I was playing soccer with friends by the lake. I had not eaten for a week, but when there is no food, you keep busy and hope to forget about it. I tried eating some grass, but it made my stomach sour.

Suddenly an unexpected thorn shoved through my foot and a terrible pain shot through me. It started in my belly and traveled to every place in my body. Falling to the ground, I cried out with all of my might. I grabbed my head and clawed the dirt and begged God to make it go away. But He didn't listen, and the pain did not leave.

"Queen Adanna! You are being summoned to your bath by your servants!" Tobile shouts.

I dream of hot water filled with lavender and rose petals, precious oils, and perfumes fit for a queen! I roll in pine needles, a substitute for a queenly bath.

"Thank you, Princess Tobile! What is that I hear? A knock on the palace door? Tobile, you are being summoned by the most handsome and mighty warrior in the kingdom for a special royal dinner! He waits for you in the banquet hall where there is lamb, potatoes, and a special dessert prepared just for you."

Sometimes, if I try hard enough, I can almost make myself believe these dreams.

I pluck a blade of dried grass from the ground, longing for the day I might have a better life. Today I cannot see it.

"Adanna, do you remember when things were different? When everyone was not hungry and dying?"

"Why are you talking like that? Happiness does not live in those words."

"But we have no crowns on our heads or paint on our fingernails." She cannot see it today, either. I feel Tobile's little body shake next to me. I know she is crying.

I put my arms around my friend.

"Things will change, Tobile. Maybe like Pastor Walter says, God will help us." I tap my fingers in the dirt. I do not believe what I say. "He will not forget about us. But I do not know how long we will have to wait."

"Maybe He is lost."

For some reason, this makes us laugh.

"Maybe He has people to take care of who are in worse situations than us."

Our silence says neither of us believes this.

Pastor Walter talked about this last Sunday in church. The title of his message scared me. He started out, "We are all dying like flies."

I'm old enough to know what death is. Pastor Walter said everyone was dying because of AIDS. Because they weren't faithful to their one wife.

He said that God would help us when we starting obeying His

Word. He held up a book. A Bible. He said when we seek God with all our heart we will find Him.

Maybe everything got bad because people stopped obeying God.

I remember when my friend Blossum and I were playing in the fields. She snuck up on me and yelled, "Tag, you're it!" I chased her through the fields and into the village. She went flying though the door of her home, and I followed. We stopped when we saw her father. He lay curled up in a heap, coughing. He moaned like an animal in great pain. Shriveled up to nothing, he looked up at us with terror in his eyes. We ran. He was the first I saw, the first of the sick.

Two days later he died.

Tobile and I lay our heads down on the riverbank. As I listen to the trickle of water, I ask God to put things back to the way they were. Maybe all we have to do is ask.

Chapter Six

Stepping off a plane in the Johannesburg, South Africa, airport in December is like walking into a packed men's locker room. My first whiff of Africa is in the walkway from the plane to the terminal, and it's like discovering food that's been left in your refrigerator for a month. The drinks and the sleeping pill I took to get me through the eighteen-hour flight are not helping.

There are two lines—one for South Africans and the other for foreign visitors. The line for visitors snakes around a series of PVC pipes, where everyone waits patiently. No one is talking except a big-haired lady with glasses who is wearing a full-length denim dress. She's going on and on about how she's going to "evangelize the heathen" and bring them all the saving knowledge of Jesus so they won't have to burn in hell for eternity. She won't shut up about how miserable her flight was and how rude the stewardesses were. Then she begins handing out Bible tracts. I grab one. It's titled "The Execution and Hell to Pay."

The official in the customs line gives me a quick smile before looking at my passport.

"Press?" She looks at me inquisitively.

"Yes, photojournalist."

She sighs heavily and shakes her head and stamps the papers twice.

"Do some good for our people, would you? God knows we need it."

"I'll do my best."

I've never actually had a customs agent speak to me before.

Two bright orange bags tumble around the corner onto the carousel looking like oversized construction pylons. No sane person would mistake them for their bland black or beige bags or try to steal them. And in this city, theft is as common as a cold.

As I continue through the customs line, I see the final agent sitting behind an old wood-laminated podium, waving everyone through as he reads a magazine. They couldn't care less what people are bringing into their country. What could anyone do that would be worse than AIDS?

The glass doors open into a large foyer where hundreds of people stand waiting for loved ones and business associates. Squinting into the crowd, I see a rickety cardboard sign with my name scribbled in black ink framed by two dark hands. Classy. I walk up, feeling like someone hit me in the head with a hangover stick. All I want is my hotel.

"Hey, I'm Stuart."

The driver immediately grabs my bags, providing some relief to my weary body.

"Good afternoon, Mr. Daniels. I trust you had a good flight?"

He speaks with a scratchy, high-pitched voice in a clear South African accent.

"I'll be your guide while you are here in Africa, and I must say I'm extremely honored. I'm familiar with your work and—"

"Thank you, thank you," I say and make a clear advance to the car. "I'm ready to get to the hotel."

"Yes, sir, Mr. Daniels. By the way, Charles is the name. I'll be happy to run you to your hotel and get you whatever else you might need. I'm at your service."

"Just get me to the hotel if you would, please."

"Right away, sir."

I look out the window to see a city in chaos. Graffiti is scribbled across every wall and buildings display a colorful array of American expletives. People walk swiftly along the streets, as if they are afraid. I notice several women holding their purses tightly to their chests and looking over their shoulders. The sun is setting, and fear is sweeping across the city with the darkness.

Disturbing images from the struggle of apartheid won't leave my mind. Many people lost their souls in that evil sent straight from the pit of hell. There's still a residual of the ugliness here, lurking in the cracks and crevasses.

I'm keenly aware of the dangers in Africa whenever I step foot on the soil. Beyond the crime, there's something more. It's like evil spirits take possession of you when your feet touch the soil. They are the living echoes of devils that for generations spread war, hate, rape, and violence throughout Africa. I have too many bad memories associated with this place, beginning with what happened in the DRC ten years ago.

I hope the hotel check-in is quick. I need sleep, right after a nightcap.

○■◊♦●———●♦◊■○

Charles stands at attention in the lobby at 8:30 a.m. sharp as I step off the elevator, dragging my luggage. He is wearing a black derby. He looks like a jockey.

Driving in the city of Johannesburg is like touring another

planet. Every home is surrounded by a wall eight to ten feet high. Shards of glass sharp as lions' teeth line the top of the walls. Metal spikes stuck in mortar jut out into the street. Electric fences snake around the top of the glass to electrocute intruders who don't bleed to death first. And as if that isn't enough, vicious attack dogs lurk behind the walls.

Charles eyes me in the rearview mirror and tips his hat in a stately manner.

"As you see, Mr. Daniels, fear is a way of a life here."

"I can see that. What does that mean to you, Charles?"

"The rich are afraid the poor will steal everything they've worked so hard to attain. The poor are afraid the rich will hoard every morsel of food and starve them to death, like the Romans did to their enemies."

We pass a building that looks a little like the Roman Coliseum. I wonder if he's practiced this speech before.

"So the South African whites have studied the tactics of the Romans?"

"It's a great strategy if you think about it. Surround entire cities and cut off the food supplies. Slowly but surely, everyone dies from starvation."

"Do you really think it's that insidious?"

I see a flash of anger in the rearview mirror, but his voice stays calm and measured.

"I grew up in those shanties and barely escaped with my life. It was the whites who almost killed me. They show no mercy, even though they have so much wealth and so much to spare."

"They choked you out? Just waited for you to die?"

"They treated me like a worthless dog. All I wanted was a chance to go to school. But the whites closed all the schools in our neighborhood. They did not want us educated. They wanted us to starve."

"Sounds like a form of genocide. Death by economics instead of guns and bombs. How convenient."

Charles nods his head. "You have got that right, Mr. Daniels."

I recall an idea tossed around by some that the South African whites invented the AIDS virus to kill off the blacks. It had always sounded like conspiracy fanaticism to me. But if the rich whites would starve them out, why not infect them? It is a sick thought, one I don't mention to Charles. God forbid, imagine if it were true.

"See for yourself. Those expensive houses on the hill—that is where the rich live. Now, look down in the valley, right below the houses. See that glittering silver? That is from the tin roofs in the shanty town, a slum where the poor die every day from starvation. The rich look down from their decks and watch them die. It is sport to them."

"You don't really believe that, do you?"

"They do it. Every day."

"I've been all over the world, Charles. Economic cruelty isn't unique to southern Africa. I've seen it in the Dominican Republic, South America, even America, for crying out loud."

"What's your point?"

"My point is, and no disrespect intended, you're not the only ones suffering. And blaming the rich won't help anybody."

"Have you ever been poor, Mr. Daniels? I don't mean the kind of poor where you cannot pay your cell-phone bill or your cable-television bill. I'm talking about the kind of poor where you wake up in the morning and wonder, for the tenth day straight, if you will go hungry again."

"No. I've not been poor. But what are you saying? That the rich are responsible to feed the poor? It's their fault?"

"Mr. Daniels, the rich do have responsibility. It comes with the power of wealth."

"People who want or want to keep power don't care who they're trying to dominate."

We drive out of the city and into the countryside. Rolling hills, rich farmland, and lush vegetation surround us. It's hard to imagine so many starving people in the midst of what looks like a place of plenty.

"The whites secretly hope we will all die from poverty or AIDS so they can remove the electric fences. I've heard some say this is God's way of destroying sinners. It's a plague like the ones sent upon the Egyptians." His high-pitched voice has reached an even higher plane.

"If what you're saying has any merit of truth, a plague has already visited the rich because they have lost their souls."

"True, Mr. Daniels, and what does it profit a man to gain the whole world and lose his soul? Still, when you live desperate like so many do here in Africa, you might just trade your soul for a crust of bread. I don't see how a merciful God could judge that sort of trade as wrong."

"How can you believe in God with what you just described? With what you see around you?"

"Oh, I believe. God is our only hope, Mr. Daniels. Don't you believe?"

"I used to, a long time ago." The truth is, I don't know what I believe anymore.

As we continue the drive into the heart of the country, smoke dragons fill the air. The remainder of last year's harvest returns to the earth to await the next cycle of winter.

"What about you, Mr. Daniels?" Charles raises his eyes to meet mine in the rearview mirror.

"What do you mean?"

"Have you lost your soul?"

"I don't even know what that means. I've seen things in your country, all over 'God's creation.'"

"I know. I have seen your photographs."

"And I have done things I am not proud of."

"Then let me ask, if I may, are you here to take photographs of our suffering people only to display them like they are animals?"

I can feel the heat rising in my face, but I corral my anger.

"Look, man, I'm here to do a job, my job—not to solve the problems in your country. I didn't start them, and I'm not responsible for them. I'm just here to do a job."

"Forgive me, Mr. Daniels."

"No, Charles, forgive me." I blurt this out in a knee-jerk reaction. I don't know why.

It will be a relief to see Gordon in Swaziland. He won't grill me like I'm some kind of criminal. There's not a writer I'd rather work with than Gordon. He is a bit of a living legend. Word has it he drinks too much and used to have a reputation as a womanizer, but that just makes him more interesting.

Silence crowds into the space between Charles and me. There's nothing left to say. So I close my eyes and go to sleep.

Chapter Seven

◆◇■ Adanna ■◇◆

I say good-bye after a day with Tobile and start toward home. The sun is a giant ball of orange fire hovering motionless in the sky. It watches me.

"God is light, and in Him is no darkness." Pastor Walter read that from the book. The Bible. He said we should all try to walk in the light. I think about how I can walk in this light, but as the sun sinks, I feel as if God has gone too.

I am the only person on the earth.

"God, are You there?" I cry aloud. "I'm hungry, do You hear me?"

Silence.

"Pastor Walter says You are good and You are light, but if You are, why do You watch us wither away and die?"

My words pierce the night, then die suddenly away in the wind. I take a deep breath.

"Pastor Walter, he's good. But You ..." I look up at the new night sky. "I'm not so sure."

I feel a chill and stop to listen. My heart races, and the pain returns to my stomach. I sit behind a small tree. I wait. I wonder if someone is following me. After a few minutes, feeling foolish, I move on.

The path home comforts me.

I bounce onto the porch and burst into the front door to find my momma. Something is not right. She stands in the corner holding onto a pole that supports the thatched roof. Why is she grabbing her side and wincing? There's a bucket below her. I notice large sores on her left arm, one blistery red and oozing blood. I've startled her and she gives me a look of surprise and sadness.

"Adanna, don't ever come running through that door again, do you hear me! How many times have I told you that?"

Why the grunting and panting in her voice?

"Momma, I'm sorry. I was just excited to see you. Where are Precious and Abu?"

She falls onto the bed and grimaces as she attempts to swing her legs onto the mattress. Her legs look like dead wood. The bed is disheveled and unmade.

"Mother, are you okay? What's wrong?"

"I'm just a little tired. Your brother and sister are with Auntie D, but they should be here soon. There's no need to worry."

My mother had hardly been sick a day in her life. She's stronger than a Cape buffalo. My mind flashes to what I heard the elders say at the kraal.

"Adanna, come sit down next to me."

I slowly shuffle my feet across the dirt floor and sit down on the bed. It creaks loudly as if it may break.

"I want you to know how much I love you and what a special girl you are. When I was carrying you in my belly, I realized there was something special about your life. God's hand was on you."

"Thank you, Momma, but why are you talking like this?"

"I want you to know the truth about who you are. I never want there to come a time when you think that things are hopeless. I do not want you to believe the lie that you will not accomplish great things in your life. I want you to believe in yourself no matter what happens."

"Oh, Momma, I do believe in myself. I am going to get a job one day and buy food so we are never hungry again."

"Yes, child, I know you will." She takes my hand and squeezes it.

"I am not talking about surviving. I am talking about doing something special with your life, about going to faraway places and fulfilling your destiny. God has shown me a vision of your life, and you are not meant to waste away in this dust bowl. You must take care of Precious and Abu. Find a way out for all of you. Do you understand what I'm saying?"

"I think so."

"No matter how bad things seem, no matter how bad they get." She hunches over and begins to cough violently.

"Momma, are you all right? Momma, can I get you something?"

"Maybe you could make dinner for us."

I kiss her. Her forehead is cold, more like winter than summer. With a pale, salty taste in my mouth, I walk outside to get wood for the fire.

Momma hasn't had good food in weeks. The store is just three kilometers away. I will go there to get Momma something good to eat. Daddy and I would go there on special occasions to get oxtail for a celebration meal. Next to the store there is a place that scares me. Strange men drink corn liquor and say mean things. They remind me of snarling animals. I try not to think about that as I make my way there.

I pass the bad place, keeping my head low. In the store several loaves of bread behind clear glass pull the saliva from my mouth. My stomach growls, like a native beating on a drum. I could steal that bread and not even feel bad.

A fat, angry-looking lady stares down at me. She obviously eats well. The counter smells of curdled milk. Suddenly I feel dirty and ashamed. I imagine I am a princess.

"Hello, ma'am. I'm wondering if I might borrow a loaf of bread."

"Borrow? Ain't nobody borrowing nothing from this store, little girl. Where's your money? That's the only thing gonna get you bread."

"I have no money. But I promise I will bring you some as soon as I do. My momma is starting to get sick, and I think it is because she has not had anything to eat."

A tall stranger dressed in black walks through the door. Outside sits a shiny silver car with a symbol on the hood that looks like a star. He turns toward me and gives me a look of disgust. I wonder why he hates me.

"We all haven't had much to eat around here. But what we do eat, we pay for. If you haven't got the money, there's nothing I can do for you."

"What can I do for the bread? Can I work for you? I am a good helper! I can clean your store."

"Not a chance, girl. But you can go ask someone next door to buy you some bread. Maybe they'll have mercy on you."

"Here's some mercy for you," laughs the rich man. He flips a coin at me.

"Thank you, sir." But it is not even enough to buy a tiny piece of gum. He turns his back on me like I don't exist.

The nasty woman behind the counter seems to find this amusing.

I have no choice but to ask the men next door. Maybe I can collect enough coins to buy a loaf of bread. I will look for a friendly face.

The small hall is thick with smoke and the rotting smell of corn liquor. I look for friendly eyes and see none.

Most of the men are old. Some are the age of my daddy. They look at me like vultures about to devour a dead animal. Every single one has a cigarette hanging out of his mouth and a drink in his hand. A few younger men are scattered in the room playing pool on a worn-out pool table.

I pass them, like a helpless goat. They laugh and point at me.

What is there to see? I am a starving twelve-year-old girl with a bloated stomach. My clothes are rags. They used to be the right size, now they hang loosely on my skinny body.

An older man with missing teeth glares at me. I see a forked tongue come from the center of his mouth. I am scared, and I turn to run. He grabs me hard and pulls me toward him by my arm.

"What is it you want, little girl? Are you looking for some time with a real man?"

I have to leave, but his grip is too tight, a ring of fire around my bony arm. The other men laugh.

I kick at his shins, but I cannot break free. I feel the sting of his open hand smack my cheek, and I fall to the floor. He spits in my face as I lay on the floor. The other animals follow his example and spit on me too. The spittle mixes with the blood coming from my nose.

He reaches down to grab me again, and my fingernails land deep in the flesh of his arms, ripping his skin, drawing blood. His grip grows tighter, and he throws his head back with enjoyment.

"That all you got?"

A scream springs from my soul. I am crying out to be rescued, but there is no prince for this princess. His arm smashes against my face sending me into a fit of dizziness. He silences me, covering my mouth with his sour, poisonous hand. Gasping for air, I choke and gag.

I bite down hard on his hand. His blood sprays in my mouth. It tastes rotten. He winces in pain, but it only further enrages this demon. He drags me like a lifeless corpse into a back room that smells of mold and urine. The laughter fades, and the door slams as he pins me against the wall.

"What do you want, little girl? Huh? Did you come here looking for a good time? I can give you a good time."

The smell of corn liquor pours out of his mouth. Gagging and choking, my mouth opens to hurl the contents of my stomach but nothing comes. He touches my lips with his forked tongue.

"I just want a loaf of bread for my sick momma!" I choke out.

"Is that all this will cost me? A loaf of bread? Do a good job, and I might give you two."

He throws me to the ground and lies on top of me, reaching for my clothes.

"This will only hurt for a little while."

I reach down deep inside myself and wail a kind of prayer.

"Oh, God, save me. Please save me."

My eyes blur. Faint shadows flicker across the ceiling. Other men have filed in to watch the show. I know I am going to die. Another scream, but my words have given up too. The world has become silent. It has transformed into still pictures. My body no longer hurts.

"Adanna. I am here with you."

I approach the golden chair.

"Am I home?"

"No, the time has not yet come."

"Please, do not make me go back."

"Remember, Adanna, who you are. Remember the meaning of your name and the gift I gave to you."

"Please make them leave me alone."

"Have faith, Adanna."

"What good is a gift if I can't understand it? What does the scroll say?"

"All I ask is for you to trust me."

"I do not know how to trust!"

I am rising over my body. Looking down, I see myself under a man who is more pig than a human. He has my skirt in his hand, tears it to pieces and throws it to the side. Two more men come into the room and catch my ripped clothing as if it were some sort of prize. They hold it and smell it.

Time leaps ahead or freezes. I see myself lying on the ground, not moving.

Quick as a cheetah, a figure darts into the room and crashes into the animal on me. The pig flies through the air as if hit by a speeding truck and crashes against the wall with a crunch. In an instant I am free. I cannot open my eyes and blood streams from my nose and mouth, but I am alive.

Glass breaks and furniture smashes into a million pieces as the other men run from the warrior. Everything around me dissolves and disappears.

Chapter Eight

After what seems like only minutes, I wake to discover that Charles has covered many miles. He tells me we're just outside the Swaziland capital, Mbabane. This looks nothing like the DRC. There are mountains and rolling hills every place the eye can see, short green grass and towering trees litter the landscape. This looks more like Ireland than the Sahara.

I hit the button, and the descending window cries out with a squeal.

Breathing deep, I'm amazed at the presence of budding flowers and clean air. It reminds me of the time I spent at a monastery in Southern California. The windows were open every evening and a continual waft of jasmine permeated the air. That may have been the only place I've felt peace.

"We're making a quick stop at the border, Mr. Daniels. In just a few minutes we'll be in the kingdom of Swaziland. Grab your passport and follow me."

"Right."

"Shouldn't take long."

My legs could use a good stretch.

The South African side of the border is a breeze to get through. They seemed happy to be rid of us. We walk a short distance to the

Swaziland side into a building. Two giant portraits hang on the wall.

"The dynamic duo you see there will be in almost every building you enter from this point forward," Charles blurts out. "Queen Mother and King Mswati."

"I guess along with royalty comes instant fame."

"You could call it that. It's more like forced worship. The queen mother runs the country; everyone knows it. Her son, the king, is merely a finger puppet."

"I'm sure he does all right for himself."

"You might say that. He has thirteen wives and all the money he could ever want."

"Everything he wants and no responsibilities. What a life."

The line is a slow-moving one since there's only one person checking passports. He sits behind the desk, smoking a cigarette, and his frown reveals how much he hates his job.

"He does have one responsibility," Charles says.

"Oh, what's that?"

"To drive across the country every year and find another wife."

"Yeah. Tough job."

"Every December, all the good-looking women he's found across the country gather to dance topless before him. The one that does the best job becomes his wife."

"You're kidding, right?"

"I am not kidding. Ancient pagan Swazi culture is still alive today in the twenty-first century."

"Being the king would be a young American fraternity boy's dream."

We finally make it to the front of the line and our passports are run through the computer and stamped. The agent never even looked at us.

The road into the capital is windy and gives me a touch of motion sickness. I reach into my bag and pop a Dramamine. One switchback after another leads us closer to town. The city is beautiful, fit for a king. It sits high on the mountain range, a fortress protected from its enemies by sheer elevation.

We quickly drive into the center of town, where large buildings loom and people cross the street in droves. Although it's filled with foreigners, it looks like other larger metropolitan areas. This should be an easy-enough story.

But as we exit the city and head toward the hotel, a dramatic shift occurs. Men and women in business suits are replaced by children. Dozens of them line the road in tattered clothing. A boy and girl no older than eight rummage through a garbage can. Their ribs poke out through the rags they've draped over their bodies.

I notice children carrying babies on their backs. They, too, look homeless and destitute. One young girl, baby strapped at her side, rushes to our car and cleans the windshield with an old shirt.

"They're wanting money. They are willing to do whatever it takes to eat. Clean the windshield, sell their body, it doesn't matter."

"How low can a human being stoop?"

"As low as it takes to survive, Mr. Daniels."

Two children, maybe three and four years old with no shoes and filthy from head to toe, stand in the street with their hands out.

"This is horrendous," I say, more to myself than to Charles.

"That's one way to describe it."

"I can't believe this is actually real."

"What do you think is happening over here? While you Americans complain that your steak isn't cooked properly, these children are starving in the streets!" Charles clearly no longer has any sense of reserve with me.

"They're everywhere—like ants." Then it hits me: There are so many children.

"Charles, where are their parents? Why so many children?"

"Mr. Daniels, the people here are lucky if they live past thirty."

We pass the hospital, a run-down three-story white building that looks like an abandoned bomb shelter from the Cold War. People lie on the ground like litter. It looks more like a soup line than a hospital waiting room.

A few elderly women stand by the street attempting to sell their handmade goods to those who pass their makeshift kiosks. Sitting at a stoplight, I look directly into an older woman's eyes. Her face is weathered, like old leather. She has the look of a horse that's been overworked to the point of utter physical exhaustion. And yet dignity and determination pour from her large, clear eyes.

The gate rattles open, welcoming us as Charles pulls up to a truly elegant hotel. It reminds me of simple '60s-style architecture in the United States—beautiful but dated.

"A little slice of America here in Swaziland, Mr. Daniels. This area is known as the Valley of Heaven."

It's nicer than I anticipated. I thought there was a good chance I'd be sleeping in the bush fighting off spitting cobras in the morning and drinking monkey blood with the natives in the evening. Thank God for small mercies. Maybe they'll even have beer on tap.

My mind flashes to my true feelings about this assignment. I don't think I can stomach taking pictures of half-dead people clutching onto their last few moments of life.

I think about what Big Bill, my boss, my friend, said before I left, and I can't help but flinch. He took me out for a liquid lunch and then dropped the bomb.

"Stuart, we'd like to keep you on here at the *Times*. Hell, everyone knows you took one of the most famous pictures of all time. You've got a great eye and nerves of steel. But your account is running low. I can't cover for you anymore. You gotta get it together, bring in some money shots, or you're done."

I just nodded my head. Then I started dumping all my marital woes on him. Even in my martini stupor, I could tell Bill didn't care. It's all business to him.

Life couldn't get much lower. Now here I am, thousands of miles from home. And yet ... I don't know what home is anymore.

"Stuart," a loud voice echoes across the lobby. It's my Swazi partner, Gordon. He gives me an enthusiastic handshake.

"Welcome to Swaziland, the land of AIDS and the highest rate of HIV infection in the world!"

"Hey, Gordon. Great to see you again." This guy is a vet. He started with the *Manchester Guardian*, then moved to the *Times*, and he traveled all over the world doing freelance gigs. He finally settled in Africa, so now he's the official South African correspondent.

The glasses he wears make him look older than he is, and his hair is completely white and a bit thinner than the last time I saw him. He's probably thinking the same thing about me, though it's still hard to tell with my midlife-crisis Jim Morrison hairdo. Gordon looks a bit like Einstein after a nap.

I've always liked him, even though he's an odd bird.

"The land of AIDS, huh? You say it like it's a medal of honor or something."

"No sense in hiding the truth, Stuart. The worst enemy is the one that's unexposed."

"True, but it's still a demented greeting."

"Oh, lots of things seemed that way when I moved here. After a time, the demented things just become a part of life. Death, starvation, disease, rape, incest—you'll get used to it."

I can't quite tell if he means it.

Something squawks a desperate plea for help behind me. I spin and see two monkeys running through the trees in hot pursuit of a third. My heart almost beats out of my chest.

Gordon erupts in laughter.

"Stuart, you look like you've seen a ghost!"

"That scared the crap out of me."

"Welcome to Africa. By the way, you don't look so hot. Why don't you get settled in your room, and I'll meet you in the lobby in an hour."

"I'm all right, just tired, man."

He gives me a pat on the shoulder.

"Make sure you have a BM."

"A what?"

"Do I need to spell it out for you, Stu? Take a good crap before we head out to the bush."

I laugh. "Yeah, I'll do that."

He turns and walks toward the bar. My kind of guy.

"I'll buy you a beer if you hurry up."

My mouth waters at the thought, and I quicken my pace.

The lobby echoes as I cross a white marble floor toward my room. A stone path lights my way, and there's a square green courtyard bordered by a few dozen rooms. I am mesmerized by the view. I see now why they call this the Valley of Heaven. Rolling hills and lush emerald green mountainsides give way to miles of fertile fields below. It's breathtaking. Who would have thought a place so filled with death could also be so beautiful?

I take a long, deep breath and exhale a few remaining carcinogens from New York. Clean air feels like a new car smells. I've almost forgotten what that's like.

The Mountain Inn is very un-African, at least the Africa I've experienced. The influence of English colonization is still strong in many places around the world. Swaziland is one of them. It's also a great way to keep the affluent happy and the undesirables away.

The room is a bit cramped and musty, but comfortable. The inside looks like a typical Motel 6. Two small beds, a lamp on a small desk, a coffeemaker with a few packets of Nescafé. I haven't seen that in years. The sounds of home reverberate via a television speaker broadcasting CNN International. Bad news is never too far away no matter how far an airplane takes you. Today it's another school shooting outside Beverly Hills.

Suddenly my BlackBerry jingles, telling me I have a new e-mail. I glance at my phone.

Bill.

All I have to do is think about this guy and he appears. Can't get away from him. I sit on the bed and take a breath before reading my impending doom.

Stuart,

Just a reminder from our last conversation: I need pictures that capture AIDS and the scope of the devastation. Get in there with the people. I know you can pull off this job!

Bill

Gotta love those backhanded compliments.

I'm still not feeling like myself, so I slip into the familiar jet-lag routine: Brush my teeth, slap ice-cold water on my face, and hope for a miracle. Charles' words echo in my ears. "Are you here to take photographs of our suffering people to display like animals?"

"You're the animal," I hear the voice in my head. "You are the animal."

Maybe I am.

My stomach suddenly tightens in a wave of fear, like a free fall in a dream. I sit in the chair and take a few sips of water. My head is throbbing, so I pop one of the anxiety pills Dr. Brandon prescribed along with an ibuprofen.

When Whitney and I first got married, we were madly in love. I had a career I loved, and money was flowing to me like a rushing river. Life could not have been better. I could do no wrong.

But then things started to change. I don't know when, exactly. It was a slow change at first. I just started to lose my motivation—for photography, travel, marriage, and life. I couldn't get out of bed in the morning and couldn't go to sleep at night. I hated the sun, didn't want to be around people, and, for reasons that continue to escape logic, couldn't care less about Whitney.

We were still sharing the same living space, but we'd been separated for weeks. I don't quite know what got me to accept this assignment—it certainly wasn't any resurgence of belief in myself. I can't even claim it was a last-ditch effort to salvage what was once a promising career. I just wanted to escape for a bit. Get some actual miles between the life I didn't recognize and an uncertain future.

If I didn't hate Africa so much, I might just stay here.

I pack my camera, lenses, and tripod into my smallest orange bag.

Downstairs, I walk backward to the lobby, taking in as much of the view as possible.

Gordon's waiting, flipping through a newspaper, the *Times of Swaziland*.

"You're looking better, Stuart. The car is waiting to take us to a place called Beckilanga. It's a care point where hundreds of kids, mostly orphans, come for food."

Guess the beer will have to wait.

We climb into a Pajero, a four-wheel-drive vehicle accustomed to taking a beating on the African terrain. Gordon and I sandwich in the back. His breath smells like gin, and his blue eyes are as bloodshot as mine.

"So what's up in the great Swaziland news today?"

"Terrible as usual. 'Man rapes eight-year-old sister.'"

"How barbaric."

"You have no idea. There's my house, right over there." Gordon points to a modest home behind an iron gate surrounded by a nine-foot wall of cinder block.

"Now that's what I call a wall. I thought it was safer here than in the big cities?"

"It is, Stu, but people here are still desperate. They try to steal the fruit from my trees, bananas, even leftover food in the garbage. I can't put trash outside a second before the trash man arrives or it will be scattered to the four winds by desperate, hungry foragers."

"How do you sleep at night? Aren't you afraid for your life?"

"Not really, but you can never really let down your guard. I certainly don't want to be stupid. Plus, my Rhodesian ridgeback scares the socks out of anyone who might be stupid enough to jump over."

"Mean as a pit bull?"

"These dogs were bred during apartheid to rip the testicles off any black men they encountered. I think they still feel the pain of the ancestors."

"Why did you move here? I mean, there are definitely shades of England, but it's not exactly as hospitable."

"Let me show you something." He pulls a wallet from a back pocket in his faded jeans and removes a picture. Looks like a family photo: Gordon, a beautiful white woman, and a gorgeous young black girl about the age of twelve with huge brown eyes. The girl is wearing flare-leg jeans, dark leather boots, and a bright striped shirt with a heart in the middle. Her skin is a medium brown and her smile could light up a city.

"This was my wife, Jo, and our daughter." He tenderly points to them both. "You might as well know."

"Know what?"

"Eh, never mind. It's a long story."

"I've got time."

Gordon takes in a long breath.

"After I did a story in Swaziland, we decided to move across the border into South Africa. At that time, it was just my wife and me. She fell in love with the place and the people. They were so warm and welcoming."

"Even as dangerous as it was?"

"It wasn't like this fifteen years ago. It was a wonderful place to live. AIDS was barely on the radar and most of the people were healthy and the culture was as rich and engaging as it had been for centuries."

Glancing out the window, the landscape drastically changes. We are no longer in the city. Rolling hills and stick-and-mud huts pepper the countryside. An iconic … and ironic pastoral scene that would be perfectly at home in *National Geographic.*

"Jo and I were high-school sweethearts. I loved her more than life itself, I tell you. We wanted a family in a terrible way, but found out we couldn't have children." He pauses, looks directly at me. "You really don't want to hear all this."

"Yes. I do. Please, keep going."

He turns to stare out of the window.

"After we moved to South Africa, we got involved in a small community with a friend of ours, Lynn. She had such a heart for kids. This area was poor, and I mean dirt poor. We started going down there every week to help them. We taught school, we cooked, we even taught them how to fish and swim. Actually, it was more like they taught us.

"As weeks turned into months, this one girl named Aisha stole our hearts. She had quite the bubbly personality and wonderful spirit. If we would have had a child, we both knew she'd be just like Aisha. Except, of course, she'd most likely be white."

We both laugh.

"Her dad had died a few years back. We never found out why. Then, her mother got sick. Within a month, she was dead. We were told it was TB. Now we wonder."

"You think it might have been AIDS."

"Yeah. Maybe. But we didn't know much about AIDS then. Anyway, we were told Aisha had no relatives, because they had migrated from Swaziland. She was left all alone. No protection, no food, nothing."

"I can't imagine a little girl having to live like that."

"It was terrible. It kept us up every night. One day, we concocted this crazy idea: What if we adopted Aisha? We went to Lynn, who had connections with the social-welfare office, and the next thing you know, she was our daughter."

"Just like that? Wow, that's incredible."

Whitney and I never were in sync about children. There was a time or two when I wanted to be a dad, but those coincided with the rare times she didn't want to be a mom.

"We had new life in our old bones. A little girl to call our own. Her name meant 'life,' and she brought so much life to us. In her smile, her funny sayings, even her temper tantrums. It was a wonderful time."

Was. Past tense. I don't like where this story is heading. Gordon takes another deep breath and his eyes begin to water.

"I was on assignment for the *Manchester Guardian* doing a story in Mozambique. There was a terrible famine that summer so I traveled north to cover it. While I was gone …"

He stops midsentence. I put my hand on his shoulder. He wipes a few tears from his eyes.

"You don't have to continue, Gordon. It's okay."

He doesn't seem to hear me.

"While I was away, a man broke into our house. Jo and Aisha weren't even supposed to be there. They were supposed to be on safari with friends from England, but they had to cancel at the last second because of a death in the family. This intruder … this demon in the guise of a man shot them both."

"I'm so sorry."

"After their deaths, I couldn't bear to live in that house anymore. I thought about moving back to England but couldn't do it. Jo and I always said we'd spend the rest of our lives in Africa and it just felt right to honor that dream. Since Aisha was from Swaziland, I decided to move here. I figured maybe I could still make a difference, you know?"

"You're a saint, Clandish."

"In the end, there was no real decision to make. It's what we would have done together. We both loved Africa, we cared about the people, and I had nowhere else to go."

"I don't think I could have done it. I don't think I could have stayed. I'd be too angry, too bent on revenge."

"It was all about the children, Stuart. I was never too much of a religious man, but through this experience, I sort of became one. And there was this verse in the Bible that stood out to me. 'Pure and undefiled religion is taking care of widows and orphans in their distress.' Well, you've seen the need. Someone had to help them. I figured I could be that someone."

"A saint, Gordon." Again he ignores my generous compliment. I suppose that's the way of saints.

As we near the community care point outside of the city of Manzini, I can't believe what I'm seeing. The wind blusters, angry at the world, throwing dust in every direction. In the distance, hundreds of children stand, lie on the ground, and rest beneath trees. It looks like a UN refugee camp. There's nothing for the children to do, no buildings, no fence to corral them, no tents, not a playground in sight, just barren land. I see the colorful headbands of two older women, sitting together in the dirt and knitting.

"What brings the children here?"

"They've come in hopes of getting a small meal," Gordon says. "But as often happens, the government and other relief agencies haven't delivered any food. When you're starving to death, even the *hope* of food is enough to make you walk five miles."

"How long has it been since they've eaten?"

"I believe it's going on four days now."

"Four days? That's insane. Why are they still here?"

"They have nowhere else to go, and the day isn't yet over. They're hoping food might still arrive. It's called hope against hope."

"This isn't at all like the lines I've seen at the soup kitchens back in the States." I barely get the words out as I'm raking a sandstorm out of my mouth.

"Soup would be a luxury here, my friend. The meal they eat is nothing more than corn with a tiny bit of beans. It's a mush called 'pap' and it's about as good as it sounds. But it's cheap. We've calculated it costs about seven cents per serving. One serving a day, five days a week, if they're lucky, comes to about a dollar forty per month."

Before I can calculate how many children I could feed simply by cutting back to one cup of Starbucks a week, a loud honk startles me and a brand-new Mercedes van speeds by on the rocky dirt road. "Food Vision" is written on the side.

"Food Vision. So where's the food?"

"That's what I want to know."

The distended stomachs of the children seem to pull the skin away from their bones. There is no light in their eyes. The thought of these kids playing soccer, going to ballet class, or eating a pot-roast dinner seems sadly laughable.

Instinct takes over, and I bring the camera up to my eye and start snapping. I offer a silent selfish prayer to a God I'm not sure I believe in. *Help these shots bring in some money. I've got to get my life back on track.*

We walk toward the trees where a hundred or more people are gathered.

"Stuart, I'd like to introduce you to Pastor Walter. He's the man responsible for the fact that all of these children are still alive, even though today things aren't working out quite so well."

Walter is short, about five-five. He hobbles over to me with a limp, and an enormous smile forms on his face revealing a row of straight white teeth. There is a big space where one of his front teeth ought to be. I find myself staring at the space instead of the man's bright eyes.

"It's a pleasure to meet you, Mr. Daniels. I've been praying for you since I heard you were coming." With his accent and clenched-mouth speech, my name sounds like "Dinnels."

"Praying for me?"

"God has something special for you here."

I sure hope so. I need that money shot.

"Well," I mumble, "I don't know what that means exactly, but it's nice to meet you anyway, Pastor. Thanks for what you're doing here."

It sounds stupid, but what else am I supposed to say? I wonder if this is what it would have been like to meet Mother Teresa. He sure doesn't look like what I'd expected, though I'm not quite sure what I expected. He just looks like an unpretentious man. Someone with no trappings.

My hand reaches for his, and he shakes mine while holding his forearm with his free hand. I seem to recall reading about this somewhere. A sign of respect? As if I know what I'm doing, I grab my forearm too.

"Thank you, thank you, my brother. All the honor is God's. Without Him, you see, we could do nothing for these wonderful children. Or for ourselves. Times are hard in our country. But we know God has not forgotten us, and He will see us through."

Walter's accent is thick and hard to understand.

Gordon says, "Walter, tell Stuart your story."

"It is not my story. It is the story of these people." He spreads his arms wide, as if reaching to the ends of the earth for a hug. There is a long pause. It is as if this says all that needs to be said. Perhaps it does.

"I think it's okay to elaborate a bit, Walter."

Walter smiles and turns toward me.

"When I started seeing the many, many people dying in our community, it broke my heart. AIDS has made life in my country very bitter. I used to stand in my church and tell the people about God's goodness. But one day I looked around and saw so many orphaned children filling my building, and every single one of them was hungry. This didn't feel like God's goodness. These children had no one to help them, no one to turn to but our church.

"One day some children were lying in the corner of our church during the service. After the service was over and everyone filtered out, one child remained. I thought to myself, this little one is so very tired. I went to wake him up, but he was not sleeping."

A gorgeous little girl skips to Walter's side, throwing her arms around his legs. She has on a filthy yellow dress, and her eyes sparkle like sunshine. Her hair is cut short. I wonder if it's to prevent lice. He puts his arm on her bony shoulder.

I can see the pain on Walter's face.

"It was a wake-up call for me. God's goodness didn't just happen because I talked about it. I realized that I had to act. So I started to pray, 'God, send me people who have the ability and the finances to help us.' And you know what God said to me? He said, 'Walter, what's in your pocket? Start giving to these children out of what you have, and I will take care of the rest.' And that's exactly what has happened. There were many nights when my own children went hungry because other children in our community would die without something to eat. Maybe my kids were a bit skinnier because of that, but we kept other children alive."

"Stuart, Pastor Walter and I were talking yesterday, and he feels it would be a good idea for you to see some of the people in his community. See what their life is like and how they live. If you want photographs of real people in real circumstances, this is the best way to go about it."

"Yes, my brother, I feel like it would be a good idea to visit my friend Samson. He suffers with the HIV virus and will talk about it. He lives just a short way up the hill."

We climb into the car, and I change lenses on my camera as we travel across the bumpy road. I could do this upside down on a roller coaster. I'm a little nervous, though. I've never actually seen a HIV-infected person up close.

A few minutes later, we pull up to a run-down shack in the middle of a small grove of short trees. Someone took a few sticks and a whole lot of mud and slapped this thing together. The corrugated tin roof on the mud hut is held down by about ten large rocks. The edges of the roof are flapping and banging in the wind, and it looks like it could fly off at any second. This is not a home fit for a human.

My camera's eye blinks rapidly, capturing every angle.

We step inside and are confronted by the acrid smell of rotten potatoes. There's a very small living area and one other room, which looks like the bedroom. The whole place is about twenty feet by twenty feet. There's no electricity. Small shafts of sunlight pouring in through holes in the roof provide the only illumination. There's no sign of life.

"Samson, my brother, are you here?" Walter says.

There's no reply.

"Samson!" Still nothing.

An eerie feeling lingers.

Walter walks into the second room, and Gordon and I sit on rickety old stools. As much as I know about how HIV works, I still can't shake the feeling that the house is contaminated. I try not to touch anything. Footsteps shuffle in the other room. We hear small whispers. Gordon is scanning the room and writing in a beat-up notebook that looks like something he's carried with him since the fifth grade.

"That's a good sign," Gordon says in a loud whisper.

A few minutes later Walter emerges.

"He's coming. He is very weak. Samson has not been doing so well these past few weeks. I'm really worried for him. He refuses to take ARVs and is totally dependent on God's healing power for his recovery. How can I convince him otherwise?"

Samson lumbers out of his bedroom to meet us. He balances his weight on a weathered cane and takes slow, painstaking steps. Gordon, who typically moves with the tact of a wild boar, walks over to him, tenderly places his arm underneath Samson's, then around the small of his back and practically carries him to the broken-down sofa chair in the corner of the room.

It seems to take him ten minutes just to sit down and gather himself.

I don't know what to say or do. I'm way out of my element.

Finally, it's Samson who speaks. His eyes are vivid, alive with life. But his body is broken, a shadow of what I imagine it used to be. He holds onto the cane to keep his body upright, but his hands are shaking. He looks like he could snap in half at any second.

"Hello, my brother. It is an honor to meet you. I have been praying for you to come all the way from the United States."

"It's good to meet you, too." He's been praying for me?

Gordon is scratching away with his pen.

"Samson is as strong as a bull in his spirit and character," Walter says. "He may not look like it from the outward appearance, but let your spirit see what your eyes cannot. Some time ago, he was not a good man. He was a truck driver, and he would sleep with women he met at rest stops. That's how he contracted the HIV virus."

"It's something I'm not proud of," Samson whispers.

"But this man loves God. He has changed his life and believes God will heal him. In this life, or the life to come." Pastor Walter sounds like Martin Luther King.

"I want the world to know I'm a human being," Samson says. "Although I have a terrible disease, I still have feelings, I still have fears, and I'm still a child of God. It's a very strange thing when you're sick and your entire community, people who have known you for years, treat you like a leper."

I nod, and my eyes focus on a handful of strange-looking spots spread out on his face. They look like boils.

"I want you to take my picture. And under the picture, I want you to write, 'The body of Christ is suffering.'"

Of all the shots I've taken, this may well be the strangest. This dying, dirty, man, stinking of death, wants me to take his portrait.

He stands up straight, bracing himself against the wall. There are two photos hanging behind him.

"Samson, who are those two people?" I need to know for the shot.

"That's my mother and father. Both dead. Both from AIDS. My

father contracted the disease and came home and passed it to my
mother."

He stands as still as he can and musters a slight smile. He wants
the world to know something.

"And now," Samson says, "I want you to pray for me."

"Oh, I'm just a photographer, from the *Times*. I really don't
know much about praying. I, I just, well, Walter will pray. He's the
pastor."

Walter looks at me. "Go on, Stuart. Pray for this man. He's been
waiting for you for weeks. We will pray with you."

I feel a tingle up my back, like the moment following a near-miss
collision with a bus. Pastor Walter grabs my hand and walks me over
to Samson. I am shaking. I haven't prayed out loud since Sunday
school.

My hand rests lightly on Samson's frail shoulder, and I open my
mouth, begging God to fill it.

Then it's over, and I'm not even sure what I said. Samson has
tears running down his face. With a heart of gratitude he places his
hand on mine.

"You have done a great service for me, and I thank you. May
God repay you for your good deed."

Good deed? I am not good. But for some reason, I feel like I am
in the presence of a great man.

Maybe God knows something about him I don't.

Chapter Nine

A hand of salvation rescues me from my prison.

Gently he pulls me into the freedom of his arms. He places his jacket over my shoulders to cover my nakedness. He's breathing hard from his battle and has a bloody scratch over his eye.

He is beautiful.

"You have nothing to fear now, little one. I am here, and I will protect you."

I fall into his arms, and see that he is Tagoze. Then everything goes dark again.

○■◇◆●——●◆◇■○

Tagoze is the brother of the village chief. One day after Daddy left, he came to check on us and bring us corn, bananas, bread, and sweets. Abu was in Momma's belly and had not yet come.

Momma said, "Mmm, that Tagoze is a good man. God has His hand on him. His reputation is clear, and his heart is gold. Adanna, there are not many men like him here in our village."

Here everyone is born poor. The only way out of this curse is to be born into the chief's family. Tagoze was one of those blessed individuals. He is like royalty.

But Tagoze refuses to live like a chief's brother. Many people believe that if it were in his power, no one would ever go hungry, and no one would ever be sick. He does not think himself better than anyone else, and he always gives to those in need.

Tagoze wasn't always this way. He used to be a bad, selfish man. Before the accident that took his family, he followed the path of many men in our town, drinking all day and night, refusing to work, and carrying on with women. Some said they often heard his wife scream from the beatings he gave her. It is hard for me to believe these stories, but Momma tells me they are true.

One day, his world was turned upside down. As we heard it told, Tagoze's son, Kgosi, who was only six years old, started a fire in their house. He was playing with the oil stove late in the evening while his sisters and mother were sleeping. They had left it on to provide heat because it was so cold outside.

The house exploded in fire. Tagoze's wife came running out of the house engulfed in flames. She died later that same night. The children were already dead.

On Sunday at church, Tagoze sobbed and sobbed, some say for over four hours. Some days passed and people wondered how he would live. But after much time with Pastor Walter, he had become someone new. Someone who cared about all of us.

O■◊♦●————●♦◊■O

My eyes will not stay open. In moments, I catch a glimpse of light through tiny slits. But everything is blurred and milky white. I should sleep.

I hear my sister and brother playing nearby. I know without

seeing what they are playing with: a weathered, rusty soda can, a faint "Coca-Cola" written on the front.

I lift my hand to rub the sleep from my eyes, but it triggers a ferocious pain, like a cat's claw down my face. I pat my cheek with my open hand. Raw and swollen, it feels twice its normal size.

Things are clearer now. I try to focus on the walls of my home. I hear voices, two men's voices and my auntie, right outside the front door.

"Why do you think the child went into that place?" It is Pastor Walter.

"Maybe she was looking for someone. Perhaps her father." I hear the deep, clear voice of Tagoze. "I have the death of another man on my soul now, but I cannot feel remorse for the creature who was defiling that little girl."

So the animal is dead. I lift my head so I can hear better. Precious and Abu see me stir and move closer. My brother, Abu, is almost three, and my sister, Precious, is four, almost five. Their presence brings a smile to my battered face.

"Hi, Abu. Precious, where is Momma?" My voice sounds as if it belongs to someone else, scratchy and deep like the lady in our village who smokes.

Abu reaches up to touch my face, and a scream bursts from my mouth.

My auntie darts through the door. Pastor Walter and Tagoze come in behind her.

Her face looks pinched and puffy, like she has been crying.

"Adanna, are you all right, my child?"

"Auntie, Auntie. Oh, it hurts so bad. What are you doing here?"

"Sweet baby, it is okay. Just lie still."

"Where is Momma?"

"She is away."

"But where is she? I need her. She should be home." I start to cry, but no tears, no sound comes out. My stomach jumps in and out, and the pain is fierce.

"Your uncle Malako and I have taken her over to our home to look after her for a bit. She is very tired, Adanna."

The great bird of fear lurks close by. Something is speaking in my ear, telling me things are not right.

She turns her eyes away. When grown-ups do this, I know things are wrong. She wrings her hands together in a strange way.

"Is something the matter? Did she touch a moon rock? Auntie, please tell me."

Pastor Walter kneels down next to my bed.

"My dear little sister, I am so sorry for what happened to you."

Auntie turns to my brother and sister. "Precious, you and Abu come outside with me and give your sister some peace and quiet!"

I have a terrible feeling inside. It is worse than the pain from what happened to me.

"Adanna, your momma did not touch a moon rock, but she is sick. We will help her and be with her, and pray to God for a miracle. But first, I want to pray for you."

Tagoze kneels beside me and closes his eyes as Pastor Walter prays.

"God, may Your mercy and blessing and healing come upon Adanna. Amen."

I turn my head toward Tagoze. I can see the mean scratches across his face. They are no longer bloody because they have been cleaned.

"Thank you."

I am more tired than I have ever been. I fall back into a dark sleep with no dreams.

I wake to a great pain in my stomach. I try to stand, but I double over, my outstretched hands narrowly stopping me from falling on my face. My mouth starts to water, and I feel like I'm going to throw up. But still there's nothing in my stomach, so it is another gagging fit. I hate these fits.

Auntie comes rushing over and helps me back onto the bed.

"There, child. Let me get you some water." She puts little drops on my lips. "You have slept for two whole days."

I try to sit up. Auntie sits beside me, lending me her big shoulder to lean against.

Life and hunger must be brother and sister.

My earliest memories of my auntie are good. She was always kind and tender. She would be considered wealthy in our community. The sign of wealth in our country is a fat woman who has plenty to eat. That's my auntie. One person said if she ever died, they'd have to bury her in an empty piano case, whatever that means. She tells us she is as poor as everyone else. That her body just works different, that's all.

Auntie brought some food for us. We won't go hungry tonight. But it is lonely without Momma here. It doesn't feel safe. Our door has no lock. I eat a small amount of food and start to feel better. My face feels more like normal, though I still cannot stand to touch it.

"Adanna, I must go to my home now and take care of things."

"Can we come with you, Auntie?"

"No, we do not have room for all of you. You are a big girl. You can watch out for your brother and sister."

"Auntie, when will we eat? Are you going to bring food to us?"

"I will try. When your uncle and I have something extra to share, I'll make sure he brings it by. You'll still need to go to school even though your mother is away. I want to make sure you and Precious are out the door on time."

"Did Momma not tell you?"

"Tell me what?"

"We have not been to school in over a month."

"Why wouldn't you be in school?"

"There is no money. Momma said she couldn't afford to send us to school so we would have to wait."

"Shame! Not sending your own children to school. I'll talk to your principal and see what I can do."

"Thank you, Auntie."

"Now, I will help you all get ready for bed, and then I must go."

After Abu and Precious are tucked away, Auntie kisses my head. Then she picks up her bags and says, "Don't come to our home unless we call for you. Understand?"

"Yes, ma'am."

"Good. Good night then, sweetheart."

"Night."

○■◇◆●———●◆◇■○

Feels strange without Momma here; it is too quiet, empty, lonely.

For two days, I have heard nothing from Auntie. No one has come to our place, and I am still so weak. Abu cries most of the day because he is hungry. I did pick some sour berries off of a tree that don't taste very good. They cure the hunger pangs, but they give us terrible diarrhea.

Abu has to eat this morning; he can't wait another day. I made a promise to myself that I wouldn't come back until I have food in my hands. Kilometers from our home, I find berries that aren't so sour, a gold mine! There are two bushes glowing with the round, green fruits. Almost two handfuls end up in my shirt and I'm proud of my find. It feels good to be a provider for my brother and sister.

But the berries will not be enough. I walk to Pastor Walter's home.

Even as I knock on Pastor Walter's door, shame overwhelms me. I should not be here. But what other choice do I have?

"Adanna, good morning. I'm glad to see you walking around today. Please come in."

"Thank you, Pastor." I stare at the floor. I am not sure what to say and am angry at myself for coming.

"Are you okay? What is the matter?"

"I didn't know where else to go. I … I was just trying to get some food. I went to that place to see if anyone would give me money. Momma needed food. I thought I would find kindness …"

"Is that what you need, dear?"

"Well, Momma is with Auntie, but Precious and Abu don't have enough to eat. I found some berries … but I don't think it will be enough."

"Sweet Adanna, just come to Pastor Walter from now on when you need something, do you understand?"

"Yes."

Pastor Walter goes to a small can in the corner of his kitchen and opens the lid. He tries to hide what he sees, but I can tell the can is nearly empty. He scoops what is left into his hands and offers it to me. I can't take it.

"Here, girl, you take this right now and go feed your family."

"But, I—"

"I'll hear nothing else, now go."

"Thank you, Pastor."

Pastor Walter just gave me the last of his food. His own children will go hungry tonight.

"Adanna? It's Uncle. Are you here?"

Uncle Malako is not at all like my uncle Sipo. He scares me. There's something about him that's just not right. He's got a strange look in his eye.

"I'm here."

"Adanna, my sweet, it's so good to see you."

He comes through the door, grabs my hand and rubs it over and over. It makes me tremble.

"Have you been missing your uncle Malako?"

I'm silent, so he sits close to me. He rubs his hand on my leg and pulls my skirt up to put his hand on my thigh. There's something wrong with him. Has he been hanging around those ugly men by the store?

"Just relax and let Uncle hold you and I will give you the biggest piece of candy you've every seen. Oh yes, I have a surprise for you."

I want to run away. I imagine kicking him or punching him and wonder if I could actually do that.

Someone makes noise outside.

"Adanna!"

Precious skips into the room.

Malako jumps to his feet so fast, it's like he just saw a cobra slither across the floor.

"Oh, hi, Uncle. Adanna, there are some foreigners in our village. Can we go see them?"

"Not just yet little one," my uncle says. "I came to take all of you to see your mother. Where is Abu?"

"He is with the white men in the village."

"Go get him and then come to my home."

"Okay, Uncle."

I start to follow Precious. Uncle Malako calls after me.

"Adanna, stay here. I want to talk to you."

Pretending not to hear him, I run down the hill.

Abu is in the arms of a tall white man. Foreigners come to visit two or three times a year. All of the children like it because they hand out candy and gifts. Candy is a rare treat, and I take it like everyone else, but it is not enough. It is not what we need. If they would just give us money instead of candy, we could buy real food.

"Abu, we have to go! Come quickly, we are off to see Mother."

He jumps down with a thud. We all grab candy from the strangers.

"Thank you," I say quietly.

"Say thank you," I urge Abu and Precious.

"Thank you," they yell out.

The tall white man catches my gaze before I turn to walk away. I cannot read the expression in his eyes. Most of these white men have big smiles and say things like "God loves you." This one says nothing.

Our uncle and auntie live about a kilometer from our home. The temporary happiness the candy provides is replaced by a sad, worrisome thought of Momma. Fear also fills my stomach because of Uncle Malako. I am terrified of what would have happened if Precious had not burst into the room.

Their home is just ahead, but I stop short of it. It's not built out of sticks and mud like our home, but out of expensive concrete blocks. It's much bigger and has two rooms instead of one. I do not want to go in because of what I might see. The thought of anything happening to Momma is too much to bear.

"Adanna, why are you standing there? Go inside. What is the matter with you?" My uncle has come out of nowhere. He pushes me through the door.

Momma is lying in the corner of the room. Her eyes have a funny yellow look, and she is as thin as a cow during a famine.

"Oh, Momma, are you okay?"

Using all the strength she can muster, she sits up in bed, then raises her hand to stroke the back of my head. She is trying to look strong. But I know what this means. My momma will die soon.

Tears pour out of my eyes. I cannot stop them. There is nothing to stop Momma from dying, and soon we will be all alone in this world. Me, Precious, and Abu. Nobody will care for us or love us again.

I wish there was something to do to make her pain go away. If only I had a magic wand, I would wave it, and my mother would be well. She would not have to die. If God really cared, He would wave His magic wand and heal her. Maybe He's too busy to see Momma. Or maybe He just doesn't care.

This world is cruel, and it is mean. And I hate it.

Chapter Ten

The sun, a gigantic orange orb, sneaks behind the mountains to get some rest. As it disappears, a remnant glow paints the sky in colors both soft and brilliant. Perhaps this was indeed the garden of Eden, as some claim.

I'm enjoying an ice-cold Heineken and checking out a brunette in a tiny red bikini while I upload the pictures I took today. The brunette doesn't seem to notice me, and I'm glad for that. I don't really want her to see me. I'm not even sure why I'm staring.

I've never seen a slower Internet connection in my life. This thing can't be uploading any faster than 14K. I've tried the company's FTP server, normally much faster. Apparently, this is not true in Africa.

Merely looking around the hotel, I could almost convince myself I was still in the good old U.S. of A. However, the picture on my laptop assures me I'm not. I'm looking at a dying man, dirty clothes hanging from skin and brittle bones, alone in a shack I wouldn't use for storing junk. But it is not the poverty that speaks to me in this photo. It is the man's smile. It is not a smile of joy, but of dignity. Dignity in the face of impending, certain death. I can't wrap my mind around this crazy photo session. And the things he said? About waiting for me to come from the United States? About God?

I wonder how a man who is barely human can speak so well of a

God who doesn't seem to care. No one should have to die like that. Alone.

This becomes my wish for this man. That he would not die alone. I think of my wish and how much it is like a prayer. But I do not lob it at God.

As I wait for the pictures to upload, I take a quick peek at my e-mails. Junk mail, spam, late-bill notices, and then one from Whitney.

I suddenly hear Coldplay blaring from my BlackBerry.

"Hello?"

"Hey, Stu. It's Gordon. Are you ready?"

"Yeah, just give me a few minutes to get my stuff together, and I'll meet you downstairs."

Gordon had lined up a dinner with someone from the Swazi government. He wants to interview her for the story.

"I've already ordered dinner for the three of us. They like to have everything made ahead of time."

"So, most of the Swazi people don't have any food, but those who do, eat like kings."

"That's pretty much the deal, Stu. And it will be some of the best food in all of Swaziland."

A half hour later, I head down, hair still wet, to join Gordon and a beautiful woman who carries herself like a queen. Her head is wrapped in a traditional silk headscarf woven with diamond patterns of purple, green, and yellow. Her dress flows to her ankles.

She stands as I approach the table.

"Stuart, this is Sipwe."

"Nice to meet you. I'm sorry I'm late." This is nothing new for me.

"No worries, dear boy, haven't you heard of African time? It's a rare occurrence when anyone is prompt."

"Yes, I have been forewarned. But I think that rule applies to Africans, not Americans. Please forgive me."

Her green eyes seem to look right into my thoughts.

Gordon had already ordered red wine, and I'm happy to have it. Sipwe's jewelry is yellow turquoise, like nothing I've ever seen, with streaks of black running in each piece. Whitney would love it.

Our waiter rounds the corner, pushing a cart carrying several large, covered silver trays. He's dressed in a busboy suit reminiscent of the 1940s—a black and white ensemble complete with bow tie, perfectly polished patent leather shoes, and a coat with tails. I'm waiting for Charlie Chaplin to come skittering around the corner. The waiters and waitresses are all African, and they call Gordon and me "boss." I don't like it. I feel like I've time-warped back to the days before the American Civil War. I am hyperaware of all this in the presence of Sipwe. I'd swear this was a movie.

The waiter meticulously sets each silver tray in front of me, his service perfect. The lifted lids reveal a smorgasbord of delectable cuisine. A Caesar salad with fresh Parmesan cheese and cracked pepper, a ten-ounce filet mignon smothered in a pepper-mushroom demi-glace, and sides of garlic mashed potatoes and fresh, grilled asparagus with lemon on the side.

A meal like this would be affordable in most places, but here in Swaziland, it costs a fortune. Thank God for expense accounts.

"Stuart, what is your view of people infected with HIV?" Sipwe turns toward me. Gordon has a smirk on his face. I can tell he loves this kind of exchange.

"I'm not sure what you mean."

"I mean what do you think about them? How do you see them? What do you say to yourself in secret that nobody else hears?"

"That's a fair question. For most of my life, I have to say I've viewed HIV as a voluntary disease, affecting homosexuals and drug users. I avoided anything to do with it like the plague. No pun intended."

I cut a huge piece of the filet and watery-red juices squirt and ooze in the center of the plate. It is cooked to perfection.

"Quite a harsh response, don't you think?"

I look over at my writer friend. "Gordon, aren't you supposed to ask the questions?"

"You should be a journalist, Sipwe," he says, but he doesn't come to my rescue.

"Yes, perhaps I should be. I think it is a fair question to ask the man who has taken pictures of suffering people what he thinks about this insidious, silent, and slow executioner."

Sipwe is all business. We start to eat. I take my first bite, steam pouring out—Gordon was right, this has to be the best food in Swaziland, maybe some of the best food I've ever tasted. But as I slowly chew the buttery-tender steak, I can't get the images of those kids out of my head. I see them sitting in their huts tonight, their bones poking out of frail skin, making them look like wooden puppets. One of the side dishes on my plate would feed a half dozen of them. I pick at the food, mulling my response for a moment. After a mouthful of potatoes, I set my fork down and begin.

"Over the years my view has changed. I'm not quite so naive as I once was. And being here for a short few days has given me a new compassion for the victims of HIV/AIDS." I picture the two young children I saw standing alone in the middle of the road on my first travel day. "It's so hard to see the children who are left alone and who are infected."

"Is it only the children you have compassion for?"

"Well, certainly them above all others. The adults? Well, I still find it hard to believe anyone practices polygamy when they know it's killing them. How do women put up with it? Surely they have a choice. It makes no sense."

"Stuart," Gordon says, "that is what Sipwe is working toward in Swaziland, in all of Africa. Women *don't* have a choice here."

Sipwe squeezes my arm, her thick bracelets pressing against me.

"There is no such thing as a woman's right. A woman doesn't have the right to make her own decisions nor to tell her husband she will not have sex with him. If she did, he would beat her, and she would be shamed."

I am left to ponder this and other difficult-to-understand truths while I push food around my plate, then finally give up on what should have been an amazing meal.

During a pause in the conversation, I'm startled by the reappearance of the waiter. He has brought dessert—a twenty-year-old tawny port and a homemade slice of New York–style cheesecake with strawberries and whipped cream. I glance down at Gordon's plate. It is empty, and he seems primed for dessert.

Perhaps you do get used to the poverty.

Sipwe lifts her wine glass, stares into it for a moment, then continues.

"People here don't realize what they're dealing with," she says. "Most people in our country are uneducated about how this virus is spread. And when you have to decide between eating food—food that your husband provides, mind you—or having him beat you and leave you to die because you won't sleep with him, what would you do?"

She takes a sip of her wine and turns toward Gordon.

"This is why we have to do a better job with education. It takes time and years of mobilized effort to overcome generations of ignorance."

Now it's Gordon's turn to fire.

"So what are your greatest needs? How would you ask the world for help?" He reopens his notepad.

"This is a complicated question. First, we need compassion. We need people to care. If they care, they will go the extra distance to join us in our struggle. Of course we need teachers to help us educate and improve our schools. Some of our best teachers have died, and the rest are dying. It's a very big problem. AIDS is a disease that kills the strong."

"But, Sipwe," I say, "how do you allay people's fear of AIDS? I mean, how do you inspire people to come when the situation is so dire, so ... and please excuse my bluntness ... so ugly."

"Is that how you are experiencing it?"

"It is hard to take. I'll admit that. I met a man today—a dying man. There is nothing that can be done for a man like that. It makes me feel helpless, and I don't like feeling helpless."

"Gordon told me about your meeting with Samson." She takes a sip of wine. "Shame, a man like that dying all alone. What's even sadder is that there are millions more like him."

"His pastor is trying to look out for him, but there are so many."

"So, Stuart," Sipwe's eyes lock into mine, "how do you see me? What do you think of me so far?"

I'm not quite sure how to respond. "You remind me of a friend I have from the DRC. Her name is Wangari, and she is working for her people as you are, trying to give people a voice and put an end to the horrible violence there. I haven't known you long, but I have a lot of respect for you."

"Thank you, Stuart. I am honored to be compared to one of your friends. Perhaps you will change your mind when you know the truth about me."

"What do you mean?"

"I am infected with HIV."

"No! But how?" I immediately wish I could take back my stupid response.

"I realize I'm not the stereotypical AIDS victim."

Gordon tries to cover for me. "It never occurs to people, to people like Stuart and me, that someone like you would have HIV." Gordon obviously already knew about Sipwe, but I appreciate his gesture.

"HIV does not care who its next victim is. I'm a respectable woman and have been a faithful wife to my husband all these years. He, on the other hand, was not so faithful. A high-powered job with the government went straight to his head. He was promising me one thing and doing another. On one very dark, very sad night, he came home to our bedroom and infected me with death. I had no idea until months later."

Gordon continues to scribble away in his notebook.

"How did you find out?"

"A common cold that wouldn't go away. I'd never really been sick much. But this cold turned into pneumonia, and I ended up at the hospital. They knew what caused it, but didn't want to tell me. It's that way with everyone who has HIV. After a few blood tests, it was confirmed."

"How did you deal with the news?"

"It has changed my life forever, no doubt. But I decided I wasn't going to waste away and die alone in some miserable corner." She places her hand on my arm again, "No disrespect to your friend Samson. Some of us have only one choice. I made up my mind the day I found out, that I would be a survivor."

"What spurs you to keep going?"

"My dream. My dream is to educate every man, woman, and child in our country about the devastating affect of AIDS. I want them to know how it spreads and how they can survive if they contract it. I want women to have the courage and support to say no to unfaithful husbands. I want to do my part to see the end of HIV's destructive power in my generation and watch as a new generation rises up to be free."

"That's quite a dream. But is it realistic?"

"Aren't we all believing in something, Stuart?" Gordon raises his eyebrows at me.

The red line swirls in the crystal glass. I bring it to my lips and drink down the last drops.

I haven't touched the cheesecake. The waiter appears suddenly again and waits for me to acknowledge him before speaking.

"Sir, is the dessert not to your liking?"

"I'm sure it's fine. Everything was fine. I'm just not very hungry tonight."

I pull out my chair. "Why don't you two finish your interview, and I'll get my camera. I'd like to take your picture outside, on the deck."

"Sure, Stu. I'll order us up some tea for outside."

"Coffee for me. Remember, I'm American."

I can't help but wonder what keeps these people going. Death lives in their bodies, it rots them away, one cell at a time. And yet, some—like Sipwe—still find reasons to hope while grasping onto the ledge with their fingernails.

The upper balcony will be perfect for the photo shoot. There is good light, even at night. The moon is full, and its rays will give the photo an ethereal quality—to match the ethereal nature of this rare woman.

The waiters have brought out tea and coffee in what looks like the queen's silver.

"Sipwe, why don't you stand over here, near the doorway."

Looking through my lens, she seems to be shrouded in other-worldly light.

I hear dogs barking in the distance. The guard dogs are keeping the enemy away. I snap off photos, more than I'll need. My instinct tells me any of these photos will work. Some people have that look.

Making a gentleman's advance, Gordon holds his hand in the air for Sipwe. She obliges, arises gracefully, and walks beside him, as if they were old friends.

"Stuart, let's walk. We can't pass up this night."

Gordon's right. The moon blazes above the mountains like a giant spotlight. For some reason it seems bigger here. We press forward into the night.

The wind blows leaves in concentric circles and brings a chill. Sipwe draws her wrap tightly around her shoulders.

I strain to hear a sound that comes and goes with the turn of the evening breeze.

"Do you two hear that?"

"What, the traffic? It never stops here," Gordon says.

"No, no, it sounds like singing."

As we walk, the two rangy white men and the African queen, the voices become more distinct.

The music is coming from a block or two up the road.

"Do you think it's a festival?" I ask Sipwe. "A wedding maybe? Certainly not a funeral."

We turn toward a building alive with the music.

Sipwe takes my arm.

"It's a church service, Stuart. All over our country, people go to the church on a Sunday night."

"So many?"

"The people here are deeply religious," Gordon says. "Many are superstitious and worship their ancestors. They're called Zionists. It's a mix between Christianity and ancestral worship. They run either to Jesus or to the witch doctors. Pastor Walter is trying to fight against this messy religion in the villages around his church."

"Mr. Daniels," Sipwe says, stopping. "Our country is experiencing so much brokenness, church is the only place people can put the broken pieces back together."

We enter a small sanctuary. It is stark, with simple chairs and no curtains on the windows.

The room is a sea of children and older women. Many are in bad shape, mere skeletons. It's the same look Samson has, bulging eyes and jutting bones. Some are content to sit in the corner on an old mat, many are standing. And every one of them is singing.

The music, the voices … I've never heard anything like it. They sing at the tops of their lungs and dance like nobody's watching. Spontaneous prayer is heartfelt and passionate.

I feel as if I've entered another world.

I think of a verse my grandmother taught me, one of the few I still remember. "Blessed are the poor in spirit, for theirs is the kingdom of heaven."

I'm standing in the kingdom of heaven.

The music comes to a crescendo, and everyone joins hands. The sick, the lame, the healthy. My heart pounds hard and fast. I do not want to hold hands with these people.

A little girl approaches me. Her dress is a corrupted version of a once-new pink princess dress, white frills at the bottom turned brown. Looking deep into my eyes and smiling, she holds out her hand. I cast an uncertain glance to Gordon. He nods. I lock hands with this little girl and close the circle.

The crowd moves to its knees in a hum of thanksgiving to their God. I move with them. My lips begin to sing, though I don't know the words or the tune. Peace and sorrow course together through my being.

Somehow, a velvet voice penetrates the din.

"Stuart, feed My sheep."

I know this voice. But it has been so long.

Tears form in my eyes, and these tiny hands, locked in mine, will not let me wipe them away.

As the service ends, we shake hands with so many people. Some offer hugs, and I accept them. Only a moment ago we were strangers, now we seem like friends.

"Anything special happen to you tonight, Stuart?" Sipwe is as observant as she is smart. My cheeks flush.

"What do you mean?"

"I know what it looks like when God speaks to a man. And that look rested on your face tonight."

A tingle races down my spine, but I have no words.

Chapter Eleven

◆◇■ Adanna ■◇◆

The early-morning screeching of chickens makes me crazy when I want to sleep. It is still dark, but not even squeezing my eyes together and tapping my foot, something that usually helps me find sleep, will stop the thoughts spinning in my mind. I do not want to get up today.

Auntie D talked to our principal, and she let me and Precious come back to school. Abu stays a couple days a week with friends who live farther away. They say this is better for Abu since I don't know how to take care of a baby anyway.

My teacher, Miss Ncondu, is no longer at the school. She was stooped over like an old woman yet she was not old. When she read stories, like my favorite, "How the Crocodile Got Its Skin," she used different voices and made funny faces. She also read us beautiful poems, and one made me cry. I remember this poem well, because I memorized it.

AFRICA

A thousand years of darkness in her face,
She turns at last from out the century's blight
Of labored moan and dull oppression's might,

To slowly mount the rugged path and trace
Her measured step unto her ancient place.
And upward, ever upward towards the light
She strains, seeing afar the day when right
Shall rule the world and justice leaven the race.

Now bare her swarthy arm and firm her sword,
She stands where Universal Freedom bleeds,
And slays in holy wrath to save the word
Of nations and their puny, boasting creeds.
Sear with the truth, O God, each doubting heart,
Of mankind's need and Africa's gloried part.

I made the mistake of asking the new teacher where Miss Ncondu had gone. This skinny man came up to me—his eyes meet mine, he is so short—and wagged his finger in my face.

"Children don't ask after adults! You can stand in the back of the room until school is finished."

Yesterday, after a terrible rage, he forced us to stare at him without looking away. Turning your head was punished by several lashes from a jacaranda switch. He reads from a book and then talks, it seems, to someone outside the window. He is not right. The other day, he slowly pulled his shirtsleeve up past his forearm, then raked his long, dirty, fingernails across the blackboard. A crazy smile crossed his face, like on one of our spooky tribal masks. We all shook in our seats. My hands wanted to cover my ears, but I fought them like they were wild animals. The first to move or make a sound was dead meat. Our class, which used to be fifteen, is now eight, and that is with the first, second, and third grades together. I feel sorry for the youngest ones in the room like Precious. Good thing she is quiet by nature. Tobile used to be in my class, but I have not seen her in weeks. I will not be asking my teacher about her!

I am in charge at home. Precious and Abu will be looking to me when they wake up, their bellies swollen and hurting, their eyes pleading for me to take care of them. Especially Abu, who is unable to understand the cupboard is bare—how do I explain to him? He cries for Momma, and it makes me feel like my head is going to pop off.

The old wool blanket filled with holes starts to stir on the floor. At first just a little, then rolls of waves toss back and forth as if a violent storm were forming in the room. Two huge, dark eyes emerge and shoot open, welcoming the morning.

The silence is broken, and the day erupts. Abu is up and running around the room.

"Hello, wild boy. Come see 'Danna." When he gets up, everyone is awake. He yells and coughs.

Momma would say, "Precious is our noontime princess." Even as a tiny baby, she wanted to sleep longer than all of us. She loves to lie around and be waited on. I have always enjoyed the quiet and colors of the early morning, but that also has changed. Now I dread the morning, because it means another day with no food, no mother.

I hear a rap on the door.

"Hello, girl. Are you here?"

The voice is scratchy and low. The door swings open and falls off the rusted hinges. I rush over to pick it up. A very old woman stands outside wearing red paint in the corners of her eyes and across her face. Multicolored beads droop from her head like bean plants, and she is dressed in a red and black cloak draped over her shoulders and tied across her chest. She is the witch doctor.

"Yes, can I help you?"

"Can you help me?" She throws back her head and laughs. "You will be thanking me that I came to help you."

"What do you mean?"

"The spirits have told me about you. Your mother is sick. Is this true?"

"It's true."

"Do you know why?"

She tells me before I can answer.

"She has made the ancestors very angry, Adanna."

How does she know my name?

"They are punishing her for her sin, and they demand payment."

"What kind of payment?"

"Blood sacrifice. If we do nothing, that sin will fall to the oldest in the family. That would be you."

"But that is not fair! I have done nothing wrong!"

"It is why I'm here, child. I know you have no animals to offer. Therefore, your blood will have to do."

"My blood?" My eyes go wide. I am afraid, then suddenly, strangely hopeful. "Will my blood save Momma?"

"When the ancestors are enraged, only blood can put them at rest. It is what they demand."

"What must I do?"

"Come to my house."

"But what about my brother and sister?"

"All of you, come to my house soon. The babies can wait outside. You know where it is?"

I nod. The hut is painted bright red, like the paint on her face. I have never been inside. Why does she want Precious and Abu to be left outside?

"Do you have anything to eat? For them?" I ask.

"Just come. I will be ready for you at noon." Then she turns into the early-morning light and is gone, her cape trailing behind.

Precious stares after her, now fully awake.

"Who was that funny old lady?" she asks.

I am suddenly dizzy, but I pick up Abu and take him to the hole we use out back as an outhouse.

My blood. To save my mother.

I remember the words of the illuminated man. "Here is your gift. It will make the way clear for you, and it will save many of your people." Is this what he was talking about? Is my gift my very life?

Precious is staring at me when I return with Abu.

"Who was she?" she asks.

"That lady was someone who wants to help Momma get better."

"She smelled stinky."

Precious is right. The witch doctor smelled like corn liquor and burnt fungus.

"C'mon, you two." I take them to the water pot. It is nearly dry, but I wipe their eyes with the damp cloth. I do not bother with my own face.

What is my life really worth anyway? I am skinny and not very pretty. Precious and Abu would be better off with Momma. If she could be well again, I would do anything.

The decision is made.

I pull back the door, now just leaning over the opening. The sunshine scatters in our home, lighting the dark corners. Dust speckles come alive and dance in the empty spaces. I want to take one last look. Abu's first steps took place by the tiny kitchen area. Right there, leaning on the wall on my bed, is where I read. I will miss Abu and Precious and Momma. And Tobile.

"Abu, Precious, come here, my sweets."

Precious walks slowly to me on tiptoes, but Abu will not listen. I take his hand and lead him outside. I wrestle the door back in front of the opening, though it leaves enough space for a small monkey to enter.

The witch doctor's house is a ten-minute walk. It is a scary house. There are stakes in the front yard, each with dozens of animal bones hanging from strings. If there's a sickness, a death, a birth, a celebration, and even if you need food or money, the witch doctor has the answer. Supposedly she gets her special powers from the spirit world. If she makes them happy, they will do what she asks. Usually they're happy with a cow. I'm not sure what is true about the witch doctor and what is made up, but I have no choice but to believe. For Momma's sake.

"Where are we going, Adanna? To get food for Momma? Will the food make her well?" Precious does not understand. It is better that way.

"Soon, she will be well."

We walk along a path I have walked nearly every day. It's lined with rocks and cacti and is not far from the beautiful baobab tree. This tree not only makes me feel proud to be African, it *is* Africa—one of our national symbols. I am holding Precious's hand, and Abu is running ahead.

I see the witch doctor's hut in the distance. The road forks off to the right—where Auntie D and Uncle Malako live.

"You two must go to Momma. I need to see the witch doctor alone."

Abu starts to dance down the road, but Precious pauses. She looks up at me with puzzlement.

My lips pucker and land on Precious's smooth, soft forehead. This little sister of mine is more valuable than a thousand jewels.

"Go now. Abu, you mind Precious. Sissy loves you more than the sun, and the animals, and everything in the world."

"Awight, Sissy."

I watch them as they disappear down the dusty road.

A cracked, tarnished mirror hangs above the bells by the door. I study my reflection. Bruised circles camp under my eyes. I look tired and sad. My skin is like the ash left on the ground after a fire. My hair is short and curly, with speckles of blonde and littered with dirt and what looks like crumbles of leaves. I try to smile. My right lip purses up but quickly falls back down.

My insides are churning as if a troll lives in my belly. He's flipping my insides with a cold steel shovel. Beads of sweat line my forehead.

I rap on the door, hoping she won't hear me, my hands trembling. There's movement inside.

"Come in, child. I've been waiting."

The home reeks of musty wood and incense.

The witch doctor sits in front of a cauldron, steam pouring over the sides like spider legs made of smoke. Candles form circles on the ground and parts of dead animals hang from the ceiling and walls.

My teeth chatter like I've been stuck outside on a cold night. I look up to see bones in a basket. Will my skull join them?

This is for Momma. I have to be strong.

The witch doctor is humming.

"Sit down. The ancestors have told me many things about you and your mother's sickness."

I sit on a small rickety stool in front of her. She waves her withered, dry hand over the vapors escaping from the pot. Sparks erupt in red and yellow. She speaks to the pot, as if someone hides there.

Bubbles float from the bottom of the pot and explode on the surface, multiplying into hundreds more. The mixture is thick and black like the color of cow's blood after it has cooled.

I jump when she shrieks, "Spirits of old, accept this sacrifice to atone for the sins of this woman."

Fear grabs my stomach, and I lurch forward as if someone has pushed me from behind. My soul burns. Something sticks deep inside me, trying to make its way back up. A cold, sweaty chill runs down my back.

"Turn your wrath away from our people—let it be quenched before the end of this night."

Her hand sways heavy in the air, then crashes downward, releasing a white powder over the fire. Immediately I'm light-headed. Everything appears murky and moves in slow motion. My head feels like a huge block of wood. All fear escapes me and rushes into the fire. The flames lick the lips of the black-sooted pot, reveling in some kind of victory. This is the end.

I picture my momma's face.

"May you receive the payment of this child's blood! Release your curse and cease your hatred of the evil in which this family has partaken."

Quick as a cobra, she grabs my arm. I yell. I am suddenly alert. And scared. I don't want to die by being thrown into a boiling pot.

With one hand she raises my arm in the air, and with her other she waves a glimmering steel blade.

No more sickness, no more death, Momma will live. I take one last deep breath and close my eyes.

A burning, searing pain shoots through my arm and engulfs the rest of my body. I want to yell again, but my mouth will not work. My lips are swollen into two large stones. Thick, wet goo pours down my arm. I open my eyes and the witch doctor is worshipping the kettle, eyes rolled in the back of her head, two white orbs twitching violently. Her mouth lies open, the pink inside alive and pulsating. Blood drips from my wrist to my elbow and splashes on the fire.

A moment later, her eyes return.

"It is finished."

She releases my arm and hands me a towel.

"Keep pressure on the wound until it stops."

I am confused. "Is that it?"

"The ancestors are pleased. They receive your sacrifice and remove their curse."

"But I thought I … the blood sacrifice. I thought …"

I am dizzy again. I look at the wound on my hand. It is small.

"What did you think?"

"That I would have to give my life as a sacrifice …"

"Goodness no, child. Go home now. Everything will be put back in its proper place."

My legs shake and wobble. When I reach the fresh, cool air, my senses start to come back to life. My head clears enough to see what's in front of me. My gait is slow and steady.

I was prepared to die. Now, a jubilation rises in me: Everything will be all right. Momma will be well, and we will all be fine!

As the fog continues to clear, my legs move faster. Momma's probably already well! The witch doctor said the ancestors were appeased. The thought of my mother regaining her strength focuses me. I can't wait to see her smile. The leaves run with me and swirl as I run to Auntie's door.

Bursting in without waiting for invitation, I call out to her.

"Momma, oh, Momma, are you well?"

I stop. Precious and Abu follow my lead and stand as still as statues. She is on that same bed. It looks as if she has not moved a centimeter. I smell the pungent stench of human waste. She is smaller than last time, her frame so frail. Her arms are twigs, like starter wood for a fire.

When she sees me, her eyes open, but only halfway. They are the yellow of pus. Her hand reaches out to me slowly, trembling and jerky, resting on my shoulder. She does not look human.

Why isn't she better? The witch doctor, the ancestors promised! Maybe it takes time. She'll be well in a few short days. Then everything will be back to normal.

Abu and Precious press up next to me. The smiles on their faces quickly turn into frown. They see what I have seen.

Abu scuttles to the corner, buries his head in his little hands, and begins to cry.

I bend down to Momma. "Everything is okay. You will be well again. I promise!"

She is whispering something, but I can't hear. I strain to hear her words.

"A-A-Add-ddaaa-nnna. I love you."

"I love you too, and it is going to be okay. The ancestors told the witch doctor. Just wait, Momma, just wait."

The pain in my arm pricks at me. Dried, speckled blood spreads out from my wrist and forearm and draws a crimson line down the middle.

"I made the sacrifice. It's done; all will be restored. She told me."

Her fingers slowly, methodically, caress my hair. Her hand and touch are familiar, and I know it is beginning. She is becoming well. My head rests on her bony frame but she grimaces in pain. Instead, I lie down on the hard, dirty floor at her feet and fall asleep.

Some time later, maybe an hour, maybe two, I'm awakened by being dragged across the floor.

"What are you doing in this house? Didn't I tell you not to come here? What's the matter with you, girl?"

Auntie D is yelling at the top of her lungs like I committed a terrible crime.

"I thought Momma would be well. The witch doctor promised."

"Did you go see the witch doctor? Because if you did, she's gonna come asking me for the money."

"No, she came to me. She told me my sacrifice would make the ancestors happy. I came here to see Momma get well. To take her home."

"What's that on your arm, girl?"

"It's nothing."

"Don't you lie to me. Let me see it."

"No, don't touch it, it hurts. The witch doctor did it."

"You don't know what you are messing with."

"She promised Momma would get well."

"Witch doctors sometimes do great things, and sometimes they do nothing. You can't depend on them." She calms down as suddenly as she had exploded in anger. I don't like how quickly she goes from angry to kind. "Adanna, I think it is time we had a talk. Your mom is very, very sick, and she will soon go to meet the ancestors. We need to discuss how things are going to be for you and your brother and sister from now on."

"But the witch doc—"

"I don't want to be hearing anything about the witch doctor. When she dies, you're gonna be all alone. Uncle Malako and I will help you as much as we can. But you know we are poor and don't have much to share."

I hardly believe that's true, but I say nothing.

"I have children of my own to take care of," Auntie continues. "But don't you worry, you will be just fine. There are people making it who are in worse shape than you."

"But—"

"No, no, no. You are a big girl, Adanna."

The witch doctor promised me everything would be okay, and

everything is falling apart. Everything is not okay. I am so sad. So confused.

Momma stirs in the corner, only slightly. More like the last twitching of a rat caught in a trap than a human being lying underneath covers. She moans, coughs, and tries to breathe; it is a struggle.

The tears burn with bitterness. And now I am angry. I am angry at the world, angry at the witch doctor, angry to be alone, even angry at the illuminated man. Especially him.

I run out the door. Stinging tears run down my face, into my mouth.

I keep running, not sure where I am heading at first. Then I know. I have to see Pastor Walter. He's the only one who will help. He will be at the care point.

I race past people going about their lives. They are a blur. I do not care who they are or if I know them. I see the empty houses of the people we used to sit with and share meals with at church. They are empty. The people, gone. Like Daddy, like Uncle Sipo, like Momma. My tears come again, and I do not care who sees me cry.

I slow when I come to the care point, but my legs are weak. I can barely walk. I stumble through a crowd of people, white men, about ten of them. They wear strange hats, like they're going on a safari. One is holding a bottle of liquid they use on their hands every time they touch one of us. One holds out his hand to me with candy. But I don't like these white people today.

Where is Pastor Walter? I walk unsteadily to the supply building.

"Adanna, what are you doing in here?"

Words won't come out of my mouth. I try, but my lips won't move, and my mind is blank.

"Are you okay?"

My shoulders heave, my nose runs, and salty water continues to pour from my eyes. I am wailing like a baby.

He is kind, like a father might be. He walks to me and holds me, silently at first. I willingly fall into his chest, and for a moment, I feel safe.

"There, there, girl, everything will be all right. Pastor Walter is here."

Chapter Twelve

◆◇■ Adanna ■◇◆

Pastor Walter wasn't always such a warm and gentle man. Years ago he was more like a painting of a person that looks good from far away but not so good when you get up close.

Before the church building was added to the care point closer to my home, we had to walk ten kilometers to church every Sunday. I had only one dress, just for Sunday. One morning, I decided to wear my dress to go out and play. Once Momma found out, she marched me right back into the house. She made it clear with a vigorous wag of her finger and her firm hand on my back that this was not a dress for play. It was white with little pink flowers and green leaves and had a pretty bow in the back. Momma soaked and scrubbed our nice clothes every Saturday using a bar of soap we didn't use for much else. I can picture all of our Sunday clothes hanging on the line outside our house—my dress, Momma's long frock with brown, orange, and green leaves scattered from top to bottom, and Precious's little pink dress. She always washed Daddy's good clothes too, even when he had not worn them. But even when he was home, Daddy never would go with us to the church. "So many lies coming out of that preacher's mouth," he always said. Momma would just cluck her tongue and shake her head, but she never argued with him about church. This was before Abu came along.

I can remember sitting with Momma in church on long benches, singing "What a Friend We Have in Jesus" and a song called "Abba, Father."

Young and old voices and hands would rise to heaven. When the people of our village got sick and started dying, even people in our church, everyone wanted answers. The grown-ups all had the same question, *Whose fault is this?* But everyone had a different answer. Some church people said we had sinned against God. Others swore the dark wave of death came from our ancestors. Some even said the white people had poured the disease into our water and poisoned our food.

We had only two places to go for answers: the witch doctor and the church. The witch doctor has been here a long time. I never quite understood how she worked, and sometimes I was scared of her, but people in our village believed she has been given great power by the ancestors.

Tobile's Uncle Sahile told her the ancestors turn people who do really bad things into zombies. The zombies come out at night and do awful things to people, though I am not sure what. For months after I heard about zombies, I could not close my eyes without picturing their decaying bodies and empty eyes.

When I asked my daddy about this, he stood up with his arms out like a big monster, opened his eyes wide, and lumbered about the house, chasing me. When he caught me, he laughed and said, "Adanna, don't believe everything you hear." But I know he visited the witch doctor at least once, after a tree from the forest fell on his leg. That was when he cut timber for the government in Bulembu. He worked sixteen hours a day with hardly any pay. He was angry and jumpy as a bush snake. His leg got better, but he always had a slight limp after that.

When I imagine the ancestors, I picture giant spirits with red eyes swirling around and watching us, waiting for someone to make a mistake. We kill our animals trying to make them happy, but I don't know what they could possibly want with dead animals.

Tobile and I were allowed to sit in the back of a circle séance one night. The witch doctor danced around like a crazy chicken, her long, pale, bony fingers pulling the unseen down into the air around us. Afterward, I could not get the sickly sweet odor of smoke off me.

My mother believes in ancestors and witch doctors, God and church, and Pastor Walter. I am still trying to figure out what I believe, but I am certain now that it won't include witch doctors.

Unless Momma suddenly gets better.

I think I believe in church, though. At least, I want to. First of all, it is free. It does not cost money or animals ... or blood sacrifice. Pastor Walter talks about blood and sacrifice sometimes, but he doesn't ask us for our animals. He says Jesus took the place of the animals. I'm not quite sure what that means, but it makes me feel better.

Before he changed, Pastor Walter scared me. After our singing time, which I loved, he would preach, sometimes for two hours! He paced back and forth at the front of the room, his face sweaty and his voice getting louder and louder. Sometimes he banged his fist, or the Word of God, on the table to wake us up.

One day, Pastor spoke about "the truth that is in Jesus."

"From the book of Ephesians," he shouted. "You must put on the new self. He who has been stealing must steal no longer! He must work that he may have something to share with those in need."

Pastor Walter talked about Jesus' church—where everyone shared with everyone else. Not only food, but homes, money, everything.

Sitting in the service that morning, my mind drifted as he spoke. I tried to think past the ache in my stomach, in my bones, even, it seemed, in my hair. I hadn't eaten in days. As Pastor spoke, I thought of fresh roasted corn, succulent fruit, tons of beans—hunks of meat—and my mouth watered. If the good news about Jesus' church was true, maybe there would be food for me someday soon.

When he was finished, I waited for Pastor at the back of the church.

"Pastor, I'm so excited about the church of Jesus!"

"Yes, dear, it is wonderful, isn't it?"

"Oh, it is, almost too good to be true."

But he was walking away. I couldn't let him go. I couldn't think of suffering through another day without eating.

"Pastor Walter, wait."

"Yes, what is it, child?"

"I-I want you to know that I am one of those people you talked about today."

"People? What do you mean?"

"I am one of the hungry. Pastor Walter, my brother, sister, and I have not eaten in days."

He looked at me with a question mark on his face. Then he gave a small smile and put his hand on my shoulder.

"Oh, that's only a story, an example of how people are *supposed* to live."

"You mean it's not true?" My lips tightened. I could feel the blood rushing out of my face.

"Oh, it's true, you just need faith to receive it."

"What do you mean?"

"Just believe! All things are possible to him who believes."

"But I've believed all this time, and I'm still hungry."

"God's just testing you to see if you really trust Him." He patted my shoulder again.

And with that, he walked off. It was plain to me that day. He was just talking dry wind to all of us.

I could not understand how people are supposed to share with those in need but God would not permit them to share with me because I'm being tested.

But Pastor Walter kept speaking these things. Often he would get all excited and start yelling at us, telling what would happen when the kingdom of God came. I started to get tired of waiting for it.

One day, that changed. Pastor Walter was in front of the church speaking, getting all excited. I could see his spit fly out toward the people in the front row. He talked about the true power of a Christian. Power to pray for things and receive them, the power of faith "calling forth things that are not as though they were." I asked someone about this, and they told me you can pray to God for something you want and He will deliver it. They said it worked for the Americans.

After church, everyone got up to leave except for one person. A little boy I have known since I was a baby remained alone, still lying next to the wall. Everyone thought he was asleep. His momma had died from the bad disease, so she was not around to wake him up. He had no one else to look out for him. Pastor Walter tried to wake him. Pastor Walter's voice made me stop and turn to look:

"Hey, boy! It's time to go now. A church is no place to sleep!

Boy, do you hear me? What's the matter with you, sleeping in God's house like this?"

He walked over to the dusty corner. The wind blew, dirt swirled, and a few leaves rested on his clothes. I can still hear the echoes of his black dress shoes stomp on the cement floor.

"I told you it's time to go home!"

He kicked at him gently with his foot, but the little boy wouldn't wake up. So Pastor Walter started dragging him by the shirt toward the door. This wouldn't have been too hard to do—Tlonge was so skinny. He was also completely filthy; he didn't own a pair of shoes, and his clothes were nothing more than used rags. My memory of his clothes and face are so clear even now.

Pastor Walter reached down with both hands to pick him up and escort him out the door. But then he froze. It must have been the touch of Tlonge's skin that did it. Cold, clammy, like the outside of a banana skin. I know because I hugged him after everyone left.

"Tlonge? Tlonge? Wake up, boy. Oh, dear Jesus!"

Walter began to cry, slowly at first. He touched Tlonge, more tenderly now, feeling his neck and the side of his face. His sobs turned into gasping heaves as he caressed Tlonge in his arms and held him close to his chest. Pastor Walter cried like I have never seen a man cry in my life. It filled the whole church and poured out into the streets.

From that day, Walter was a different man. He even looked different. His eyes and face were softer. He brought food from his house to share after every service, feeding as many children as he could. There were times when my only meal for the week came after those Sunday-morning services. Once in a while he even came to my home with a small meal for our family. It wasn't much, he said, but it was all he had. I believed him.

Tlonge's death snapped something inside Pastor Walter that needed to be broken.

This is the Pastor Walter whose arms embrace me now.

"Adanna, dear, dear. What's the matter, my child?"

My lips attempt to form words, but nothing comes out. My nose runs like a river and tears are as big as raindrops.

"There, there. You tell Pastor Walter everything. I am here for you."

After what seems like hours, the words finally pour out.

"My momma, she is sick, Pastor Walter! She has the deadly disease. I went to the witch doctor." I show him my arm, the blood now congealed in an ugly, jagged line. "But it did not help and now Momma is going to die!"

"Oh, Adanna. What has been done to you?" He shakes his head, and his eyes tear up. Tears for me.

"I have prayed for you and spent many nights awake thinking about what to do. It's a terrible thing, but God will see you through."

"I am so scared to be alone. What will I do? How will I take care of Precious and Abu? How will I feed them?"

"These are hard times. But I will do all I can to be by your side. To help you, to love you, to take care of you." He takes his face in my hands. "You can count on it."

All of this is hard to believe. I feel as if I am trapped in a nightmare and cannot wake up. My fingers claw at my skin with all their might, but to no use. I will not wake up because this is not a dream.

Pastor Walter hands me a bundle.

"Take this maize and beans. It's not much but some foreigners were kind enough to bring it so we have hope for a few days."

The words "Thank you" escape my mouth and I'm grateful for these minutes with Walter. I feel loved and protected. The warmth of his hands, the way he looks into my eyes, and the gentle caressing of my back gives me a glimpse into a father's heart. I could get by on less food if that kind of love was a part of my life all the time.

Having a father like that would mean never being scared again.

I let the best memories of my own father fill my head. I remember the last day I saw him. It was like any other day. He got up early, and he fixed breakfast for the family—he even had special rolls he'd brought back from the city. He kissed Momma good-bye, and never came back. My last memory of him is with his back turned, walking away.

After this memory fades, I look up to see that a white man has stepped into the room with Pastor Walter and me. He has dark wavy hair, down past his neck, pulled back into a ponytail.

He walks to where Pastor and I are sitting.

"Hi, Walter." Pastor grabs his hand and pumps it up and down.

"Stuart, so good to see you."

Then his chalky white hand thrusts through the air like someone jabbing a stick at me.

"*Saw—Sawubona.*" He is trying to say hello in S'swati.

I do the American thing like Pastor Walter and shake his hand, with my right hand, not my left.

"Hello to you. I speak English."

"You do. Yes, and very well, I see."

"I studied English in school."

"My name is Stuart. What's yours?"

"I am Adanna."

"I am sorry your mom is sick."

I look up at him and nod. I cannot imagine why he is talking to me. My foot kicks the ground lazily and dust flies in the air.

Pastor Walter stands up.

"Adanna, Stuart is from the United States. He is here with Gordon—maybe you have seen Gordon with me. The tall white man who sometimes comes to our church."

"He's very loud," the man named Stuart says. He looks at me, not in a bad way, but I can tell he is studying me. It makes me aware of the rags I am wearing and the dirt crusted on my arms and legs. He is wearing a blue T-shirt with a horse and rider on his chest.

"Oh, maybe." I wish I could just disappear.

The white man speaks kindly, but it seems to take effort.

"Mr. Gordon is a writer, and I am a photographer. We are here to do a story about your beautiful country and your people for a newspaper back in the U.S."

"Our country is not as pretty as it used to be."

"Maybe things can change, become better for you and your people."

He answers quickly, like someone trying to catch overflowing water from one pot to another. I am not feeling polite today. Can he not see the difference between his perfect, clean clothes and these filthy things I have on?

"Look around." My voice is scratchy, but I am surprised at how strong it sounds. "Everyone is dying; we have no food to eat."

"I really can't begin to imagine how hard it must be." He bends down close to me. "I know we just met, but can I give you something?"

"Okay."

He takes a bright orange daypack off his back.

"This backpack has some food in it—crackers, bread, and cheese. It's not much, but I want you to have it."

"Thank you, mister." Maybe I misjudged him.

I stand up to go, but I am very wobbly. The white man puts his arm around my shoulder and guides me into a chair. His hand brushes across the fresh knife wound on my arm, and I wince.

"Sorry. I'm so sorry." His eyes fix on the cut.

"What happened to your arm?"

Pastor Walter steps up. "Adanna, why don't you put your head down here for a few minutes. I will help you get home after you have some rest."

I lie like a worm on a worn mat, holding onto the stained, orange backpack.

Pastor Walter moves to the back of the room and motions for Stuart to join him. They talk in low voices, but I can hear them.

"Stuart, this child is at the end of herself. You cannot believe what she has endured. Today, she got it into her mind to see the witch doctor, to give a blood sacrifice—she believed this would make her mother well. Her mother is very sick with AIDS and could die any day now."

"A witch doctor did that to her?"

"I am fighting against this kind of superstition, but it is strong with our people. We need to make sure she gets the knife wound cleaned, so it doesn't get infected."

I realize now that another man has joined them. This must be Gordon. He is indeed loud.

"I have a first-aid kit in the car," says the man who must be Gordon. "There's some disinfectant and antibiotic in there. I'll go get it."

"Yes, yes, good idea. Please do."

The white men spread a jelly and solution on my arm that burns me. I can't help but wince, though I try not to show it. Then they place a big brown bandage over it.

"There you go, good as new," Stuart says.

"Thank you."

"You are more than welcome," Gordon says.

"Why don't we all escort you home," Pastor Walter says.

"Okay."

I'm not sure I want them to see my home. There's nothing to see. Not much of anything really. On the walk over, I think it's a good idea to keep them outside. Less questions, less I have to say.

When we arrive, I know it was the right decision. The white men—especially the dark-haired one—try to hide their dismay, but I can see it in their eyes. "Thank you all so much. Perhaps I will see you again soon."

"Oh, okay. Yeah. That would be nice." The man named Stuart is very strange.

"*Sala kahle.*" I say.

"Good-bye, dear," Pastor Walter says. And they walk away.

Chapter Thirteen

Gordon drops me back at the hotel.

"Meet you in the morning for breakfast, partner," he yells as he pulls away. That man is tireless.

I head up to my room and lie back on the bed. I am wiped out, but I can't sleep. I still haven't recovered from the jet lag. The kids at the care point are messing with my heart. I'm not supposed to get close to these people. That's how I stay sane. But then again ... I haven't been sane for a long time. I think of Adanna—the long scar on her arm. I think of the crazy church service and those words "Feed My sheep." Did that even happen, or was I caught up in the moment?

Whitney has had me bent over laughing with stories of growing up in her Southern pew-jumping church—it was something like "Attapulgus Free Church of the Gospel, Holy Spirit." On revival Sunday, about once a month, she and her brothers were "encouraged" to go to the front of the church and get thumped on the forehead. Something about being slammed by the Spirit. Or slain. Either way, it sounds violent and wrong. But Whit and her closest brother didn't really feel anything during those moments. They just played along, like it was a game. They'd lie there on the ground for a while, then peek at each other and nod when they thought it was okay to get up.

I wonder how many people just play along in non-pew-jumping churches.

I miss Whitney. I need to talk to her, to hear her voice.

I dig the phone out of my bag. It still has a little charge left in it. I take the elevator up to the pool and walk over to a chair on the far side. A white-haired man and a much younger blonde woman are treading water near each other in the deep end. He is clearly flirting with her, and it is obvious to me that it's working.

The phone rings once, twice.

"Hello?"

"Whit, hey, it's Stuart."

"You made it! I was starting to worry since I hadn't heard from you."

"Just so you know, cell service here is hit and miss. I can only get one bar up here by the pool. I could lose you any second."

"It's good to hear your voice."

"Oh, and my battery is low. So this will probably have to be quick."

"Okay …"

"Sorry, I just wanted to get that out of the way. Um … it's really good to hear your voice, too." I'm really not sure what to say. I guess that's because I'm not sure how I feel.

"Is everything okay?"

"Gordon and I went to a care point today, to talk to the kids and take pictures. It's hard for me to even describe the scene. These kids, they have no one."

"What do you mean, 'no one'?"

"I mean *no one*. Their parents and uncles and aunts have all died. There are seven-year-old kids parenting siblings. I met this one girl,

Adanna, she's probably no older than eleven or twelve, and her mom is dying of AIDS, so what does she do? She goes to the witch doctor. And all that did was get her a nice scar on her wrist where the quack sliced her open to spill her blood."

"That's horrible."

"Pastor Walter, the guy who's trying to help a lot of these kids here—man, you should hear his story—he is working with aid organizations to help kids get food, but they're not very reliable. Gordon and I gave this Adanna some crackers and a few little things I had. But it hardly feels like we did anything at all."

"It sounds unreal, Stu." Her voice is quiet.

"This whole trip is unreal."

There is an awkward silence. I know she wants to talk about "us," but I'm not ready to go there. Not yet. There's too much swirling in my mind.

"I went to church," I finally say.

"Did you say 'church'?"

I laugh. "Well I didn't plan on it. It just happened. Gordon and I interviewed this incredible Swazi woman—reminded me a lot of Wangari."

"So she took you to church?"

"Well, after we ate dinner, we went for a walk. By the way, this is a really beautiful place, you know, aside from the starvation and AIDS wiping out most of the population."

"Lovely word picture. Don't quit your day job." She lets those words simmer for a moment before continuing. "So what happened at church?"

"The place was packed, but it wasn't like any church service

I've been to. Mostly it was children and older women—I think the grandmotherly types are called *gogos* or something like that. Anyway, they were singing, that's what caught our attention while we were out walking. I have to admit, it almost choked me up it was so beautiful."

More silence.

"Stu? Are you still there? You're breaking up a bit."

"Sorry. I can tell you about it another time. But it was … surreal. And a bit freaky, too, because I heard a voice …"

"Stu, I didn't catch that last bit …"

"I said it was a bit freaky. That's all."

"I'm glad you went to church. I think that's a good thing. Maybe it will help you … us. I mean, it would at least put us in the same place on Sundays."

"Yeah." When was the last time I went to church with Whitney? Months ago? Years? Whitney breaks yet another silence.

"Stuart, this isn't exactly how I pictured telling you what I'm about to say … but I have some important news …"

"Okay." That sounds ominous. Is this about us? Or a friend? Is someone sick … or dead?

"Is everything okay?"

"Yes, except I'm—" She stops talking.

"Whit, are you still there?"

"Stuart, I, I mean we, are going to have a baby."

I drop the phone. It bounces once, then skitters toward the pool, stopping short of falling in. I quickly pick it up and hold the receiver to my ear.

"Whit, are you still there? Whitney?"

Silence.

Chapter Fourteen

◆◇■ Adanna ■◇◆

My journal was a gift from a lovely grandmother named Frida who came from a place called Finland. On the cover of the journal there is the face of a woman with shiny silver hair that flows from the front to the back of the book. She has deep blue eyes, like my friend Frida, and her eyelids are shaded in blue, teal, and silver. Two small teardrops run from her left eye, and two elegant birds rest atop her head, their beaks meeting in the middle to create a queenly crown. I have never seen anything so beautiful. Frida said the woman on the book is a Nordic ice queen.

I have only seen ice once in my life, in a cup of Coca-Cola. I asked if I could touch it, and a nice white man said yes. He poured the Coke into his hand until two perfectly clear cubes fell out and the brown, syrupy liquid oozed between his fingers and onto the ground. He handed me one and threw the other in his mouth and crunched it between his teeth. This little square burned my hand and made me tingle when I held it too long. I put it in my mouth too and bore down on it with my teeth like the white man.

Frida's language sounded strange to me. I told her so, and she laughed. "Your language sounds like Greek to me!" She knows English, and so do I, so we would talk about all kinds of things together. When Frida would come, my momma would smile, and they would exchange a warm Swazi greeting. Precious would come running, and Frida would welcome her; but Momma knew this was my special time, and she would keep Precious and baby Abu away. She knew Frida was a special teacher, and my mother wanted me to learn as much as I could.

Frida told me her home was as different from mine as night is from day. She said it was cold, ten times as cold as it has ever been here! She also spoke of something called snow that falls from the sky. It is like a blanket of frozen white cotton all over the ground. I told her I've never seen cotton.

There are words written in Frida's language on my journal. Frida told me they were from a poem called "Tears," by a woman from England named Elizabeth Barrett Browning. She lived a long time ago, and she and her husband both wrote many poems about life, and especially about love. Frida told me what the words on my book say: *Soon in long rivers down the lifted face, / And leave the vision clear for stars and sun.* Frida told me what comes before these lines in the poem, so I wrote them all on the first page of my journal, in my language and in English.

> Those tears will run
> Soon in long rivers down the lifted face,
> And leave the vision clear for stars and sun.

Frida came to visit our village twice a week for three months. She always came to my home to find me so we could talk about poetry. She told me the "Tears" poem is about life and sadness, but that it is also about being able to see things more clearly because of the tears. All we have to do to see is lift our faces up to heaven, to God. Frida believes in God and talked about Him often. She said He is the author of life, creative power, and words. He gives these things and is these things. I do not completely understand this mystery, as Frida called it, but her thoughts bring me comfort, like life is somehow bigger than I know.

"Poetry is a beautiful art form, Adanna."

"I thought art was something you look at."

"Well, art is a way of looking at life and expressing what you see, from your perspective, through *your* eyes. With poetry, you use the power of words instead of a paintbrush to express the beauty and awe of life, and also things that bring pain and sadness."

"Kind of like a thunderstorm?" I exclaimed. This made sense to me.

"Yes, *exactly* like a thunderstorm." Frida's blue eyes lit up when she was excited. Talking about poetry made her eyes very bright.

"You know how, in the midst of the frightening thunderstorm, you stop to enjoy its beauty? You marvel at the power of the lightning strike, you ponder the life the rain brings to the ground to bring forth food, and you wonder who made it all?" She said all this with her arm around me, looking toward the heavens.

"I do wonder about those things."

"That's poetry."

She taught me about poetry and language, about words, verse, and meter, the rhythm of language, and helped me learn how to express my deepest thoughts. She knew many poems by heart. I had a thousand questions, but Frida was always patient and kind. She said she loved my curiosity. I cried the day she was leaving. Frida cried too. But I am glad I got to say good-bye to her.

Before she left, she wrote a note in my journal:

> *Adanna, it was a gift for me to meet you, and you are a gift to the world. Keep pondering the deep things of life. Keep using your gift to express your wonderful thoughts.*
>
> *Your friend,*
> *Frida*

I was lonely when she left, even though she said she would return some day.

I have named my journal Frida after the kind woman who gave it to me. Frida is a source of comfort when life hurts, like a hot cup of tea on a cold, wet day. And that is a real luxury. When I open my journal and see a blank page, my pen goes to work. As I write, a world emerges that is my own. Something about this fills me, even as I let go of my thoughts and feelings.

My favorite thing to do in the whole world is write poetry. Momma says it was my grandma's gift too. I wrote a poem for Frida in my journal. Maybe I will give it to her some day.

I wrote this one just a few days ago:

> I see the path, edged with tall grass
> Where you walked, to come home.
> And I wait.
> For your big loving smile, strong arms

To protect me from harm. Wait—
I see you coming as you did, calling my name,
Eyes toward home. My heart leaps,
And then falls when I wake.
Father of my dreams.
The dirt path is empty, and so is my heart.

That's a poem about my daddy. He'll never get to read it, but I wrote it for him anyway. Or maybe I wrote it for me. Either way, it is what I would want to say to him if he were here. Maybe one day, he will come back to get me. I hope he still remembers he has a daughter.

Sometimes at night I am scared, but Frida keeps me company. I sit against my bed and write as long as I can after Precious and Abu are asleep, except for the times when I do not have anything to write with or a candle to give me light to work by. Candles are expensive, but Pastor Walter gave me a package of them he got from an aid organization. I use them only a little at a time so I can stretch their life as long as possible. When it's windy, the air blows right through my house. It causes the candle flame to bend, making the wax run, and ruining it. I never read or write in a storm. I have only one candle left.

"Abu, Precious, come eat your breakfast." It is the last of the food the white men gave us.

"Adanna, the food has been so nice! Do you think the white people will give us more?"

"It is hard to say, Precious. One day food is here, the next it is gone. That is our life. With God's help, we will have enough for tomorrow." This is something Momma would tell me. After Daddy left us, she started answering a lot of her questions by saying, "With God's help …"

"Are we going to see Momma today? I miss her." Precious starts to cry, and so does Abu. I hate when they cry.

"Okay, no more crying." I do not care what Auntie D says; we want to see our mother.

"Yes, today, we will go to see her."

Smiles light their faces.

"Just make sure you put on your warm clothes."

"But we don't have any warm clothes," Precious reminds me.

"Just put on Momma's green sweater."

"But she'll get mad."

"Just do what I say. And make sure Abu is wrapped in the blanket."

The walk to Auntie D's takes longer than usual. The weather is changing and the temperature is dropping, and we must walk against the wind. Dirt sticks in our eyes and coats our throats. Leaves rocket through the air as if they're arrows. Gnarled, ancient trees line the path. People say they are thousands of years old and our greatest treasures. A few even believe the dead live in those trees and watch our every move. Whatever they are, I do not like them much. They scare me.

When we round the bend, I can tell something strange is going on. Narrowing my eyes to focus reveals flashes of color. I grab Abu by his tiny, bony hand, and my walk turns to a jog.

"Adanna, don't go so fast. 'Low down, okay?"

"Just hurry up. C'mon, Precious."

A figure runs toward us.

"Adanna, you must have heard. I was just on my way to get you. Come quickly." Beads of sweat are forming on Uncle Malako's brow and he's breathing hard.

"What is wrong, Uncle?" But I already know.

"Hurry along. You'll soon see."

My world becomes a blur. Uncle Malako pulls me by the arm so hard my shoulder is about to come out of its socket. The jerk opens my wound and small droplets of blood drip down my arm.

Several small groups of people stand in front of the house weeping, moaning, lifting their hands to the sky, and muttering prayers to ancestors or gods.

I maneuver between them with my head down, not wanting anyone to see who I am. It works.

The inside of the house is flooded with people. Our village elder grabs me, holds me, and kisses me. I twist to get away. Where is my momma? Women have grabbed Precious and Abu, but I take Abu into my own arms and pull Precious by her little hand.

After pressing and squeezing through the crowd, we emerge as if from an underground cave to her bedside.

"Is that Momma?" Precious looks up at me with a quivering lip.

That's not our Momma. The flesh is falling off of her face. Her skin is not the beautiful brown of my momma's. It looks more like melted candle wax. Bones stick out where they shouldn't. Two huge lumps hang lazily over her eyes, a once well-rounded chin now hangs lifeless like a rock, her mouth gaped open exposing teeth like a dead cow's.

My belly starts to erupt. I turn and in one motion hand Abu to a woman behind me and pull Precious with all my force through the bodies and outside. Vomit spews, the acid burns my throat and ignites in my mouth like fire. This is the taste of my life.

I drop to my knees and pound my fists against the hard earth. The cold wind whips the dirt and dust around me. From somewhere inside, my voice rises.

"Momma! Momma!" I scream.

Ten fingers close on my shoulders, a grip as strong as a gorilla, and pull me up. It's Uncle Malako. The vomit, now matted with dirt and sand, still trickles from my mouth as I'm forced to my feet. Everyone is staring at me.

"Go pay respects to your mother." Uncle Malako leads me back into the house. I do not know where Precious and Abu have gone.

I bring my arms up to cover my face. Hands grip the back of my neck. It's Auntie D.

"Dear, dear child. My prayers were that this day would never come. I am so sad for you, so brokenhearted for your family." She says it loudly so everyone can hear.

I say nothing. There are no words in my mind, no feelings in my heart. I am numb all over. Nothing works right. I am not sure my heart is beating, if my legs can walk, or my mouth can talk. It is finished. And now life will never be the same.

Auntie D shakes her head, fake tears in her voice.

"Don't you worry, because Uncle Malako and I will help you, protect you, and care for you."

Every word she says is a lie. I think I'm going to be sick again.

"You hear me, child?"

I nod.

After being tossed around from relative to stranger, and stranger to friend, I sneak away, quiet as a cockroach, and edge toward the door. Even standing on my tiptoes, I am not tall enough to see over the ocean of bodies. Where are Abu and Precious?

Oh, I wish I could talk with that man in my dream. He said his name was "Whatever You Need." I need someone to tell me what to do. I need someone to show me how to survive. I need help. I throw a desperate prayer to the wind in hopes that he is close. That he hears. *Please, Illuminated Man, ruler of everything, help me!*

I hear nothing as I walk away from my mother.

The sun burns bright, but the air is frigid. The wind has stopped, but there is a new coldness now that Momma is gone. I feel it deep down in my soul. Everything inside of me is being rearranged. Every particle and every speck of dust that makes up who I am is changing.

My eyes scan the horizon. The world around me looks the same as it was yesterday but it does not seem the same to me in this moment. I do not want to go on. When everyone leaves, I will sneak back into the house and lie next to Momma. Then I can die too.

Two small figures escape the swarm of mourners like fish escaping a hook. Abu and Precious run to me. I wonder what they are thinking. Abu is just a baby. He only knows that his mommy is not moving. He kept trying to talk to her. Nobody noticed him as he poked her and asked if he could have something to drink.

He has no idea of the event that has occurred. Abu will not

remember his mother, how she used to kiss him on the forehead
every night before he went to sleep, or how she would explode in
laughter when he tried to form words. He won't know how great her
love was for him. He won't know how everyone in this community
loved her and looked up to her. But I will tell him.

We are empty, without words. I look into their eyes, wipe away
their tears, and hug them. I want to tell them everything will be okay.
It is what they want to hear. I form the words in my thoughts but
cannot speak them.

I grab their hands, and we walk. I am not sure where to go, but
we have to get away from Auntie's. It has become a place for the
dead, not the living.

"Good-bye, my sweet Momma." I am done with tears today.

We walk for hours, up hills, through the dry, wintered grass,
across the sandy riverbed where crystal water one flowed. Even Abu
does not care where we are or what we are doing.

As we near our home, I pick up Abu. It is dark now, and this
time I am not afraid. If a wild beast eats me, it would be a comfort.
If I step on a black mamba, or if the ancestors devour me because I
step on their graves, let it be so.

We stumble like drunk men into our home. Abu and Precious
walk to their mats and collapse. No good-night wishes or words of
sweet dreams are spoken.

I feel half dead myself, but I am not ready to sleep. Grabbing
Frida, I begin to write.

> I had a dream, Momma,
> and in it the sky was blue as water;

I was thirsty, but it was too high
for me to lift my face and drink.
Patches of green were scattered
like emeralds over the red earth,
but I had no hands
and could not gather a treasure of grass
to hold against my baby bird-like chest.

Nothing was sound,
and everything was broken.
I looked for you, Momma,
but you had gone.
I woke up and lay on my mat
weaving your name into a blanket
to keep me warm.

I tell myself
that you aren't gone,
you've only flown away,
like a shining black bird
and all your days are spent
breaking twigs with your beak
off the sticks that maim and beat
To build a nest for your Precious,
And for me and Abu.

And we wait, mouths open
Screeching with our dry mouths

past the screams lodged deep
inside our tiny throats.

Come back for us.
Take us beyond the sky
where you are.

I fall into the deepest sleep.

I see a small room filled with bones, shoes, clothes, and human hair. An evil presence is near, a presence of destruction and death. There are no living people, only the remnants of people. It is a lonely place. I believe I am the last person on earth.

Screaming and yelling rip through my home, but where is it coming from? Voices pass through the walls and get louder and louder. Now they're wailing and shouting my name.

"Adannnnnaaaa, Adannnnnaaaa." What do they want with me? Why can't I make them go away?

With a jolt, my feet hit the floor. My body is wide awake. There is a familiar voice coming from outside.

"Adanna, open this door! It's Uncle Malako."

Why does he sound so angry?

With caution, I open the half-mended rusty gate that makes up the front door. He could easily tear it down if he wanted.

"Sorry, I was sleeping. How are you, Uncle?" My eye peers through a crack in the door to make sure it is really him. "Uncle, are you okay? You do not look so good."

"Get out of my way. You have things in this house that belong to me."

"What are you talking about? Nothing in here is yours." I say the words with boldness, but fear shoots through me.

The whole house is awake. Abu wipes the sleep from his eyes and is about to unleash a battle cry because he is hungry. I know that look.

Uncle pushes me out of the way with such force I almost fall to the ground. He steps in, carrying a large white bag made of canvas and looks like the Devil clothed in flesh.

"Uncle, this is our home, not yours!"

"Shut up. That worthless mother of yours stole things that belong to me. Now she's dead, and I'm taking what's rightfully mine."

Deep anger rises in my chest.

"Don't you talk about my momma like that!"

Abu and Precious cower in the corner, holding on to each other. Abu lets out a scream. We are terrified.

"You are not welcome here with your cruel words about our momma." I reach for all the inner strength I can gather to sound older than I am. "Please, just go ..."

"Don't tell me what to do, little girl. One more word, and I'll make you sorry you ever lived. Abu, Precious, go play somewhere far away."

"But we don't want—"

"Get out!"

He grabs them both by their shirts and practically drags them outside. My anger explodes like hurling knives. My hands fly up so fast I can't stop them. The strike lands like a hammer on his back and neck.

"Get away from me, you stupid child."

He doubles his fist and hits me squarely in the mouth. I fly into the wall and slam against it with a sick thud. My eyes won't work right. I am hurt. I am bleeding and helpless.

"These things belong to me."

He is stealing everything in the house. There isn't much to take except all my momma's special things—her brush, a silver necklace with a red stone, our pots and pans. He stuffs them all into his soiled and stained white bag.

A few words gurgle out, "Why are you taking all of our things? I thought you were going to help us?"

"Help you? I've never liked your rotten family. You're vile rats. Good for nothing."

The bag draped over his shoulder is filled with everything we own, and I am helpless to do anything about it.

"If you say a word about this to anyone, I will kill you with my bare hands. Do you understand me?"

I nod in assent, knowing he means it. But he doesn't leave. He stands in the doorway, staring like he might put me in that grimy bag next.

"You really are quite the pretty little thing, aren't you?"

He lets the bag fall to the ground and skulks toward me like a wolf. His anger has become something else. Something far more evil.

"Let me see that shoulder of yours. So beautiful and golden brown, just like the girls I see in the big city."

I clench my jaw and speak.

"Just take that bag and leave."

"I will take and do whatever I want."

Quick as a diving hawk, he swings at me and rips my top off. He touches me in places he shouldn't. My body shakes with panic. I'm afraid he will kill me if I cry out.

"You just obey your uncle and everything will be fine."

I cry out for the illuminated man. "Where are you?"

And then I see his face. So pure, so kind, filled with love and light. I remember his gift. The scroll he put in my hand. But how does it work? How can I use it to save me? What magic spell do I have to say to escape this nightmare?

I open my eyes, and Malako is putting his pants back on. He's not my uncle anymore. He won't look at me, but I look at him. He is not human. He is a demon.

My body throbs with pain that I am certain will never go away. He lifts the bag onto his shoulder and escapes like a cat.

I'm left quivering on the floor, unable to move, wishing I were dead.

Chapter Fifteen

The sunrise paints orange streams across the empty lobby as we walk into the restaurant. It's been only days, but it feels like months have passed since that strange night in the church. I grab a coffee and walk outside to meet Gordon.

I usually don't like to sit in on interviews, but Gordon has again insisted that this is one I don't want to miss. "What else would I be doing at 6:00 a.m.?" I had said to Gordon last night.

"Stuart, a man like Tagoze is worth getting up for," he responded.

Whitney's bombshell kept me awake all night. And no matter how hard I tried, I couldn't get the phone to work again.

A mist has settled in the valley this morning. The clouds pass quickly in front of the mountains as if they are late to an appointment. The sun may not make it out today.

In a matter of moments, Gordon pulls up in his Land Cruiser.

"Good morning, my American friend."

I jump into the passenger seat.

I scowl a "Good morning," and we're off. I've never been a morning person. If it wasn't for the rotgut coffee, I don't think I could form words at all.

We drive down the familiar paved roads until they intersect with dirt paths that are more potholes than roads.

"Sleep well?"

"Yeah. Like a baby."

"I know sarcasm when I hear it, my friend. And I know the hotel isn't up to your impossible American standards, but it's not really that bad, is it?"

"No, the hotel is fine. It's great, actually." I don't really want to have this conversation, but words spill out anyway. "It's just that there's a lot on my mind, you know?"

"This place will do that to you."

"Yeah. That ... and I got a bit of surprising news last night."

"News?"

"My wife ... she's pregnant."

"That's fantastic, man. Congratulations!" He thrusts out his hand to give me a handshake, and the car swerves. He corrects but doesn't seem fazed. "Is this your first?"

"Yeah." First. It seems a rather unusual choice of words. Ominous, in a way, like it's inevitable that we will have two, three, or a dozen more.

"I'm happy for you, my friend."

"Thing is ... I dropped my cell phone right after she told me, and I couldn't get it to work after that. I thought it was just the battery, but I think I jarred something loose inside. I'm sure she thinks I'm a real prize right now—having disappeared off the face of the earth after hearing the news."

"I'm sure she'll understand."

"I'm not so sure. Things haven't been exactly ... um ... great between us lately." Something occurs to me, and my stomach bottoms. "Man, I hope it's mine."

"Wow, you two are really having problems. Do you really think she would … I'll just shut up. It's none of my business." But he can't shut up. He's a reporter. "How far along is she?"

"I don't even know. I thought about sending her an e-mail, but the Internet wasn't working. And I have a feeling she doesn't want to continue the conversation via e-mail."

"Do you think she would cheat on you?"

"I think *I* would cheat on me at this point. But … I don't know. I don't think so." We ride in silence, the clouds still hugging the terrain and the dew falling on the windshield like rain. I've lost track of the days, but I think it is Saturday.

Loyalty is ingrained in Whitney's Southern fibers. She wouldn't cheat on me. Besides, that would only give me one more reason to leave. And if I know one thing about her in this time, it's that she is still hoping for us to find a way.

We pull up to a house that looks vastly different from the others I've seen. In America, this would be considered a dump in the middle of a dump. But here, it is one of the nicer homes you'll find. It is built from concrete blocks. It's small, maybe twelve by eight feet, and the tin roof is held down by about twenty-five large rocks. Rocks seem to be the nail of choice in Africa. Ahead, I see the silhouette of a large man. At a distance, he reminds me of an African god.

"Here's our man," Gordon says. We step out of the car. I grab my bag from the backseat and sling it over my shoulder.

Tagoze has come to greet us. He is dressed in Western clothes—brown pants and an untucked white button-down shirt with wide green and blue stripes. His arms bulge out of his short sleeves. He looks like a black Arnold Schwarzenegger. I would not want to arm wrestle this guy. He stands with confidence but not swagger. I like him even before I meet him, which usually isn't my approach to new people. Whitney said once that everyone in my general area is a jerk until proven otherwise.

He and Gordon exchange the traditional Swazi greeting.

"*Sawubona, babay.*"

"*Yeybo. Sawubona.*"

"Tagoze, this is Stuart."

Tagoze takes my hand and waffle-irons it between his huge mitts. "Stuart, so nice to meet you. So good to meet you."

"Thank you, Tagoze. It's great to meet you."

"Come into my house. I've made some tea." Gordon pulls out a bag of rolls, some cheese, and cut-up fruit.

"I brought along a little something as well," Gordon says. He is a master, I've come to see, at navigating interviews and friendships here in Swaziland, bringing along just the right things. In this land, it would be easy to bring too much, but there's a fine line between appropriate and offense.

"You can leave the camera bag in the car if you want. Tagoze will join us at the care point later today. I thought that might be the best place to take photographs."

"Sounds good." I leave the bag on my shoulder. Gordon shrugs and enters Tagoze's house.

"Make sure you get my good side." Tagoze laughs and turns his head to display his scars, three lines along his upper cheek bone that look like they were drawn by an angry cat.

"Yeah, that's definitely your best side. Were you sparring with a lion?"

"I think my entire face would be gone if that were the case. But you are not so far off."

"Stu," Gordon turns toward me, "Tagoze got those scratches when he—"

Tagoze waves his huge hand through the air. "Let's wait for that story. You know me, once I get going …"

"Yes, I do. That's why I brought this." Gordon produces a micro recorder from a pocket and sets it on the table. Then he pulls out his much-used notebook. That's one thing I've learned from hanging out with writers: The pen is trustier than technology.

Tagoze's house is sparsely furnished. There is a very old, torn love seat against one wall, a small table to the right, two wooden desk chairs adjacent to the coach, and another table made from cardboard boxes that has been covered by a colorful tablecloth. Two pictures hang above the couch, one of the queen mother, the other a very young king with three red feathers sticking up from a small crown. A chicken walks through the living area and into the kitchen like it owns the place.

"Please, sit down. May I offer you some tea?"

"That would be great, Tagoze, for both of us." Gordon gives me a snide look and bumps me with his elbow.

Tagoze walks into the only other room in the house and hollers out, "Stuart, is this your first time in Africa?"

"No, I've traveled all over Africa, but never to Swaziland. You live in a beautiful country."

"It was once a wonderful place to live. Not only beautiful to the eye, but to the soul. Now, all has been polluted."

"I wanted to talk about that," Gordon says. "What changed?"

"Today, it is nearly impossible for a man to be a man."

He comes around the corner with three steaming cups of tea and milk and sugar.

"Thank you." Gordon clicks on the recorder and picks up his pen.

"The African man has been reduced to an animal. Poverty has reduced him to one who must survive at any cost. The duty of 'man the provider' has been discarded. No longer can our men provide the things our families and loved ones need. This used to be simple; now it's nearly impossible. Men need to provide money, but there is no work. They need to provide food but don't have a job and can't buy food."

Tagoze pushes his plate away.

"Too many men in our community choose the ugly path of violence. That is what happens when all hope has disappeared. Nobody cares anymore. Men don't care who gets taken advantage of or who dies. It doesn't matter how innocent, how young, or how vulnerable. This is an ugly truth.

"Things are not soon going to get better, either. Look at all the young men. Every value we have upheld over the centuries has been destroyed. The days of father and son working side by side, sons learning trades and traditions from their fathers—those days are nearly gone. And so the young men do not have any understanding of how to treat our women and no model of a healthy family. Instead, they become directionless and take on the values of hooligans.

"We must find a way to change this. But how do we do this? How do we give hope to men who have lost all hope?"

Tagoze sits back in his chair and crosses his legs. He stares into some distant, hopeful future, looking more like a sage than a muscle-bound man who could wrestle lions.

"I want to tell you a story about a herd of elephants," he continues. "During a time of great drought, many of the herd died, including all of the older bull elephants. The bull elephants had been the leaders—the teachers of the young. Over a period of time, with no example to show them how to live, the younger bull elephants started to go crazy. They tormented the rest of the herd, fighting and injuring the females and offspring. They acted like warriors who had no war and so decided to simply kill for killing's sake. Well, one day these wild elephants stormed a village. Many people died in that village, stomped by elephants or gored by their tusks. My friends, elephants do not usually act this way. While they have great power, we have lived in harmony with them for many generations. Their terror was a tragic, terrible thing.

"I am certain smart men like you don't need me to tell you how these young bull elephants are like the young men in our country. These are the worst of times. Death and disease have broken down everything we have worked so hard to build. So what keeps the young bull elephants—the young men who have no direction—from raping and plundering our homes and families? Nothing. Our hope for change is hanging on by a hair.

"This is also my life. Wanting to be a man. I hate this feeling of powerlessness and helplessness. Before my wife died, she used to say, 'Tagoze, you are God's answer. You can only say yes to His plans for your life, and you don't always know how He is working. You have to trust.'"

"How did your wife die?" I ask, and the moment I ask it, I wish

I hadn't. Tagoze turns to me, looks me in the eyes, and speaks with an intensity that unsettles me.

"I did not lose her to the plague. I lost her and all my children in a terrible fire. Everyone called the fire an accident, but I am to blame."

"I'm so sorry."

"The night before, I had been drinking again. I had said many terrible things to my wife. We fought, and I'm ashamed to say that I hit her. More than once. On the night of the fire, I was drinking at the Shabine, the local bar. I saw the flames as I staggered down the road toward home. People were yelling in the distance, '*Simo bucayi, simo bucayi!*' 'Emergency, emergency!' I arrived just in time to see my wife tear out of the house, her whole body engulfed in blue and orange flames."

He turns away for a moment, but when he returns his gaze to me, his intensity has been replaced by something else. Resolve, perhaps.

"At first, I wanted to die. I thought about killing myself. But Pastor Walter kept checking in on me, praying for me, with me. His friendship changed my life forever. I gave my life to God, and the Lord made me into a new person."

He stands and collects the now-empty teacups.

"I lost my family to a fire. But now a fire burns in me to do what I can for my people. Though I am but one man, I will not stop trying."

Gordon stands, walks over to Tagoze, and embraces him. This is no embarrassed man-hug that calls for violent patting of the back and a quick release. It is a true picture of compassion. My throat tightens up, and I snap a mental photo of this scene.

Gordon takes the teacups from Tagoze and heads into the other room. Tagoze sits back down at the small table.

"Gordon tells me you have met my little friend Adanna," he says, a broken smile growing on his weathered face.

"Yes … just the other day. She had a scar on her arm …"

Tagoze reaches up and touches the scars on his own face.

"I remember when she worked in a neighbor's fields. Seven days she plowed the ground, planted corn, and carefully watered each and every tiny mound where the seed was sleeping. She had earned enough money to buy some food, so she headed to the village store. I happened to be coming home from a long, tiring day working in the orchards. There was Adanna, skipping and smiling as if she was about to be the guest of honor at a birthday party. There was reason to celebrate indeed.

"She wasn't in the store but a moment before she burst out with a green apple in her hand, and a grin on her face as wide as the Maputo River. I was mesmerized by her joy. I watched as she skipped proudly down the road, toward home. But something stopped her in her tracks.

"Just ahead of her, lying beneath a tree, was a little boy named Tembe. Everyone knew Tembe. Both his parents had died from AIDS, and little Tembe was dying of starvation. Many of us gave him the crumbs from our tables, but it wasn't enough to defeat disease and sickness.

"Like a tender, loving doctor, Adanna crouched on one knee and placed her hand on his forehead. He didn't move. She looked at the apple in her right hand and back to Tembe. There was no doubt what she would do. With her mouth still salivating from the thought of that first bite, she brought the apple low to the ground into Tembe's line of sight. Slowly, as if waking from a deep sleep, he sat up and gratefully took the apple from her hand. That, my friend, is the heart of this dear girl."

He touches the scars again.

"You asked about these scars," he says, and his smile fades. "You do all you can to protect the children. But it is never enough.""

Gordon returns with fresh cups of tea.

"I heard a scream coming from the back of the bar as I was walking by. I did not think twice—I knew what sort of men hung out there. Bad men, men like I once was. When I saw what was happening, I exploded in rage. I pulled a demon off of Adanna and beat him until he died."

I am stunned, wide-eyed, and my heart has snapped in half. That poor little girl. I swallow hard.

"These scars are new, but the evil that caused them is not. And I will continue to fight against it."

I take a deep breath. "Lucky for Adanna you happened to be passing by. I can't imagine what would have happened if you weren't ..."

"I do not believe in luck, Mr. Stuart."

"There's more to Adanna's story, Stuart." Gordon turns to me and places his hand on my shoulder. "Her mother died yesterday."

A strange blend of ache and anger fills me. I want to hit something or someone. And I want to crawl into a hole and hide.

"I wish I could say this kind of thing does not happen here," Tagoze says, "but the sad truth is, it happens far too often. We have become more like animals than men, and even to say this is unfair to the animals.

"Light has to be sown in the middle of this miserable darkness. So I do my part. Whatever I can." Tagoze sees me look at his scars. "Whatever I must."

"What will become of Adanna?" I ask.

"I will help her and her brother and sister as I can. I am certain Pastor Walter will too. Her physical scars will heal in time, but I do not know about the scars inside."

"She is strong, Tagoze. I saw it in her eyes," Gordon says.

"She is just a little girl, but our God is a very big God," Tagoze says. "I have to trust that He will take care of her when we cannot."

Gordon reaches over and clicks off the tape recorder. Our breakfast meeting is over. As we walk back to the Land Cruiser, Tagoze stops us to add an addendum to one of his stories.

"The story of the elephants has an interesting ending," he begins. "A group of scientists got together and decided there was only one thing that could be done to help the elephants. They found three bull elephants from another herd and relocated them to the out-of-control herd.

"An amazing thing happened. The seasoned bull elephants stood together, side by side. They watched as the younger elephants wreaked havoc. After they saw enough, the older elephants simultaneously left each other's sides and challenged the younger bulls in battle. The older elephants drove the younger into the ground with brute force and superior skill. They pinned them there, refusing to let them move. This went on for sixteen hours.

"After that time, they let the rebels up. The younger elephants cowered at the sides of the older, stronger bulls. And that was it. They never exhibited the crazy, carousing, out-of-control behavior again. Peace and order had been restored to the herd.

"This, too, is my prayer for our people. That the older elephants would rise up and do what is good, what is moral, what is African. But where are those men?

"I, at least, will be one."

Chapter Sixteen

I look out the side mirror and see Tagoze's massive figure becoming a speck as we drive down the main road. In Swaziland, there are only two main roads. One runs north to south, the other east to west. They are new, smooth roads not unlike any well-traveled highway in America. But once you turn off from the main roads, you're in for an entirely different experience.

The sound of shredding metal raking across the surface of the asphalt as we turn off the main road is a vivid reminder that this is not America. One second you're cruising at sixty miles per hour, and the next your vehicle is crawling like a moon rover over millions of rocks and boulders as you dodge potholes as big as your vehicle. No wonder nobody drives at night around here.

No matter where you go in this country, if you are white, people will notice you. They stop whatever they're doing, smile like they're posing for a glamour shot, then wave enthusiastically in your direction. Perhaps they think we are bringing food, medicine, clothes. They know we are here because we choose to be. We could be doing a thousand other things in a thousand other places. Instead, here we are, the pale ghosts of hope.

There are scattered cornfields on the slopes of these hills, but they are mostly an exercise in frustration. There has been too little rain. The corn comes up but can't produce a viable crop. Futile fields are abandoned, left alone to be attacked by disease and parasites.

I look at Gordon, who's been uncharacteristically quiet.

"Where are we headed?"

"Another care point."

"Could we stop by Walter's place instead? I'd like to get some more pictures of Walter, and ..."

"And?"

"I also want to see how Adanna is doing."

Gordon turns and raises his eyebrows.

"Careful, Stuart. You're about to break the golden rule here in Africa."

"Golden rule? What, loving my neighbor?"

"No, I'm talking about focusing too much on one particular child instead of the overall situation—the crisis in this country. Don't get sucked in. Remember, you're a journalist."

"A journalist. Yeah. I am certainly that."

But is that all I am? "I don't know how you do it, Gordon. How you can live here among all the poverty and desperation without going crazy. Everywhere I turn, there's another sad story. Poverty is like a stray, starving dog you fed once and now follows you everywhere."

"Hey!" He grabs his notebook and throws it at me. The pen drops onto the floor and rolls under my feet. "Write that down, what you just said about poverty and a starving dog."

I struggle to write as the car jerks and bounces.

"I've lived here for some time," Gordon says, "trying to wrap my brain around this situation and find a way to help. I'm not saying there isn't value in helping an individual child. Of course that's important.

It's critically important. My point is that you have to juggle two realities—the big picture and the small one. If you lose sight of the big one, you might just miss opportunities to help in small ways."

I think about this, and I hear the words "Feed My sheep."

"What is it about this place, Gordon? It twists you all up inside and messes with your head."

"And your heart."

"Yeah, that, too."

"In this place, Stu, God has a way of bringing people down to the essence of who they are."

I wonder about the people who live here. What is their essence?

The homesteads along this road are peppered across the hills like ships scattered across the sea. It is a far cry from the crowded cityscape of New York or even the cut-and-paste communities of American suburbia. If the homes were huge, it might remind me a little of the ranches of Montana. But these homes are sticks and rocks and mud. And there are no SUVs parked along snaking driveways.

"Gordon, I'd like to pull over at the next store."

"Stores are hard to come by around here."

"How far?"

"At least an hour. Forget your hairspray or something?"

"Very funny. No, I want to get some things to hand out to the kids. It's the least I can do."

"Stuart, that's very noble of you. But we've got to stay on course here. I do still need to get paid for this project, and so do you."

The car makes a sudden swing around. A few hundred yards later, Gordon turns down a road I never would have known existed.

"But then again, maybe that is just what we need to do after all."

The store is not at all like your local Safeway. It's tiny with four or five isles. As soon as I step inside, I am accosted by the pungent smell of unrefrigerated meat. Flies are hovering around lamb, beef, and chicken, landing now and then to take a few bites.

Gordon walks ahead of me.

"The sugar cane workers shop here. They're mostly white men in management jobs. They're the ones with the coin. The blacks could hardly afford to buy anything here with the slave wage they receive for hacking through cane twelve hours a day."

Perusing the shelves, I quickly realize I don't have the faintest idea what half of this stuff is: gravy powders, curry, piri-piri oil, biltong—a meat of some kind—mielie-meal, and huge bags of beans and rice.

The packaging looks like most American products ... from ten years ago. This stuff has been sitting around for ages. I pick up a package in search of an expiration date. Three years beyond "sell by" date.

"Gordon, what is this stuff?"

"This must look like Chinese to you."

I read the label out loud. "'Biltong.' Even sounds a little like Chinese. What is it?"

"They're strips of sun-dried, spiced meat. Just like your beef jerky."

"Beef jerky can stay good for years. I think I should get some."

"I remember the first time a came into a shop like this. My daughter pulled things down from the shelves as fast as she could and piled them into my wife's basket. I was so overwhelmed by the whole situation, I just let her go. You can't believe how much we spent that day!" He laughs, but I can see the sadness on his face. "Now, I'm a pro. Let me help you out."

Without missing a beat, Gordon throws a myriad of strange

boxes in the cart. I recognize the basics—corn, rice, and tea—but other than that, I have no idea what the stuff is.

Four staff huddle together in the corner by the cash register, watching us with great amusement. They laugh and point, covering their mouths sheepishly. If that happened in my local Safeway, I'd definitely complain to the manager.

"Why are those clerks gawking at us?"

"Well, to you, this may seem like a typical shopping day, but here, nobody shops like this."

"Because they don't have money?"

A white couple walks by, staring at our cart without inhibition. They have three things in their hands and it looks like they're done shopping.

"In part because of that, but also because of culture. In Africa you only live for the day. No one would buy this quantity of food unless they were having a huge party."

"I guess that makes sense. But it's hard to fathom something as basic as food being a luxury."

"T.I.A., my friend."

"What?"

"T.I.A.: This is Africa."

"Got it."

We place the items on the counter. There's a single bag of wet wipes next to a first-aid kit, so I swipe them both. The clerks huddle together with big smiles on their faces and nods of excitement. One starts to ring us up, and the others watch with great interest, happy as larks.

"Okay, what's the damage? I hope I have enough cash; this looks like a fortune."

The cashier's voice breaks off in accented English, "Seven hundred and ten rand."

Turning to Gordon, I ask, "How much is that?"

"Let's see. One hundred and one dollars."

"That's it? For this much food! I'd spend this much on dinner with a decent bottle of wine."

"You and a million other Westerners."

"Okay, you can pull the knife out of my chest now."

Moments later we are outside, packing the food in the Land Cruiser. Hoisting fifty-kilogram bags of food over my shoulder isn't something I've done very often, but I can imagine it would have been easier a few years ago. When I was not so out of shape.

"Ow!" My hand grabs hold of my lower back. That didn't feel so good.

"You all right, old man?"

"Old man? You're twice my age."

"You couldn't tell by the way you lift those bags."

As the dust spits behind the tires, we finally round the corner toward the care point—Pastor Walter's care point. My heart starts to beat a little faster, and my palms sweat.

The place looks exactly like we left it yesterday. The same children sit under the trees. The same widows huddle next to the rotting pyramid of wood wondering when they will next cook a meal. A spirit of despair loiters here like an unwanted guest.

Our arrival changes everything. People jump up as if jarred by electricity. They head toward us, some hobbling, others jogging. The first bag of food pokes its head out of the vehicle like a man emerging from beneath the water, and the whole community comes to life.

Women clap, run to us, and lift their hands to heaven crying, "Praise God, thank God!" In a nanosecond, children bear in on us like heat-seeking missiles and shout, "Please, mister. Me, mister, please!"

The gratitude gushing out of their souls is like a sudden rainstorm in the midst of a draught. And we bring so little.

The gogos, busy as a swarm of bees, arrange wood and light a fire. They've been waiting for days, so they're not going to waste a second.

Every face is filled with beauty and the anticipation of a good meal. But I don't see the face I'm looking for. Adanna is nowhere to be found.

"Gordon, could you ask someone to take me to Adanna's place? I don't see her anywhere."

"Sure. Eshe, run with Stuart and find Adanna would you?"

A lovely college-aged girl with short hair and a glowing face looks our direction. She's wearing a T-shirt that says "Children's HopeChest."

"No problem, Gordon. Mr. Daniels, are you ready?"

How does she know who I am?

"Let me just gather what I want to give her from the car." I grab what I can and it really doesn't seem like much, but I suspect it's enough food to last her family a week.

"Do I need to be on the lookout for snakes, Eshe?" I hate snakes.

"Not in the winter. Now, if it was summer, you would be in big trouble!"

"Big trouble?"

"Yes. You're really afraid of snakes aren't you?"

"You have no idea."

"Last year, the men killed a nine-foot black mamba."

"Where?"

"Right over there by the hut. You look so surprised. You should not be—after all, they were here first."

She smiles at me, clearly pleased with herself for making me squirm. But it is a sweet smile. I think she is just teasing me.

As we walk, I begin to notice things I hadn't the other day. There is trash littered across the dirt paths—everything from tin cans to scattered animal bones. Cacti grow like they're on steroids along with something I think must be called a "devilbush." This bush is more prominent than weeds and far more intimidating. Hooked thorns hang by the hundreds off its branches, just waiting for careless passersby to become entangled … and probably bleed to death.

Gordon told me this area is known as "the valley of a thousand hills," and I see why. When we crest the top of a hill, you can see hundreds more kaleidoscoping in every direction.

"An interesting landscape you have here, Eshe."

"You think so? Why do you say that?"

"There are so many beautiful things about it on one hand and on the other …"

"So many ugly things?"

"Hmm … maybe not ugly. Contradictory."

"What does that mean?"

"Like beauty and ashes or light and dark. There's so many incredible things about your country and so many terrible things."

Soon, we arrive at Adanna's. I recognize the two tree limbs standing guard to the open door.

I knock on the broken door that rests up against the house. No answer.

"Hello?" Eshe says. "Adanna?"

She pushes the door aside and I follow.

It's dark. The smell of burnt wood hits me in the face. I notice there's no hole to ventilate the place. The ceiling is pitch black from soot. There are smoldering ashes in the middle of the room.

"Adanna?"

"Hello? Anyone here?"

There's the faint sound of sniffling. My eyes quickly adjust to the darkness, and I spot a child curled up in the fetal position.

"Adanna?" Precious and Abu are sitting on the opposite side of the room, huddled together. They're a mess. What has happened here?

Without a second thought, I gather her in my arms.

"Are you okay?" I look at her legs, "You're bleeding! Eshe, help!"

Adanna is not comforted by my presence. A look of fear rests in her eyes. I take a quick inventory of the room and wonder if there has been a fight. A broken cup and some things I don't recognize are scattered across the floor. Then I realize … the room is almost completely empty. Can a family really have nothing?

Eshe is by my side, stroking Adanna's hair and speaking soothing words to her in S'swati.

"Ask her what happened."

"I have, but she will not say. I can tell you one thing though."

"What's that?"

"Somebody very bad did this to her."

Chapter Seventeen

She's been beaten pretty badly. She is shivering from head to toe like someone just pulled her out of a frozen lake. There are bruises on her skinny arms and one on her foot. The goose egg over her left eye is swollen and red, and her lips are crusted with blood. My stomach tightens when I remember what Tagoze told me this morning.

She won't utter a word. From the looks of her body and torn clothes, I have some idea of what took place. My brain takes orbit in a new planetary sphere, one I cannot fathom. I am shaking my head back and forth over and over as I look at this child, her brother and sister huddled in the corner, in this barren hut. Where is God in this?

"Eshe, what do you do in a place like this to get help? Do you call the police?" As the words leave my mouth, I already know the answer.

"The police don't care."

I pick up the little boy, who has started to cry, and walk outside the door. Precious follows behind.

She says something in S'swati, and I don't understand her, but I hear Adanna's name.

I am surprised when Abu puts his head on my shoulder. I pat his back and sit down in front of their hut. The girl, who I'm guessing is about four, sits next to me. She is dressed in a dirty pink skirt and red shirt. She smoothes out her skirt like a lady, something she no doubt saw her mother do many times. Her tiny nails are dirty. Still, she is beautiful, like her sister.

"What is your name?" I say to her. She just looks at me, so I point to myself and say, "Stuart." Then I point behind me into the house and say, "Adanna." Then I repeat the exercise.

A big smile crosses her face. She points to me and says, "Duard," then inside and says, "Adanna." Then she proudly points to herself, "Precious."

"What a beautiful name." Somehow, she understands and sits a little taller. Then she points to her brother and says, "Abu." I'm not sure if that's his name, or if it means baby. I wish I could sweep them all away.

I look at the dirt path leading to this home, isolated and totally unprotected. There's no alarm system to set, no way to even bolt and lock the door. I can picture the perpetrator warning Adanna to stay quiet or he will hurt her more next time. There is no justice here. Only fear. I am convinced this is the very root of wickedness. Precious leans into me, quiet as a mouse. Birds chirp in the distance. The baby sighs. And I am suffocated with my inability to help these children.

After a few minutes—though time has no measure in this surreal place—Abu has fallen asleep. I stand carefully and walk back inside. His sister follows and points to a mat, and I lay him down. My heart is breaking.

Eshe is sitting next to Adanna, her hand gently placed on Adanna's back. Eshe knows how to handle this.

I bend down beside her. Precious follows me like a shadow. "Adanna, I'm so sorry. I will do what I can to help you."

She looks up at me with big brown eyes that reveal more pain and loss than I've ever known but says nothing.

"I know you're scared. I will protect you." I feel the anger rising up. I don't feel as patient as Eshe. "Tell us who did this to you."

Silence.

"She's too scared, Stuart. And you're just a stranger. There's no way she'll tell us who's responsible. It could even be a relative."

A relative? God forbid.

Her clothes are badly ripped. I look for something she can put on but find nothing. I take off my shirt and offer it to her. Precious covers her mouth with two hands and laughs at the sight of my bare white torso and hairy chest.

Adanna shakes her head. She won't take the shirt.

"Eshe, will you please ask her to put this on?"

Surprisingly, Adanna lets her.

"Is there anything we can do to help you?"

Nothing.

"Can we take you to someone? Is there somewhere you want to go?"

Still nothing. I stand and brush the dirt from my pants. It won't brush off because it is not only dirt but also blood. Adanna's blood.

I pick up the first-aid kit and open it. The cold pack inside snaps in my hand, and Adanna is startled.

"I'm sorry. This is a cold pack for your head. It may not feel good at first, but you need to let Eshe hold it so the swelling will go down." Eshe takes it and slowly works it onto her head like an expert. Adanna doesn't move.

"Precious, would you help me?" Eshe repeats the phrase in S'swati so Precious can understand.

Precious smiles. "I know what you say." Clever girl. Apparently, she knows some English.

I spot a small ramshackle cabinet on the opposite side of the room. It creaks as I open it. The room instantly fills with dancing specks of dust reflecting in the light. This obviously hasn't been used in quite some time. I use one of the wipes to clean the inside of the cabinet. When I finish, it is almost completely black from dirt and soot. I offer another wipe to Precious. She starts to clean alongside me.

"No, honey. For your face and hands." She looks confused, so I bend down and wipe her hands. Then I take another and gently wipe her face. She stays very still.

I empty the bags of food onto the floor and hand them to Precious to put away. Soup. Tea. Sugar. Canned meat. Oranges. She organizes them neatly inside the cupboard, except for one orange, which she hides behind her back.

"You don't have to hide it—it's for you. Do you want me to peel it?" She looks up at me and nods. As I take off the skin, she grabs the peel from my hand and stuffs it in her mouth.

"No, no, wait." She laughs and keeps chewing. I give her the orange in quarters, and she eats it.

Eshe continues to talk to Adanna, trying to soothe her, and begins to dab at her cuts with the little antiseptic pads from the first-aid kit.

At last she is looking up at us. I can tell she is thankful, but that thankfulness is quickly pushed aside by shock, grief, and a soul-deep devastation.

A rage begins to boil in me. Real rage, rage that could kill. There will be a white-hot place in hell for the worthless pigs who do things like this.

"Eshe, would you be willing to stay here while I go find Walter?" I hate to leave her here, but I can't think of what else to do. "I'll come right back with him or my friend Gordon."

"I go with you," Precious says and steps next to me like a little soldier.

I hear a scratchy, weak voice say, "No. Precious, you stay here with me."

It's Adanna's voice.

Closing in on the care point, I spot Gordon playing soccer with some of the kids. He stops when he sees me.

"Stuart, what is it? Where is your shirt?" His face twists with concern.

"It's Adanna, Gordon. She's been hurt. Bad. We need to get Walter."

Pastor Walter is sitting on concrete steps outside of the church. He looks intense. I can tell he's teaching a young woman about something important, maybe helping her deal with a husband who has ten other wives and could be bringing the AIDS virus to her bed, or about malnutrition, or about how to get rid of the worms in her belly she's picked up from drinking contaminated water.

I rush up, Gordon following, and interrupt their teaching time. He and the woman look at me, and the woman covers her mouth. She hides a smile behind her hand. I had forgotten for a moment that I was shirtless.

"Pastor Walter—we need your help." I am out of breath, realizing for the second time today that I have a long way to go to get back into shape.

"Yes, my brother. What is it?"

"Could I talk to you in private?"

"Sister, give me just one moment, would you?"

We walk inside and to the back of the room.

"Stuart, where is your shirt?"

"I gave it to Adanna. Eshe and I just went to visit her—to take her some food. But when we got there ..."

He grabs the back of his head with his right hand. "Is she okay?"

"I don't know."

"What happened?"

"She wouldn't talk. It looked like someone broke in and stole things from the house. It's been picked clean. And Walter ... Adanna is a mess—beaten up badly. Bleeding in places." Gordon cranes his neck to listen in.

Walter is shaking his head. "Can things get any worse for that poor child?"

"I think they are worse," I say, unsure what words to use. "Walter ... her clothes were shredded."

"Oh, dear God in heaven. Not again."

"Eshe is with her now. I'm afraid for them to be alone. What if the monster who did this comes back?"

"Run back to her house right away. Gordon, you go too. Then send Eshe back. I will come as quickly as I can."

"Do we need anything, Stuart?" Gordon grabs his backpack from the Land Cruiser.

I grab an extra shirt from my bag and struggle into it as we jog toward Adanna's house.

"No, I already brought her food—and for some reason had the first-aid kit with me too. It's already being put to use."

We start down the narrow dirt path, shoulder to shoulder.

"I would call that providential, Stuart."

"Providence. Yeah, let's talk about the providence of being raped, Gordon. What about that providence? I can't imagine how God can sit up in the heavens, watch this happen, and do nothing. Where's the rain of fire and brimstone to defeat the evil?"

"God is grieved."

"Then why won't He act?"

Gordon sighs loudly.

"That is a tricky question, one I've thought about a lot."

"Of course, Gordon. I'm sorry ... I wasn't thinking ..."

"No, it's good to wrestle with these questions. There was a time when I nearly lost my faith over them—but now ... now I am content to rest in the mystery of it all."

"Content? Really? But it's all so senseless—you, a good man, losing your family. Adanna ... I can't even say it. Why would anyone do that to a little girl ... she's just a little girl, Gordon!"

"Oh, I am not content with the evil—I hate the evil. And I will do anything I can to fight it. But the mystery—how God is working in all this ... that I have learned to trust."

Three kids pass us holding hands, heading to the care point. The youngest can't be older than two, and the oldest only around five. They are barefoot and caked in dirt.

"After seeing all this ugliness … I just don't know if I can trust in anything, Gordon."

"It's taken me years to come to this, but here is what I've concluded: The utter depravity of these terrible acts, the sheer poverty and sickness, death, and sadness—these things can weigh down your soul and render it weak and useless, or they can stir your soul to life in a way that changes you. And other people as a result.

"I believe this is God's way. His heart is broken over what happened to Adanna, this I know. But look at your feet, Stuart, you are racing to her aid. You are God's feet. You are showing kindness. You are God's hands. You have fed her and her family. You are feeding His sheep."

These familiar words punch my gut and stir my soul. The growing wind blows tears from my face onto the scorched earth. The wind is carrying something else, a sound.

"Gordon, do you hear that?"

"Yes. It's voices. Screaming."

We both start running. I race as if a lion is chasing me. Up ahead is the hut, the door wide open. A stuffed white burlap sack is resting against the side of the house. The red label from a package of rice pokes out through the opening.

Eshe is screaming in S'swati. I can only make out the word "No." Inside, a large man is pushing Eshe up against the wall. He is hitting her and ripping at her clothes.

My eye catches a form moving on the other side of the room. Adanna is stumbling across the room, a tin cup in her hand up over her head. She sees me, our eyes catch, and she freezes. Fresh blood flows from her nose and lip. A searing flash of red rips through my cortex, and I lunge forward.

I grab the beast from behind. He's got to be twice my size, but I pull him to the floor. My fists pound with a fury I've never known. Each blast rings true. Flesh and bone ripping and cracking beneath my fists. I can't stop myself. He tries to escape, but trips over the burlap bag. I leap onto him again and grab his neck. I want to squeeze the life out of him. A hand grabs the back of my shirt and tugs me away.

"Stuart, stop. You're going to kill him."

"I don't care."

"There are laws in this country, and they won't work in your favor. You've made him pay a price. Now leave it alone."

I look at the blood pouring from his nose and mouth. The right side of his face is badly swollen. I never imagined I would ever be angry enough to want to kill a man.

Gordon says something in S'swati. The man hoists himself up. He gives me a piercing stare—a Charles Manson stare. I feel a power deep inside me, and I do not look away. Gordon speaks to him again, and the man shouts something, then turns and shuffles away.

"What did he say?"

"It's not worth repeating."

"What did you say to him?"

"I told him, 'God sees what you've done, you snake. You will not go unpunished.'" He pauses. "Then I told him to get out of here and never come back."

My mind starts to clear. We step into the house.

"Eshe, are you okay?"

She is crying and has her arms around Adanna, who is also sobbing.

"Adanna. Are you okay?"

Eshe looks at me. She has scratches on her face, but otherwise seems unharmed.

"He meant to steal everything you brought," she says. "He was so angry and started to beat Adanna again. I tried to stop him, but I could not."

Adanna's sobs become a low, guttural moan. How much does one girl have to suffer?

"Where are Precious and Abu? Do you see the little ones anywhere, Gordon?"

"He told them to run away." Adanna sobs louder.

"I'll find them," Gordon says. He steps out of the hut and begins calling their names.

I put my hand on Adanna's shoulder. "I will do all I can to make sure that man will never hurt you again." My voice is quiet. I can offer more than a tenuous hope.

Suddenly I hear the bang of the door and a thud. Eshe yells something in S'swati.

Before I can turn around, hot burning fire is lodged in my back. I reach behind myself and feel something hot and wet. Blood. Everything begins to cloud over.

The evil man scrambles out of the hut, grabs the white bag, and disappears. Gordon comes running moments later.

"Gordon, I think I've been stabbed."

Chapter Eighteen

God only knows where that knife has been. The wound on my back pulsates in waves.

Gordon is by my side. "Stuart, oh man, you're bleeding really bad."

Eshe is holding Abu. Precious is standing next to her, a look of horror on her face. Adanna springs back to life and kneels next to me like an angel in prayer.

Gordon reaches over and turns my head so he can look me in the eyes. I am having trouble focusing.

"I'm going to peel up your shirt so I can get a better look," he says. I wince as he carefully rolls up the back of my T-shirt.

"He got you good. It looks deep."

My head is a cantaloupe, and I can barely hold it up.

"Eshe, run back to the care point. Tell Walter to drive up here with my car as fast as he can. Hurry!" He throws her the keys, she sets down Abu, and she's gone. Gordon walks around the hut, looking for something. He mutters, "That devil must have taken the first-aid kit."

I hear ripping sounds. Gordon ties two ends of his shirt together. "I'm going to wrap this around your torso, Stuart. Adanna, put your hand on it and press down. We have to stop the bleeding."

She puts her hand on my back. I scream in pain. It is a sound I have never heard escape my own lips.

Precious comes over and tries to help, but Adanna shakes her head and motions for her to back away. Precious sits down right in front of me, a pouty, sympathetic look on her face. I muster a smile that quickly morphs into a wince. Scooting closer to me, she eyes her sister to measure her response. When she gets none, leans against me, offering her closeness as a hug.

"Who was that man?" Gordon asks.

Adanna does not respond.

"Please, Adanna, we must know. He has done very bad things."

Precious answers instead.

"Uncle Malako."

"Your uncle?"

"He's my aunt's husband and nothing more." I turn at the sound of Adanna's scratchy, low voice. She is talking through clenched teeth. "I am sorry for what he did to you," she says to me.

"I am sorry for what he did to *you*, for everything." My body starts to slump over. The last thing I remember before blacking out is seeing Walter standing in the doorway.

The doctors shout in English. This is good.

"He's lost a lot of blood!" I barely make out what looks like the face of a young African doctor. He's wearing a white coat with a stethoscope around his neck. Like any doc you'd see in a movie.

Lights flash and monitors beep like an untrained handbell choir. The gurney I'm lying on flies down the hall. We pass people who are nothing more than blurs and swirls to my semiconscious brain. I am holding tight to my orange pack, which has somehow made it onto this crazy train.

This looks nothing like an American hospital. People are stacked everywhere, like rows of hot-dog buns; on the floors, two to a bed, and under the beds. I come to a rest in a room that is surprisingly empty. I can't tell if it's an operating room … or a morgue.

The walls are made from gray cinder blocks and match the clammy metal fixtures perfectly. I expect to see an IV line in my arm, but there is none. A black cat darts through the hall. Tremors run up and down my spine. If blood loss doesn't kill me, surely a staph infection will.

I'm not ready to die.

Where is Gordon?

"Hello, Mr. Daniels, I'm Dr. Smith."

I lift my hand to shake his and pain jets through my back.

"Just try to stay still."

"You don't sound African. Neither does your name." My words drip slowly from my mouth as if through molasses.

"Nope. I'm American. Moved here ten years ago to help establish this hospital."

"You came here on purpose?"

He laughs.

"Yes, on purpose." He is holding up an X-ray, studying it against the flickering fluorescent lights. "I have good news for you. We were worried that the knife had punctured one of your kidneys. I'm happy to tell you that's not the case. It was a near miss."

"Thank God."

"Another few millimeters to the left and it would have been a different story."

Gordon appears behind the doctor. He is wearing a look of concern.

"Is he okay, Doc?"

I see another figure trailing behind him. Adanna.

"Eshe and Walter took the little ones for the night, but we decided Adanna could use a bit of attention at the hospital too."

"Hello again." I must sound delirious. Perhaps I am.

The doctor walks around the gurney and checks my vitals. He smiles at Adanna.

"I see you have good friends looking out for you," he says to me. "We are concerned about infection setting in so we're going to have you on some strong antibiotics. Other than that, you should be fine."

"Thanks, Doc."

"We'll get you some fresh blood and finish sewing you up and then you can be on your way. Looks like you'll need about twenty stitches."

"You mean I haven't been stitched up yet?"

"Not yet. Don't worry. We've got a pressure bandage holding you together for the moment."

"Okay."

He leaves for more than a few minutes, during which I fade in and out of consciousness. Every time my eyes open, I see Adanna standing beside Gordon. And every time she sees me looking at her, she brings a smile to her face.

Dr. Smith comes back, and I feel every stitch as it goes in, muted only slightly by local anesthetics. When he is finished, I half expect him to slap me on the back and say, "All done!" Instead, he strips off his rubber gloves and walks around so he can look me in the eye.

"Nineteen," he says.

"Nineteen?"

"Stitches. That's how many it took. No need for a twentieth, even if it would have made me particularly pleased to have guessed exactly right."

I think he is being funny so I smile.

"Now, be sure you keep your stitches and the wound clean at all times. And don't go swimming for a while. That would be a very bad idea."

"Got it. No swimming."

"One more thing."

"Yes?"

"Please try to stay away from crazies wielding knives."

"Yeah. That's my plan."

"We'll need to see you back here in a few days, to check the wound."

"Of course."

"Now, young lady," he turns to Adanna. "Do you think you could come with me to get Mr. Daniels' medicine?"

He looks at Gordon, "Is this okay with you?"

"Certainly, if it's okay with Adanna."

"It's fine," she says, and walks with the doctor. I can hear him saying, "Maybe we can find some medicine for you, too."

"Tomorrow, we must go and file a police report," I say.

"That would be like throwing a complaint into a hurricane."

"Why?"

He lowers his voice. "Well, first they won't believe that he raped the girl. In this country it's always the adult's word over the child's. They'd never believe her in a thousand years."

"So there's nothing that can be done?"

"Nothing. And you wonder why there's an AIDS problem?"

"Not anymore, I don't. But what about the fact that he stabbed me?"

"It's his word against yours. He'll say it was self-defense because you were beating the crap out of him. You may get in more trouble than he would. At the very least, it would waste an entire day."

"There is no justice in this country."

A U2 song emanates from my backpack. "Gordon, can you fish that out of my pack?" He hands me my suddenly functioning cell phone.

"Hello?"

"It's Whitney. Good morning."

"Uh, yeah, good morning. It's morning here? Or there?"

"Stuart, you sound terrible. What's wrong?"

"Nothing. Well, not much. What makes you think something's wrong?"

"Where are you? I hear a lot of noise in the background. What's that beeping?"

"Well, it's a long story, Whit. But it's nothing to worry about." Gordon turns his back to me, shaking his head.

"Would you just tell me, please?"

"I'm at the hospital. I was stabbed. But I'm okay now."

Chapter Nineteen

"This isn't funny, Stuart. Are you being serious, or is this one of your badly timed jokes?"

"I wish it were a joke. Wait, no, I don't really mean that. I wouldn't joke about things like this … I …"

"Just tell me what happened."

"Well … I was visiting the home of this young girl—her name is Adanna—anyway, she has had it really rough because her mother just died from AIDS and Adanna had been attacked once by an evil man and just before I got to her house—I was bringing her food and stuff—she had been attacked again, but this time by her uncle so when he came back later and I walked in on him, I beat him up real good and told him never to come back but then later he did and snuck up behind me and stabbed me.…"

"Oh, is that all?"

"Yeah, that pretty much covers it."

"Stuart …"

"Wait, I forgot to mention that Adanna is, like maybe twelve years old and that she has two younger siblings who were there too."

"Those poor children. Are they okay? And are you really okay?"

"I'm about as okay as a man can be with a stab wound in his

back. Adanna … she's been through a lot, but I think she's going to be okay too. And the other two are fine."

I can hear a sigh that is both relief and resignation. "You can be such an idiot sometimes, Stuart." She's not angry. She knows me better than I know myself. "I was all ready to yell at you for hanging up on me the other night, but how can I possibly be angry at someone who risks his life to save helpless children?"

Children. Whitney.

"You're going to have a baby!"

"Why, yes *we* are. Glad you finally caught on."

"Babe … Whitney, I am so sorry. I dropped the phone and couldn't get it to work again. The Internet was down and all the phones went out and I have no idea why the cell phone is suddenly working now but I'm so glad it is.…"

"Whoa … slow down. It's okay, Stuart. Relax."

"I think the pain medication is starting to kick in because I'm starting to feel a little loopy."

"Starting to?" She laughs, and it makes me smile. "We don't have to talk now. It can wait. I'm just glad you're okay … and that you didn't hang up on me. Right now you just need to heal."

In more ways than one. But for the first time in a long time, I actually think it might just be possible.

"Is there a doctor or nurse nearby?"

"Um … yeah. I think the doctor is just outside. He was here a minute ago.…"

"Let me talk to him."

"Okay."

"And, Stuart …"

"Yes?"

"I love you."

Despite the drugs, or perhaps because of them, I don't hesitate. "I love you too."

Gordon has already gone after Dr. Smith. He takes the phone and tells Whitney about my injury and the prognosis for recovery.

"Of course, Mrs. Daniels. We will indeed. Do you need to talk to your husband again?" He laughs. "Okay, I'll tell him."

Dr. Smith closes the phone and hands it to me.

"What did she say?"

"She said, and this is a bit of a paraphrase, 'You tell him not to do anything stupid again or I'll kick him in the … gluteus maximus.'"

"She didn't say 'gluteus maximus,' did she?"

"No."

He walks back out into the hallway. I zone out for what seems like minutes but might have been much more. When I look up, Adanna is talking with Dr. Smith again. She's showing him a small book with what looks like a woman's face on it.

My heart hurts when I see Adanna's face, especially when she smiles. I want to help her, to make her life better. But what can I do?

Gordon grabs my backpack.

"The doctor said if you're feeling up to it, we can go. Actually, he said we have to go. They need the bed."

Gordon helps me sit up. The pain in my back is numbed, but I still feel it. My head spins, but I am determined to stand.

"Where are we headed?"

"We need to take Adanna to Walter's place. Then we'll get you to the hotel." We walk slowly into the hallway.

"This is one special young lady here," the doctor says. He looks in Adanna's direction, and she puts her head down.

"Yes, I know."

Gordon is at the wheel, and a quiet Adanna sits in the back, looking out the window. The afternoon sky is unusually dark. Thick clouds have interrupted the sun without announcement or apology. There's a crack of thunder that makes us all jump, and the sky opens. We are not introduced gently to this storm. There is no drizzle or light rain. There is only a sudden downpour. Immediately torrents flash down across our path.

"I've never seen rain like this," I yell to Gordon, who's craning his neck forward, trying to see. I look back at Adanna. She continues to stare out the window.

The sound of the rain pelting the car is deafening, like rocks on a tin roof.

I've been through a few Texas thunderstorms, potato wagons and all, but this is different. The rain is falling with such force, a fog envelops the car in minutes, and we can't see five feet in front of us.

Gordon yells, "We're going have to pull over until this lets up. I can't see a thing."

We pull over, but not far, fearing we might slip down the edge of the road into a gully. Within minutes, small rivers of runoff have formed in the streets. *Rivers.*

"This is unbelievable. It's never rained this hard since I've lived here. I don't trust this storm." Gordon fumbles with the radio dial.

The second it clicks on, there are several raps with loud, consecutive beeps.

"Swazi Radio AM 1060. This is a severe-weather alert. A flash-flood warning has been issued for the city of Manzini and surrounding areas through tomorrow morning. This storm will hit particularly hard in the area of Matsapha. There will be severe flooding in Matsapha and all areas around Manzini. Take to higher ground immediately to avoid this potential threat. Repeat, flee to higher ground immediately."

Adanna raises her voice to a level of alarm. "Matsapha? That's where my brother and sister are. We have to go find them."

She starts coughing. She's been coughing a lot today.

Gordon speaks firmly. "We can't go anywhere right now."

"But there's no choice, Mr. Gordon. Abu and Precious could drown. Please, we have to do something."

"We'll go, just as soon as this lets up."

"No, I'm going now. There is no time to wait."

And with that, the door clicks, the rain pours in, and she's off like a bullet.

I can't believe she's just run out of the car. "I'm going after her."

Before Gordon can stop me, I'm outside chasing Adanna.

In two seconds, I'm soaked to the bone. This must have been what it was like when God flooded the earth. Running after a hazy figure, my foot slips on a rock and I go tumbling like a log down a hill. A deluge of water yanks my other foot out from under me. A second later, I'm lying on my stomach.

At this point, a random, unexpected sense of gratitude for pain pills wells up in my soul. I could die here and not even care. There's mud in my eyes. Everything is shapeless. I'm being absolutely hammered by drops of rain. A strange thought crosses my mind, how in the world can people living in these mud huts stay dry during a rainstorm like this?

"Adanna!" I'm not sure she can hear me. "Adanna, help me!"

"Stuart? Where are you?" It's her voice.

"Over here, Adanna, down in the gully."

"Oh my, how did you get there? Are you okay?"

"I'm not sure, I haven't tried to move."

"Let me help you up. Ready?"

"Ouch! Nope, that's not gonna work. Get Gordon."

"Okay, stay put. I'll be right back."

"I'm won't go anywhere, I promise!"

The raging water is getting higher. If it continues to rise, I will be completely buried in minutes.

Gordon's booming voice is music to my ears.

"I can't leave you alone for a second."

With Gordon's help, I'm able to get to my feet. Thank God for that. We're all drenched as we make our way back to the Land Cruiser.

"I know you're not going to like this, Gordon, but I think Adanna is right after all. We really need to go to Matsapha." Gordon looks out the rear window. "Either direction we go, we're gonna be in the flood zone, so we might as well drive toward Matsapha." Gordon guns the Land Cruiser into reverse and then quickly forward.

Adanna is sitting in the middle of the backseat, leaning forward. We're all leaning forward, straining to see out the front window covered in an oily gray glaze.

The drive to Matsapha isn't easy. We can barely distinguish the road from the water. The village looks like a ghost town. The rain shows no sign of letting up.

"Gordon, watch out!"

"What the—"

The brakes lock up, and we're skiing on mud. Sliding to the right, then the left. Gordon has no control of the vehicle.

"Hold on."

Adanna screams.

"Hold on, honey."

As we complete a 360, the vehicle smashes into a huge green Dumpster. Gordon's hair is wild, and it looks like he's hit his head on the steering wheel. We all look out and see a steep embankment just beyond the Dumpster.

"Is everyone all right?" I shout louder than I need to, even with the noise. Mercifully, I wouldn't know if I had hurt myself.

"I'm all right. I never thought I'd be thanking God for a rubbish bin," Gordon says.

"Adanna, how about you?" She's holding her head.

"I am fine. Can we please just try to go?"

"Move your hand, let me see."

She reveals a small bump above her eye. That will surely turn into quite a shiner.

"Ouch. Honey, that's a good one."

"I'll be okay." Of course she will. This is nothing compared to what her body has already suffered.

The rain continues to pound.

"Are we stuck?"

"I don't think so. But there's another problem. Look."

A wall of water appears magically, like on that tour at Universal Studios, except this flood won't be redirected last-minute, leaving us with quickened heartbeats and damp shirts. We're about to discover the immense power of Mother Nature's secret weapon.

"What do we do?"

"We have no choice. Surely it's not as deep as it looks. Okay, Adanna, your job is to hold on and pray. This could get wild."

Gordon yells, "Hold on, everyone." Gordon points us toward the wall of water. As soon as we hit it, we start to float. Our Land Cruiser has been transformed into a boat. The sensation would be exhilarating if it weren't so frightening. We're out of control, and there's nothing we can do about it.

"So, maybe it is a little deeper than it looks. How's that praying going, Adanna?"

In a matter of seconds the water carries us into a deeper tributary of this brand-new river, and we are flying at high speed, pushed by the force of the current.

"Gordon, you have to do something, or we're going to die!" I yell. He looks like he's seen a ghost.

"I'm doing everything I know to do. Nothing's working."

An uprooted tree slams into the side of our vehicle with a crunching thud.

"If we get pulled under, we won't stand a chance."

"I'm trying!"

Adanna places a hand on my shoulder; the other is wrapped securely around my headrest. She says, calmly, "Okay. I'm doing my job. I said a prayer, and everything will be fine."

I'm not sure if she really believes this or is trying to make us all feel better.

"We're going to hit a tree! Hold on!"

A screen of gray rushing water appears out of the left corner of the windshield. It's filled with tree limbs and trash. It slams into the middle of the car and pushes us away from the unmoving tree and to the edge of the water.

Then we stop, just as suddenly as we were swept away.

"Whoa, this thing really is an amphibious vehicle."

"Oh, I had it under control the whole time," Gordon laughs nervously.

"Someone had it under control, but I don't think it was you, Gordon."

I look at Adanna. She's smiling.

"You are right. And I saw him too" she says. "The illuminated man, right there in the water. He knew what we needed."

Gordon and I look at each other and give a shrug. But I don't question it. Maybe God is finally making an appearance in this little girl's life. It's about time.

The tires grip the mud and pull us to safety. Gordon's driving leg is shaking. In spite of the narcotics, my hands vibrate like I've downed ten cups of coffee.

Ordinarily, the trip to Matsapha wouldn't take long at all— maybe ten or fifteen minutes. But we've been slowed down terribly. We could have walked faster. Well, except for the flood, of course. Finally, we close in.

The area is unrecognizable.

"Adanna, is this it?"

"Yes, this is it. But I've never seen so much water. The creek is now a river."

A very angry river.

"Stuart, do you see that? There are people trapped in the river," Gordon cries out.

"Where? I can't see."

"Right there. Look at the crowd; they're trying to fish people out of the water with those sticks."

"Lord in heaven, I see it. Let's go."

Before another word is spoken, Adanna is out of the vehicle and running toward the gathered crowd.

"Adanna, wait!"

But she isn't listening.

We're all running fast on the slippery surface, like ducks skimming the water before takeoff. We arrive at what is now the riverbank. There are six, maybe eight, homes poking through the raging current, and the leftovers of several other homes float down the river at high speed. But the most horrendous site is the children, dozens of them, stuck in the current, lodged in trees, grasping onto buildings, floating on wood, clinging to life.

Chapter Twenty

◆◇■ Tagoze ■◇◆

The day begins like any other, a typical African day—boring, long, and dry.

But as the afternoon rolls in, the temperature becomes unusually cool, and the wind starts to howl. I look up and am shocked at how fast the clouds are filling the sky. The swirls of gray and white twist and turn, running into each other like an angry mob. A storm is brewing.

A deafening crack of thunder gives way to a bright white streak, warning everyone to get inside. I grab the chessboard and pieces and tuck them under my arm. I will invite the chief to play another day.

Very little light shines through the walls in my house, just enough so I can read on a bright day. But all light is extinguished in a matter of minutes on this day.

It seems a good day for an early nap.

I lie down on my mat and begin to drift into dreams. Thunder pulls me awake now and again, but it is a more unusual sound that snaps me to alertness—the sound of people yelling and screaming. I stand, go to the door and peer through the pouring rain.

I step into the downpour and follow the sound. Before my eyes, a wall of water races toward a small crowd, chasing them. The water is uprooting trees and swallowing homes.

They will not be able to outrun it.

Without thinking, I take off running to homes still in the path of the raging flood. A dozen small children stand frozen before me.

"Run! Run this way!" I yell to them. But they can't hear me.

I run toward them, waving my arms. But the wall of water is too swift, and it devours them.

I stop, uncertain for a moment where to run, how to act. Then I whisper a quiet prayer.

"Lord, have mercy. Lord, have mercy. Please help."

It is total and utter chaos at the water's edge. A mother is fighting the current, holding tight to her two children. She will not be able to hold them for much longer.

I take a step toward the rushing water. Tree limbs are snapping like toothpicks, people are screaming for their lives.

"Tagoze! No, wait. What are you doing?"

It's Adanna. I offer a quick wave, then turn and dive into the water. It sweeps me under, and for a moment I am caught by it. I spin out of control, knocked by branches and uprooted thorn bushes. Suddenly I surface—just feet from the mother and her children. She is swept off her feet.

I launch myself in her direction. The debris grabs at my feet and smacks against my chest. A bramble races by, clawing new scars across my face. Blood mingles with murky water, but still I fight forward.

"Dear God, give me strength!"

I stand against the current, and the woman slams into me. Quickly, I wrap my arms around her and her frightened children. Together, we are pulled downstream.

"God, please help us."

I turn my head to see a tree standing tall and strong in the middle of the river. Its old roots must have spent hundred of years digging into the crust of the earth. It's the last one standing in the path of nature's fury.

"Lady, hold on to me, and hold tight to your children," I say. With one arm free, I pull at the water, steering, fighting, wrestling with invisible foes.

The tree arrives faster than anticipated. I hold tight to the woman and swing myself around to take the brunt of the hit. *Bam!* My body crunches against the tree. I am momentarily dazed.

I reach up out of the water and catch a sturdy branch. With a surge of energy, I pull myself toward the tree trunk, but the force of the water spins me around, and the woman slips out of my arms. I lunge for her and grasp the collar of her dress. Mustering all of my strength, I pull her back toward the tree, praying that the cloth will not tear.

Her children are trailing behind her, one held by each of her weary arms, but the smallest is slipping. My muscles straining, I manage to pull her against the crashing current back toward the tree. She is within reach. She could grab it, but her arms are still wrapped around her children.

"You have to grab the branch. I need you to grab the branch!"

"I can't!" she screams.

"The current is too strong. I can't hold you here for long. You must grab the branch."

"But my children!"

"I will count to three. When I get to three, let go of your son and grab the branch. I will catch him. I promise I will catch him."

"I am afraid!"

"God is with us. Be strong! Hold tight to the little girl. I will help her next. Ready?"

The woman nods.

"Remember … on 'three,' use your right arm to grab the branch. And hold on for life."

"One, two, three!"

She lets go of her son and reaches for the branch. My long reach enables me to grab the boy by the arm. But as the woman pulls herself up onto the branch, a sudden surge rips her little daughter away from her grasp.

"Bisa, no!"

A log appears out of nowhere and hits the flailing girl with the force of a charging rhino. She is swept downstream.

"Grab the limbs and climb into the tree," I yell. The little boy clambers onto my shoulders and up into the high branches. His mother stares downstream, wailing.

"Climb into the tree now!" I find strength I did not know I had and pull her up, out of the water, laying her across a branch that has not yet been submerged by the flood.

I am too tired to climb up into the branches with them so I hang on tight instead.

Chapter Twenty-one

The rain has slowed to a steady drizzle, but the water continues to rise in the valley. Adanna, Gordon, and I stand on the bank scanning the gnarled trees one by one for any sign of Precious and Abu. I am looking under the cover of a bright yellow poncho through the lens of my camera. Old women and mothers are clutching babies, telling one another to hold on. Old men perch on branches, and children lean into the trees in defense against the wind.

I snap a photo of a bicycle being carried by the current. It is upright, as if ridden by an invisible man.

Gordon turns to me. The wind and rain have matted and twisted his white hair. His left eye swollen shut.

"Nobody deserves this." His typical optimism has long since departed. I keep snapping. I focus on each frame independently, considering light, perspective, and subject matter, independent from context and yet conveying it at the same time. This is why I'm good at my job. This is why I won an award.

This is who I am.

Adanna steps into frame. "They are not there," she says, pointing toward the raging river.

I can see the photo caption: *Village girl looks into the trees for lost brother and sister.* I focus for a close shot.

Her face bears the marks of the abuse she has suffered, a crusted-over cut next to her eye, a swollen lip. Her clothes, now soaked, hang like rags on her undernourished body. Her eyes hold rivers of blue sorrow. Even so, the lens reveals a girl with a curious dignity, one that can come only from a spirit of fire.

She looks right at the camera and says in a clear, strong voice, "I am going to look for Pastor Walter and see if he has seen Abu and Precious." I snap her picture. She ignores the camera.

"Stuart, will you please help me?"

I pull off my poncho, look at Gordon, and he nods. I hand him the camera and follow Adanna.

The rain has picked up again and beats down around us. We're headed to the river and right into the middle of the devastation.

"Adanna, wait!"

The water is like a herd of crazed elephants destroying everything in its path. A house with a thatched roof floats down the river at the mercy of the current.

I see something else floating next to a log.

"Oh, no!" It's a tiny head bobbing up and down and tossed in the waves like a rag doll.

I back up from the water's edge, and then like a long jumper, I run, plant, and hurl myself into the raging river.

My head smacks against something hard, blurring my vision. I see two of everything. Focusing with all my energy on the child still bobbing toward me, I maneuver against the current, positioning myself to catch the child.

I will have only one chance at this.

Here she comes …

I reach over and grab her by the back of the shirt, then pull her into my arms. A sudden wave knocks me off my feet and for a moment we are both underwater. The wave turns away, and we pop up to the surface.

"God, for the sake of this child, give me strength."

She is shivering but still breathing.

With every ounce of strength, I rocket toward the bank, clawing at the water with one arm while holding tight to the little girl with the other. Every second is critical. The edge is drawing closer and closer. Suddenly my work is made light as a current sweeps us close to the bank. A man is standing there, holding a long branch out for me to grab.

He looks out of place. His hair is white, and his ebony skin almost seems to glow. He has light blue eyes, lighter than Whitney's, and he is smiling. I grab the branch with my free arm and lock it in place. He easily pulls us to safety. I'm bent over, gasping and coughing up water that tastes like dirt and sweat.

The little girl is crying. When I turn to thank the blue-eyed man, he is gone. The child and I are alone. I climb to my feet and, holding the little girl's hand, start walking along the bank upstream.

The child is whimpering.

"It's okay. You're gonna be okay." Something sticky drips down my face. I swipe at it and look at my hand. This country is taking a lot of my blood.

The area around the river looks like a war zone. Trees are uprooted; rocks, tin, and straw are cast aside in piles, the remnants of what use to be homes. Dead animals pepper the area, victims of the initial flood surge.

Ahead of me I see lines of people along the shore, reaching into the river with large sticks, perhaps saving lives. Perhaps watching loved ones die.

This child and I are soaked to the core, and she begins to shake violently. What I wouldn't give for a down comforter to wrap her in. Instead, I lift her up and pull her close. I feel a tearing in my back and for the first time since the rain began am reminded of my stab wound.

I start toward a small crowd that has gathered ahead. Maybe somebody will recognize her. I wonder where Adanna has gone.

A Swazi man up ahead looks at me and stares. I turn my body so he can see the girl's face and shout, "Do you know this little girl?"

He shakes his head no. My steps become harder to take, and the weight of the little one heavier. I want to tell this girl that we'll find her mommy, but I don't know her language.

And I don't know if her mommy is still alive.

Out of the blue, a song comes to me. It is a song I haven't sung in decades, but one I have never forgotten. Perhaps the melody came from the wind in the trees, or maybe I heard it in the child's rhythmic whimper.

I start to hum "Amazing Grace." The little girl looks up at me. I smile, and she rests her head back on my chest. She seems calmer.

As I get closer to the crowd, I hear Swazi voices and see people pointing toward the water. Two people are stuck in a towering tree in the middle of the now raging river. It is a woman and a child. No, wait … there is a third. A man, still in the water, hanging on for life to a branch that is almost completely submerged.

Even at a distance, I know this man.

Tagoze.

"Stuart, Stuart, over here!"

Peering over the crowd, I see Adanna smiling with Precious and Abu at her side. Thank God. Precious and Abu run toward me, and Precious hugs my wet leg.

"Oh, Adanna, I'm so happy." I start to cry.

"Stuart, you have blood all over your face. What happened to you?"

"Something hit me while I was trying to save this little girl. Do you know who she is?" I turn the shivering child around.

Her eyes light up and she blurts out, "Yes! That's Mrs. Malaza's little girl, Bisa. Come, come! You must come with me." She starts toward the crowd and motions for me to follow.

"Who is Mrs. Malaza?" Why does that name sound familiar?

"She's Pastor Walter's wife's sister. And she's over there." Adanna points to the tree in the middle of the river. "In the tree with Tagoze."

I move as close as possible to the bank. Adanna, Precious, and Abu trail behind.

"Stay away from the current," I tell them, as I lift this little girl into the air.

"Mrs. Malaza! It's Bisa! Bisa!"

The sound of the water is so overbearing that even though I'm screaming at the top of my lungs, I am sure Mrs. Malaza can't hear me. I start jumping around like a mad man, waving one arm wildly.

I can feel the emotion of the crowd behind me changing, with cascading exclamations of "Oh!" rippling out around me. Others begin to yell Bisa's name and point. I hold the little girl higher. She sees her mom, and she is crying out, "Momma!"

The voices continue to shout out around me in a wild antiphonal chorus. Finally, I see Tagoze point, and Mrs. Malaza looks toward us to finally notice her daughter. I cannot see Mrs. Malaza's face clearly, but I can tell life has returned, her body suddenly stronger, taller as she holds tight to the tree branches.

Swazi women come and embrace me, kiss my bloodied cheek. Men grab my shoulder then my hand in a traditional gesture, only this time, they bow. The highest honor they could pay.

"Stuart, you have done something very good today. Very, very good." Adanna, holding Abu, has come beside me. Precious stands on the other side, and along with the crowd we all look out toward the ancient tree.

Now, how do we get them to shore?

The crowd turns into a wave as a series of ancient army green vehicles pull up from the muddy main road, brakes squealing loudly. Men in light blue uniforms pour out. They start unloading lifesaving devices that look like they've come from a World War II movie—canoes, stretchers, boxes of who knows what, and rope. They are all carrying handguns, and one guy is even carrying a World War II machine gun.

Most of the rescuers are walking, not running, so the villagers help drag the supplies to the riverbank across from the great tree. Everyone is talking in S'swati; some of the men in blue seem to be arguing. I sit with the child, who hasn't left me since I pulled her out of the water. The current is still swift, but it seems the river is no longer rising.

Even though I don't understand them, I can tell the rescuers are confused. They're firing questions and suggestions back and forth, and the villagers are joining in the discussion.

"What are they saying?" Adanna is sitting next to me with her legs crossed.

"A man in blue is saying, 'How long do we wait before the rescue begins?' And a villager is saying, 'You have waited long enough, now go ahead.' Then the man in blue says, 'But wouldn't it be better for the river to slow down first?' And the man in the white shirt is saying, 'No, that would mean we wait for days!' He is angry."

I can see the fury build in this villager.

"Now, they are talking about people getting the chills from being in the water too long."

"Ah, hypothermia."

"Yes, they are saying they must have the strongest men help, so they can pull them out of the water fast."

I've been told this is the coldest it's been in Africa for fifty years, so hypothermia is a real possibility. But it seems ridiculous. To me, it's just a cool summer day.

This discussion goes on for well over fifteen minutes, until the man with the most medals across his chest makes a decision. The rescue will commence—now.

They throw the rope several times before Tagoze is able to catch it. The rope is tied around the young boy first.

"Hold onto the rope as tightly as you can." The crowd repeats the command.

Adanna stands to get a better look, but I remain seated. My back is pulsing with pain.

"Bisa, look—here comes your brother." Her eyes are fixed on the tree.

Looking upstream for dangerous debris and finding the coast

clear, the light blue men give the signal. The boy leaps from the tree branches, and five men pull him through the water as quickly as possible. The little boy looks like a lure spinning on the top of the water, and in about thirty seconds, he is safely ashore. Everyone cheers. Village women pass him around, planting kisses on his wet cheek, then deliver him to me.

"Here, Stuart, let me take the boy." Walter is suddenly beside me. He lifts the boy into his arms and wraps him in a joyous hug.

"Hello, Walter. Bisa is safe too." Bisa stays still in my arms.

They toss the rope out to the tree again. It takes four tries before Tagoze is able to grab it. When the woman has tied herself in the rope, she is given the signal to jump.

As she jumps, five men pull and she flies through the air as if shot out of a cannon. She hits the water with a thud, and the rope makes an ominous snapping sound. But moments later, she is pulled safely to shore.

"Here comes your momma," I whisper to Bisa.

Adanna and I walk toward her. Dripping wet and covered in river plants and twigs, she makes a beeline in our direction. She runs more like an Olympic athlete than a woman who's almost lost her daughter or even her own life. I place the little girl in her arms. She buries the little girl in her chest, heaving between her sobs. A twinge of sadness escapes from my heart when I let her go.

"Jesus heard my prayer. He saved you; He saved you," she says.

The women gather around us, and shouts of "Praise the Lord" and "Hallelujah" fill the valley like a chorus of angels. I am crying again. Africa has opened the valve to my tear ducts, and now it won't shut.

She says something to Adanna, and Adanna answers.

"She asked if you saved her. I told her yes."

The woman drops to her knees and grabs my legs with one arm. "Thank you, thank you, thank you," she says in English. Her gratitude is more than I can bear. I am unraveling.

I put one hand on her head, the other on Bisa's. The only thing I can think of to say is, "God bless you. He is good." I don't stop to question the reason for the flood or the lives that have been lost or man's inhumanity to man. I just do my very best to believe—if only for a moment—in God's goodness.

As we are rejoicing, there is a terrible sound. At first it is like thunder, but it echoes louder and longer than any thunder I have heard. Everyone turns toward the river to see this magnificent tree—this ancient, deeply rooted symbol of security and hope—snap in two. The river carries the broken tree away with ease.

A chorus of anxious cries pours out across the river. All that is left of the tree is a ten- or twelve-foot-tall section of trunk, rising above the water and one short, twisted branch that rests perpendicular against it near the top. It is in the very same moment when I notice how much the broken tree resembles a cross that I realize Tagoze is nowhere to be seen.

He has been washed away.

Chapter Twenty-two

It takes two village men and four of the blue suits to pull Tagoze's bloated body onto the riverbank. When we hear the shouts, everyone runs downriver. The villagers circle around Tagoze. Some bend down to touch his forehead. There's no such thing as distance from death or the dying here.

A good man has died. In his wake, everything has stopped—even the rescuers pause. The women cry out, releasing their grief for Tagoze and for their land and their people. The few men standing around him fall to their knees, shout, and extend their hands to God.

I keep my distance, but I feel his loss as if we had been brothers. There is a great heaviness in my heart, but it is not just over Tagoze. I grieve for these people. And there is something else tugging at me. Something in my own heart. Something from long years ago.

Suddenly I realize how completely exhausted I am. I fall to my knees, then curl up on the muddy ground and am whisked away into a feverish memory.

I am closed away in my room, listening to the sounds of booming thunder and machine-gun rain pounding the dilapidated metal shed outside my window. We had moved to California because my mom had just married my new dad.

Don had been an E-9 Master Chief in the navy. He had all kinds of medals and flags he wore like prizes on his silky white uniform. He also sported a white hat with a shiny black bill. He looked every bit the patriot and military officer. But he didn't look so stately those times mom and I came home to find him passed out, slumped in the chair on the front porch, drool running down the front of that white uniform.

He was a big man, bigger than most adult men I had ever met. At six foot three inches tall, he towered over my boyish frame. He had a kind face and a thick brown mustache. I remember his walk, long, with his feet pointed out like a waddling duck. When he pushed the rototiller through the garden, he left huge footprints in the freshly turned dirt. I followed behind, matching my footsteps to his. I wanted to be just like him.

His arms were hairy, scarred, and tattooed. On his right arm was a tattoo of the Seabee emblem. It made me think of honeybees. Honeybees toting machine guns. His arms were strong, like cannons. If he was on your side, you were in great shape. If not, then you had much to fear.

One night our new family went to the CPO club on the naval base. That was before he and my mom got married. I was feeling like a big man, dancing my heart out on the dance floor with a pretty lady, a blonde with long dark eyelashes and golden skin. She reminded me of a swimsuit model. She must've been at least thirty, and she made my young heart beat fast. I was in love.

I was sure I would marry her or maybe my new fourth-grade teacher, Mrs. McNulty. I was on the dance floor, practicing my *American Bandstand* routine. I worked out the beginning of a spin but couldn't quite plant it, and I ended up face-first on the floor. My red-faced humiliation was interrupted by movement over by the bar.

To my right, a fight exploded. My soon-to-be dad was in the middle of it. His shirt was ripped apart, but he had one of the men in the air. The man went flying over the bar like one of my paper airplanes and crashed on the floor. He didn't move. Another guy came charging at Don, and one punch later, he was on the floor looking just like my dead grandpa I had seen in a wooden box a few weeks earlier, minus the brown suit. That's the moment Don became a hero to me. He was Conan the Barbarian. He grabbed my mom's arm on one side and mine on the other, and he marched us out of there like the Law in one of those Westerns he used to fall asleep to on Saturday afternoons.

I am back in my room now, and the rain is still pouring down. My mom and Don have been arguing in the kitchen. I walk down the hall to see what is going on. They don't see me peering in from behind the door. He is yelling terrible words at her at the top of his lungs.

"You worthless whore! I hate you and that stupid kid of yours."

With that, he spits at her, raises his fist in the air, and starts pounding her like a jackhammer. One blow lands on her nose and blood splatters across the kitchen. I don't know what else to do; I am scared. My hero has become my enemy.

I charge at him, both fists flailing in the air and landing on his legs and midsection. I wish I were fifty feet tall so I could beat the crap out of him and he would never come back.

"Leave her alone! Leave her alone," I yell. "Why are you doing this, Dad?"

I wish I could take back my words. He is not my dad. He is a monster and I hate him.

He looks down at me with rage in his eyes. He hates me; I know it. There is nothing I can do to change that.

His fist comes down so fast I don't have time to move. It catches me smack in the mouth. I fly across the room like one of the rocks I used to launch at the moon with my slingshot, and I land against a dining-room chair as it collapses under me.

Reaching up to my mouth, I open my lips and spit a tooth into my cupped hand. It mingles with streaky lines of red spit and dark blood. Then blood begins to pour out of my mouth. My mother runs over to me to help as best she can; both of us are bleeding and scared.

As soon as I can, I run away to my room. I sit there for hours until I hear the thunder. Then I quietly walk past my mom's closed door—I can still hear her sniffling and groaning—then through the kitchen and out the back door. I stand in the summer rain, letting it wash over me. I start to walk, and as I do, I get angry. Angry at everything and everyone and especially God. Why didn't God stop Don from hurting us?

"Stuart, are you okay?"

It's Gordon, and he's covered with mud.

"I'm … I'm fine. No … I'm exhausted."

"What's going on over there?" He nods his head toward the crowd.

"It's Tagoze. He's dead."

"Oh, sweet Jesus, no."

"He saved the lives of a mother and son, Gordon. He risked his own life … he lost his own life … to save them."

I think back to what he said the other day. Was it yesterday?

"A fire burns in me to do what I can for my people. Though I am but one man, I will not stop trying."

Gordon shakes his head.

I put my hand on his shoulder, and we both walk toward the crowd, now quieting down.

"Gordon, what will they do next?"

"I don't know, Stuart. I just don't know."

Mrs. Malaza sees me. She says something to Gordon in S'swati.

"Stuart, you saved this woman's child!"

I suddenly remember the strange man on the bank. "I had some help." I smile at the woman and at her daughter, Bisa, who looks shyly at me.

As the crowd disburses, we see Pastor Walter and Adanna standing over Tagoze. A little girl who looks about Adanna's age runs up and wraps her arms around her. She is barefoot, her clothes are shredded, and blood is dripping from her leg.

Adanna wraps her arms around the girl. "Tobile!"

Tobile looks down and apparently recognizes Tagoze.

"Why does God have to take the good people? Why can't He take a bad man?" Tobile cries.

I've been asking myself the same question.

Gordon has taken out his notebook and is writing in it. But this time he is not writing quickly, a mad dash to make sure his pen keeps up with his thoughts. Instead, he is writing slowly, deliberately. I wonder what words could possibly capture the magnitude of this disaster.

"Get your camera," he says. It is not a command. There is sadness in his voice. I start to balk, then pause.

He's right.

I need to get a picture of Tagoze's face. I need to get photos of Pastor Walter's sister, and Bisa. I need to capture the bodies, the mess, this inverted hell where water tortures and destroys. This is why I'm here. It is my job.

I walk down the bank toward the car. I feel as if my feet are made of cement. I step past bodies, some lying as if taking an afternoon nap. One stops me in my tracks.

A woman is standing near this body. She has been helping others carry the dead. To where? I'm not sure. Perhaps she knows.

"Excuse me? Do you speak English?"

"Yes."

"Do you know this man?"

"I do, that's Malako Umbeni."

I knew it. Adanna's uncle. He has scratches and bruise marks on his bloated face. Not all of those came from being battered by the floodwaters.

"He was an evil man," she says, then looks down at him as if to spit.

"Yes, I know." I feel some satisfaction in his death, but I am also surprised by a quiet sadness that sneaks into my heart. Perhaps he has gotten what he deserved. But now, there is no chance for his redemption.

The woman's gaze moves to someone behind me, and I turn to look. It's a large woman with cold eyes. She looks me up and down.

"D, I am sorry about your husband," the woman says in front of me.

So this is Adanna's aunt. I nod at her and step aside.

Looking at her face, I see no tears, no sense of remorse. She pushes him with her foot, as if trying to make sure he's really dead. There's almost a look of relief.

My shoes sink several inches into the mud with each step back up the hill. My body is covered from head to toe in black African soil.

"Stuart!" I turn to see Adanna running toward me. She stops short when she sees her aunt … and her uncle.

She stands, staring at her aunt, neither of them moving. Then Adanna moves forward and puts her frail arm around her aunt's big torso. Her aunt is stiff at first, but she begins to soften. She hugs Adanna and then kisses her head over and over.

I scrape the caked dirt from my hands as best I can with a cloth from the car and pull out my gear. My body is so weary, I could crawl into the car and sleep for a year, but I latch my camera to the tripod, walk back down toward the riverbank, set it down, and begin to shoot.

Frame after frame, I chronicle a people's despair. Tagoze is on his back, his face swollen and barrel-sized chest bloated. Someone has placed his hands on his midsection. With one click, I capture the death of a hero. I turn the camera to see Walter talking with his wife and sister-in-law. They don't notice me, but when I look through the lens, I see Bisa, her eyes staring right at me. Behind her I make out a familiar figure: white hair, black skin, blue eyes. The man who helped me out of the river. He's smiling. I click the shutter. A lingering crack of thunder turns my head away for a moment, and when I turn back, Bisa smiles at me, but the man is gone.

"We need to get this story out there fast, Stu. These people need help." We are driving through the muck and water-filled potholes, headed back to the hotel.

"Yeah. Hey, Gordon, have you ever seen a man in the village with white hair and blue eyes?"

"What, like a colored? They don't have those around here, only in South Africa."

"A what? No, very black skin."

"Never saw him. You can ask Walter when we go back—he seems to know everyone."

The brakes grind as we come to a halt in front of the Mountain Inn and wait for the gate to open. There's a smell of burning oil coming from the car. The concierge greets us, looking the same as always, apparently unchanged by the day's events. He gives us a funny look when we step out of the vehicle. Gordon and I are covered with mud and muck from the river.

"The flood," I say.

He just looks at us inquisitively.

"The flood in Matsapha," as if I owe him an explanation.

"Well, it's lovely to see you back, sir."

Chapter Twenty-three

Looking out the window from my hotel room the next morning, the only evidence of rain I can see is the steam rising out of the saturated ground. The earth looks as if it's taking a smoke break.

I can't believe how late it is—nine o'clock. It feels like someone shoved gunpowder in the wound on my back and lit it on fire. I can't imagine what it was exposed to in that floodwater. I step into the bathroom. The remnants of last night's shower remain in the bottom of the tub, black organic material that seems to be affixed with Bondo. Running my hands through my hair, I am reminded of the baseball that's formed on my forehead.

My cell rings.

"Hello."

"Hey, Stuart! How you faring today, man?" It's Gordon, and he's back to his chipper self.

"More than a little hungover from that beating yesterday. You?"

"About the same. I'll bring you some yarrow-herb salve I made for your nasty back wound. It'll help it heal and prevent infection."

"Just some coffee and Advil will be good for me, thanks all the same."

He laughs. "You can have 'em all. I'll be there around noon, and we can head back to Walter's care point. I've got someone working on the car now, so we should be good to go. I've been writing since six this morning, and I want to get this article out."

"Yeah, I need to look over these photos and download them to the server in the States. Send me the article when you're ready?"

"Right. God, let's hope this does some good." Sounds more like a prayer than a statement.

"I'm with you on that, my friend."

I call down for coffee, boot up my computer, and pull out my gear. Before I can even plug my camera into my laptop, I hear a polite knock on the door.

"Coffee, boss."

I open the door, and the white-suited hotel hop wheels in a cart with a silver coffeepot, sugar bowl, creamer, and cup meticulously placed on a tray. They've included a dish of fruit and two pastries, cheese, and some sort of berry.

"Thank you." I dig in my pocket for some *emalangeni* and hand him a tip.

"Oh, thank you, sir. Let me know if you need anything more." Ever obsequious, ever efficient, these hotel staff.

I transfer the photos, taking care not to get my laptop sticky, and scan through them. Some of the flood shots are perfect for the *Times*. A mother and her baby in a tree, hanging over the rushing water. More people hanging onto trees, desperation etched on their faces. The one with the floating bicycle could be a prizewinner.

I get to the photo I took right just as the sun was setting. The one of Pastor Walter, his sister, and her children. It is a compelling shot, full of emotion and packed with riveting detail. I can see the sweat and dirt caked on Walter's face. But the black man with the blue eyes is missing. I zoom in to the section of the photo where he should be, but it is just a blur. A trick of the light? But I was certain I saw him.

My phone rings again.

"Stuart here."

"Just sent the article off to Bill and to you. You should get it any second. See you at noon."

"I'll look at it now. Hello?" Gordon rarely says good-bye, so I'm never really sure when the conversation is over until I find myself talking into a dead phone. I breeze through the first part of the article and finish downloading my photos.

> Matsapha, Swaziland, Feb. 14—A flash flood in the southern quadrant of Manzini, Swaziland, the worst since a devastating flood in 2000, has forced scores out of their homes to seek higher ground. For hundreds in the area of Mankayane, this meant scrambling up trees to avoid the rushing waters of the river below.
>
> The death toll is believed in the hundreds, but local relief workers fear it will reach thousands. The affected area is already impoverished, with nearly half its population infected with HIV-AIDS. Now residents are without means for basic survival.
>
> The government of Swaziland says it has no need yet for international aid.
>
> Just halfway through the rainy season, forecasters predicted heavy rains, but no flood warnings went out to local residents. The region has been plagued by drought in recent years.

"I have never seen anything like this here. It came like a giant wave, sweeping away much of our community," says resident Walter Malaza, who operates a care point to help orphans in his area. "We have been losing so many people to AIDS, we hardly had time to bury our dead before the flood, but now ..." The river bank is lined with hundreds of bodies dragged or washed up out of the waters.

As I read the article, I realize that there truly are no words that can completely capture the events of the past few days. The picture will certainly help, but I am beginning to wonder if stories like this really do any good.

Promptly at noon, Gordon pulls up in his Land Cruiser, and I hop in beside him. He tosses a little container at me.

"Put some of this on your back right now. It's concentrated, so you don't need much. It will smart a bit, but then it will start to heal. And it keeps infection away."

The container holds something that looks like clear yellow frosting and smells like the vitamin section of Vita-Cottage. That place makes me think of people who join communes. Whitney likes to shop there.

"It's a yarrow paste. There are some other things in it, crushed chrysanthemum, nettle—just try it."

I take a good amount, reach around, and dab it onto my back. "Ahh ... ow!" The stuff stings like fire.

Gordon laughs. "It'll get better, and you'll be thanking me by tomorrow."

The sting is already subsiding.

"Good work on that article," I say through a wince.

"What photos did you send?" The car jerks and bumps as Gordon tries to keep on the high ground.

"Some of the people hanging out of the trees. And a great one of Walter and his sister-in-law and the girls."

"And Tagoze?"

"I didn't send it. The image wasn't sharp enough." This is a lie. The image was stunningly sharp. Brilliant and haunting. I've never held back a photo I knew was perfect … until last night. "But about the other one—the one with Bisa … "

"Yeah?" he looks over at me.

"Remember how I asked if you knew the guy, the one who helped us out of the river?"

"The one that sounded like a colored. Mmm-hmm."

"Well, I was sure I saw him standing in the background when I took that picture. But when I looked at it, he wasn't there."

"What do you mean?"

"I mean he wasn't there."

"Maybe you took your eyes off the shot, and he walked away before you clicked the shutter."

"No. I was looking through the eyepiece when I clicked it. That's sort of how I do my job."

"Whoa … didn't mean to rattle your cage." We hit a particularly deep pothole and my head nearly hits the roof.

"Well, he was there and now he's not. That's all I know."

"Maybe he was a ghost … or an angel."

"Yeah. I see dead people." I realize the inappropriateness of my words as soon as they spill out of my mouth. But Gordon doesn't seem bothered. In fact, he chuckles softly.

"This is a rare experience for you, isn't it."

"What do you mean? Nearly drowning or having a man disappear from my photo?"

"Both. And more. This whole trip ... it's a one-of-a-kind adventure for you."

"I've been doing this for a long time, Gordon. Every trip is different."

"Ah ... but this one is different ... in a different way."

"How so?"

"You've been all over the world, right?"

"Yeah."

"And you've seen all kinds of things—the best and the worst our world has to offer."

"Especially the worst."

"So ... what's on your mind, Stuart. What have you been thinking about these past days?"

"Huh ... wait, I don't understand."

"What's been uppermost in your thoughts, your feelings?"

"What are you, a shrink all of a sudden?"

"Africa demands you become lots of things in order to survive. So ... yeah, consider me your therapist for the day."

"Well ... I've been thinking about big things. My purpose, I suppose. And wondering where God is in all this. I mean ... He watches as the world falls apart, but then ... when Adanna prayed for us on our drive? I was certain He listened."

"So you're confused ..."

"That's putting it mildly."

"… and wondering …"

"Yes."

"… and searching?"

Yes. But for what?

"The Bible says God has a hope and future for every person and that He suffers right beside the suffering."

He throws me a book that I recognize from the hospital. It is Adanna's journal.

"Adanna left it my car, and I couldn't resist looking through it. She is an amazing writer and poet. I'm overwhelmed by her gift. Read the page I have marked."

I saw the bright path before me, and the illuminated man stretched out his hand. My body was being smothered and torn by an evil man, an animal, but I could sense love from the illuminated man. I asked the man, "Can I come home?" And he said, "No, this is not the time. Remember your gift, your purpose." And then he sent Tagoze to save me.

I flip through the book, the pages filled with words.

"This is really good stuff."

"We need to do a story about her, Stu. I think that should be the last in our series. And there's something else, too."

We pull up to the clearing, and our conversation stops short.

Gordon is as stunned as I am. Most of the people are huddled around the church building—men, women, and children. Nobody is running around playing games. They all sit still, quiet, like hopeless people confined to a refugee camp. The looks on their faces reveal a submission to the immutable power of death. I've seen it in war-torn countries too many times.

To my right are as many as fifty freshly dug graves with mounds of dirt lying beside each hole. We sit for a moment in the car. All the color has left Gordon's face.

"Oh, this is so much worse than I thought."

The second the door opens and my foot hits the ground I am rushed by a group of women and children. Several of them I know, including the two head gogos who distribute food here … when it's available.

"Please help us," they cry. I feel my insides gathering in twisted knots.

"What do you need?" Gordon has shifted into reporter mode.

One of the gogos steps up to Gordon.

"We need fresh water. We need food. Like this, we can't survive. And look at our children."

Many of them look sick and dehydrated. A few sit completely naked on the ground, others are battered by cuts and scratches. Two young children are lying together on their backs by the tree. I wonder if they're already dead.

The rain has washed away the few crops they had. The small cornfield behind the mud hut is completely gone. The hut itself has taken so much of a pounding, it has practically melted away. All that remains are the broken pieces of the foundation, a number of stones, and the tin roof.

"I'll see what I can do." Gordon has pulled out his bulky satellite phone. Those things can get a signal anywhere.

The crowd parts to allow us out of the vehicle.

Walter makes a beeline for me. He looks like he's been through the wringer. I can only imagine what the last twenty-four hours have been like for him.

"Stuart, thank God you came back."

"Walter." I put my arm around him. "I wish the circumstances were better, but I'm glad to see you again." His orange plaid shirt is covered with dried-on muck and leaves. I look down at my clean arms, freshly laundered shirt, and I feel shame. What I must look like to him, to all these people. Walter doesn't seem to take notice.

"Yes, thank you, my brother. And thank you for saving my niece, Bisa. You spared my family even more grief."

"I wish I could help more."

"I'm sure you know that many of the people in this community haven't had much food in a very long time."

I nod.

"This flood has made things so much worse. There is absolutely no food, and we have been told all the wells are contaminated and we cannot drink the water in the river for the same reason."

"So there's really no food. None at all? And no water?"

"Nothing. We've got to do something. There are so many villages around here—and so many people, children who need help. Many will die unless we do something. We are like sheep forgotten by our government."

I think of New Orleans after hurricane Katrina—the horrible devastation, the bungled relief effort—but at least people were trying to help. At least the media was covering it. I get the sense that isn't the case in this country.

"All we can do when the children come to us for help is send them away with the hope that tomorrow we'll have something."

Gordon walks up from the car with a train of women and children following behind him. "I've just made a call to some of my contacts in Mbabane and New York, but I don't have any confirmation of help. I'm sorry."

"Thank you. You are a fellow believer and an important man. I know you have a lot of influence. God will yet use you to help us."

"How many people are we talking about who need assistance?" Gordon tries to get to the facts.

Walter turns to look behind him and waves his hand. As if on cue, dozens of people crest the hill from the surrounding villages, heading in our direction.

"It's like someone sounded a call," I say.

"Yes," Walter smiles in spite of the situation. "We have a very sophisticated system of communication here. A young boy ran as soon as you arrived and alerted one crowd. Someone ran to another, and here they are."

Gordon turns to me. "In this country, white people mean either oppression or hope. And when you're desperate, it is hope they choose to believe."

"But we have no hope to give. Not even a drop."

Pastor Walter is shaking his head. "What are we going to do?"

The three of us stand dumbfounded as the wave of people approaches. It is a bizarre scene, looking like something out of *Dawn of the Dead*.

I scan the crowd.

"Have you seen Adanna, or her brother and sister?"

Gordon is looking across the crowd, sizing up the situation. "I was just looking for them myself."

"I haven't seen that child today," Walter answers and starts to walk toward the crowd. Gordon follows behind him.

"I'm going to check in on her." I shoulder my camera bag and start walking.

Gordon looks back at me, "Bring them here, if they'll come. I hate to think of them alone."

"Right. I'll be back as soon as I can."

The ten-minute walk to Adanna's hut takes twenty minutes. The storm has flung mud everywhere; on the trees, the cacti, the devilbushes, and the rocks. Thousands of waterholes have formed on the path, and I'm forced to dodge them every tenth step.

Looking down into the small valley, I get a new perspective of the destruction. Where homes use to stand are piles of broken wood and twigs. Enormous trees look as if they've been yanked out of the ground by some primordial giant and flicked to the side like unwanted weeds.

I see Adanna's house in the distance. It is one of the few that has weathered the storm well.

"Thank You, God," I whisper.

As I get closer, I can't believe what I'm seeing. Outside of her home are about two dozen children sitting together in clusters of three or four, eating what looks like a home-cooked meal. Out of the front door glides Adanna, as if she were the fairy godmother from the Make-A-Wish Foundation. She has a stack of bread and a jar of jelly.

"Adanna!" I call out to announce myself, and all of the heads turn toward me.

"Mr. Stuart! What are you doing here?" I'm hit headlong by Precious, and then Abu, who hug my legs. I laugh for the first time in days. I give Precious a squeeze around the shoulder and take Abu into my arm. I ignore the pain as my camera bag scrapes around my back.

"What are you doing, Adanna? You look like you're running a bed-and-breakfast."

"A what?"

"It's a place where people go to sleep overnight, and they get breakfast in the morning." I realize how ridiculous this sounds.

"Oh. Well, you gave me all this food, so I'm sharing it."

"But that food was for you. Did you use it all?"

She nods.

"What are you, Abu, and Precious going to eat tomorrow?"

"I don't know. I didn't think about it. These children were hungry too." She waves her hand across the group, as if she is blessing them. "It's okay, Mr. Stuart, because God will take care of us."

"You didn't save anything?"

"No."

I shake my head and sigh.

"Are you mad at me?"

"Of course not." I feel horrible for my response. "Honey, how could I ever be mad at you? We'll just have to figure out something else."

I put Abu down, give him a pat on the rear, and he runs back to his playmates. Precious stays at my side, mimicking every one of Adanna's words and expressions toward me.

"Adanna, do you mind if I take some pictures of you and these children?"

She looks sheepish and instinctively starts to smooth her skirt. I can tell she made an effort to clean it.

"Okay. It's okay," she says, as if confirming the answer to herself. Through the lens, I see her stooping down to help a child not much younger than she is. Adanna seems so much older today and yet so frail. I step back to capture the whole scene. The kids are so focused on eating, they no longer pay attention to me, except Precious, who stays by my side.

"Precious, beautiful girl, why don't you go help your sissy so I can take your picture too?"

"Precious, come," Adanna calls like a mother. Precious stamps her foot hard and won't move. I laugh.

"It's okay," I say to Adanna. Precious looks up at me and smiles. I snap off dozens of shots, children of skin and bones, dried mud and hanging clothes, grateful for a bit of food. They are living in this moment only. To look back would be too painful; to look forward, pointless. I have never felt so completely enveloped and powerless.

I bend down to let Precious look through the lens.

"Put your hand here, look through this little window, and then press when you see the picture you want to take." Like Adanna, she is tiny, but her constitution is steel. No one can rush her. She scans with the camera slowly, stopping when she sees her sister, who is looking at us with a quizzical eye.

"There." She pushes the button. In America, I'd say she'd be running her own company by the time she was fifteen. Here, I can't even imagine a future. I am forced by the immediacy of this situation to live in the moment right along with the children. It is strangely calming.

I think about Gordon wanting to do a story on Adanna. Her journal is still in the car.

"Good work, Miss Assistant," I say to Precious, and Adanna smiles.

Suddenly a flash catches my eye, and I whirl around. A small boy and girl run like streaks through the group, yelling as if there's a fire.

"They're here! They're here. Come quickly!"

"Who's here?"

"The big trucks. They're here, and they've come to save us."

Finally! The cavalry has arrived. Help has come.

Chapter Twenty-four

Every step is like trying to break free from a giant suction cup.

"I'll come in a few minutes, Mr. Stuart," Adanna calls to me as I slog away, feet slapping through the muddy ground. The two messengers take off like a shot, spraying clumps of mud through the air, and I can't keep up.

It feels strange, leaving Adanna and the children there. Of course, they aren't in any hurry to leave. They have good food and a safe, quiet place to rest. By the time I crest the hill, my shoes are caked in mud, but the scene before me makes me forget all about them.

Two giant eighteen-wheelers dominate the landscape. On the side of each truck, painted in bold blue letters, are the words "A Helping Hand." They must have had quite a journey getting here over the bumps and rocks.

The children are gawking at the huge vehicles in silence, as if they were saucers that just swooped in from outer space. The women huddle together in circles, hands linked and jumping up and down in celebration. More and more people are gathering, and the hum of energy is growing.

Gordon has his notebook out. He's talking to a guy wearing a suit and carrying a clipboard. He still has the Bluetooth headset on his ear. I pull out my camera. The saints have landed, and they're bringing gifts from the heavenly city. What a day. This is going to make a great story.

A squad of about twenty men dressed in blue pants and white shirts gets to work like a professional rigging crew. They move in machinelike fashion, putting together tables and roping off areas. I walk over toward Gordon.

"This is incredible, Gordon. I can't believe help arrived so quickly."

"Don't believe everything you see."

"What are you talking about?"

"There's some kind of an agenda here."

"Agenda? What kind of agenda could there be in helping people and giving them food?"

"Not sure. Maybe they're the king's people on some kind of a publicity stunt."

"You're too suspicious."

"Let's hope so."

Within moments, the supplies are unloaded. Oddly, a perimeter has been set up to keep people away from the provisions. Long tables manned by the men and women in blue and white are flagged with banners prominently displaying the name of the organization in gigantic blue letters: "A Helping Hand." The subtitle below reads, "The touch of loving-kindness." Still larger banners unfurl from the top of the 18-wheelers, covering the whole side of the tractor-trailer.

A young Swazi boy runs to Gordon's side and reaches up to grab his hand.

"Isn't it wonderful, Mr. Gordon? Look, they even have toys in the trailer. I can see them."

"Yes, Zineela. Wonderful indeed." He pats the top of the boy's dirty head in a fatherly fashion.

Two representatives approach Pastor Walter. I can't hear what they're saying, but from the looks of it, they want him to rally the group.

I take a picture of Walter talking with these two men.

"What's going on?" I ask Pastor Walter a moment later.

"They want the people in lines to receive the aid in specific order: first children, youngest to oldest; second, women and children; and third, men."

Walter's tired face holds an expression of joy. This is exactly what he's been praying for. One of the men hands Walter a bullhorn, and the crowd immediately quiets as Walter's familiar voice blares out the instructions.

"I don't know why you're so worried, Gordon. This is exactly what these people need." Gordon doesn't respond.

I scan the goods through my camera lens—huge crates of food, water, clothing, and other supplies that look like soap, first-aid kits, chlorine, detergent, and water-filtration systems of some type.

The people from the villages fall into a practiced formation, the older children guiding the younger. Then women followed by men.

A large black four-wheel-drive van pulls up behind the trucks. The windows are tinted dark. Even though the black exterior is splattered with mud, I can see it is a nearly new vehicle. And an expensive one. About ten nicely dressed men with walkie-talkies and earpieces jump out of the cars and take up their positions, as if they're clearing the perimeter for the arrival of an imperial guest.

"Gordon, are you watching all of this?" I can't believe how subdued the people are, talking quietly and waiting in lines like sheep.

"This is starting to take a weird turn. Keep shooting photos until someone tells you to stop. I'm guessing it won't be long before they do."

"Yeah, either that or gun me down." I point at some of the men armed with handguns. Now that the people are moving into lines, Gordon and I stand out like we're wearing orange prison jumpsuits.

"Let's move toward the back." He motions for me to walk with him.

"The only time I've seen this kind of a setup is when a head of state or president of a country was going to show."

"Maybe the king is making an appearance." I am starting to understand Gordon's apprehension. I can't shake the sense that something is amiss.

"It would be good PR for him, at the very least. But I don't think that's what's going on. This organization may be run locally by Swazis, but I wouldn't be surprised if they're merely local puppets for some American group."

The crowd noise begins to swell again, and the CIA looking guys get a little jumpy and start pulling out their radios and talking frantically to one another.

"I wish I could hear what they're saying." Gordon is looking past the trucks and has a worried look on his face.

"Stuart, look at that, down the road." Removed from the circus, we can finally see down the road. I spot two expensive white Mercedes-Benz vans bumping steadily toward us. They pull up behind the one that arrived earlier.

"Aid work must be good business." I whisper to Gordon. I raise my camera as a group of men wearing slick designer suits and black silk ties emerge. Next come women dressed in business attire, each wearing brightly colored scarves around their necks that float behind them in the growing breeze.

Gordon makes a note on his pad.

The door opens on van number two, and out come photographers and people with video cameras perched on their shoulders like parrots. They take their places to capture the full range of today's events.

The security force escorts them down to a special platform in front of the tables. It certainly looks impressive: huge trucks, signs, important people in fancy clothes, video cameras and photographers, and a bunch of starving Africans scratching in the dirt.

Several of the official-looking men come down to the tables and start handing out prepackaged gift baskets. Before the basket is released into outstretched hands, a conveniently placed cameraman has them pose for a picture. The shot is taken, and they are allowed to walk away.

More people filter into line. Now, there are hundreds of desperate, hungry men, women, and children.

The video cameras catch the entire escapade. A few suits come out from behind the table and start to mingle with the people. They shake hands, say something with a smile, and move on to the next person. The video cameras keep rolling.

Now there is no doubt in my mind that the Helping Hand folks are here not merely for generosity's sake, but for a much more nefarious purpose. I've never felt so much turmoil, watching these people subjected to such a contrived handout.

Gordon is standing and shaking his head.

"This is nothing short of ridiculous." We look on as a slick *GQ*-type, wearing a thousand-dollar suit doles out a pittance to someone who won't earn a thousand dollars in his whole life.

The rest of the Mercedes-Benz contingent hand out baskets—maybe twenty or so each, pausing for every photo opportunity along the way. Then, suddenly, and without warning, the security guards start gathering the suits and corralling them back toward the vehicles. The men and women in fancy clothes wave, make one more appearance on the podium, wave again, and head back to their van. The door closes and they're gone—just like that.

I look at Gordon. "Is this an aid mission or a political campaign?"

"Bizarre stuff, I tell you. I don't think I've ever seen anything so wacky. But whatever it takes for these people to get food."

Out come a dozen or so large duffle bags. Half of the security guards start handing out small paper bags, each about the size of a lunch bag.

At the same time, the other goons and workers start loading the supplies and tables back into the semis with the same cold efficiency with which it was unloaded.

One of the gift bags falls to the ground and the contents spill out, revealing a pathetic array. I count among the supplies a tiny bag of rice no larger than my hand, a packet of seasoning the size of a quarter, a tea bag, and a bar of soap—and something that looks like a Bible tract.

Walter catches my eye. He looks like he's in ruins.

I'm incensed. "Gordon, who are they? What are they doing?"

The words spill out of my mouth. "This is immoral, ungodly—how could they do something like this? That food is their only hope."

"I know." Gordon begins to charge forward, and I follow, snapping pictures along the way.

"Excuse me, sir?" Gordon's face and ears are beet red.

The suit stays calm and says in a measured voice, "Sorry, no interviews, no questions."

"Like hell I'm not going to ask questions. My name is Gordon Clandish, and I'm with the *New York Times*. What do you think you're doing?"

"No comment." A few more security guards start to wander closer to us.

"You can't say 'No comment.' These people are starving, and you've obviously brought plenty of provisions. But now you're loading everything back into the truck? What in God's name is that all about?" Gordon's voice is louder than I've ever heard it.

"Many people have been affected by the flood, sir. Obligation and care for them all compels us to move on. We've done what we can do here." He says something to another suit and points toward me. Then the second suit walks toward me.

"Put your camera down," he says in a low, quiet voice. My camera's not coming down.

Gordon is following the first guy, getting in his face.

"You've got to be kidding me. You know exactly what you've done. Exploited these people, taken your crappy pictures and video so you can raise more money in order to line your filthy pockets!"

"Sir, step aside." It is a threat, not a request.

"I won't step aside, you scum."

I continue to take pictures, backing away from the man who's coming toward me. I think I'm about to get decked, when another of the men, the apparent ringleader, calls out to him.

"Come. Let's go now."

They all turn at once toward their vans.

Gordon shouts. "You can count on seeing this charade in the *New York Times*!"

"Have a nice day, sir," the driver says right before he closes his door.

"Burn in hell," Gordon says. But his words are drowned out by the sounds of sixteen cylinders growling to life.

Chapter Twenty-five

The crowd at Walter's care point has scattered. Some have gone back to their villages, but most have remained, sitting in groups. I am amazed at how quickly the gogos collected all the paltry bags of rice and pooled them to cook a meal for one day. The only meal for the day once again.

"Walter." Gordon puts his hand on his friend's shoulders. "We are going to find some real help for you."

I can tell Walter wants to believe this, but his words carry little hope. He seems defeated, deflated.

"Thank you, my friends. God bless you. Without help, I don't know what we will do." He has aged fifteen years in one day.

Gordon and I head back to the Land Cruiser.

"Stuart, how much cash do you have?"

"I have about $1,000; what are you thinking?"

"Let's see, $610. We'll need to exchange yours into emalangeni."

I look back at the care point as we pull away. There's hardly any movement, except for the gogos watching over the pot and the steam curling up into the sky.

"Make sure that water boils good and long, Walter," Gordon had told him, "or you'll all be sick."

We drive away, dodging the rocks and clothes, sticks, tin cans, and other rubbish that has surfaced from the roads now that the ground is starting to dry out.

"I've never been so angry." Gordon yanks the wheel to the right, avoiding a dazed-looking chicken.

The Helping Hand farce has stolen some of his optimism, but he is determined to do something that matters.

"There's a huge SPAR grocery store that will have everything we need. We'll be there in about an hour. But we'll need to swing by my place first and pick up a trailer. There's no way we'll get that much food into the vehicle."

Gordon is still steamed. He beats a hand on the steering wheel. "Calculated, so exploitative. Imagine the lengths they went to, driving those rigs all the way out here in this mess." The color has risen once again in his face. "Because they are snakes, coming in the name of our God. Wolves in sheep's clothing."

I remember that phrase. Whitney used it once to describe the execs at her previous network when she was told over a very nice dinner that she'd been passed up for a promotion. "You're so good," they told her, "we need you to stay right where you are." As Whitney tells it, she nodded politely and smiled at her superiors, one not much older than she. Then, after her shift that night, she told her boss, using her best Southern manners, that she indeed was not going to stay "right where she was" but would in fact, not be returning to their network with its insipid executives and inferior ratings. Whitney almost never swears, but, man, is she ever good at shooting steel arrows through her eyes while speaking with a voice that is much too polite for the circumstance. She hits you twice—first with the laserlike stare, then with pangs of guilt for having wronged such a generous, unselfish woman.

I look over at Gordon, who is deep in his thoughts.

"So are you thinking you can get this article together for the *Times* tonight?"

"We've clearly been spending too much time together, Stu. You read my mind."

I think about Adanna feeding those children at her house.

"I have another element I want to add to the story, if you're okay with it."

"Yeah, what's that?" He shifts his eyes toward me for a second and then back to the obstacle course ahead of us.

"Adanna." That gets his attention.

"Okay. I thought we might do that as a separate story ... but what are you thinking?"

"When I went to her house today, she had a circle of kids outside her door and was feeding them all the food I gave to her—food that was meant for her, Precious, and Abu. She used it all, Gordon. She said, 'They were here, so I fed them.'"

Gordon chuckles. "You know, these Swazis think one day at a time. Still, it's remarkable that a child her age would reach out like that so unselfishly. Especially considering what she's been through these past days."

Days. Has it only been days? It feels like a dozen lifetimes.

"Yeah, I felt like a heel. She thought I was mad at her for giving the food away. Of course, I wasn't. I was just worried about her and Precious and Abu."

Gordon picks up Adanna's journal from the center floorboard and hands it to me.

"Maybe we can use something from here in the article too. With her permission, of course."

I feel a little like I'm committing a white-collar crime, but I open it to the first page and read.

> *My memories of my father are few. My mother tells me he was an important man who had very big things to do. I do not know if that is true, but I do know he was gone all the time. My daddy was very good to me. He would take me fishing, and he brought home presents, little treats, from the city, food and even a pretty dress, white with pink flowers on it. But sometimes he would come home smelling of corn liquor and foul smoke, and do things to me that fathers do not do to their daughters, things you do not write about. Those times, I hated him. I wished him dead. And then he would come home after being gone, singing and bringing treats for us, treating me like his daughter again. Then I had two minds: I wanted the bad person to go, and I wanted my good daddy to stay. These are things I would never speak of, Frida. Never.*

Her precise writing covers every square inch of the page. Of course, that makes sense. Adanna would understand the rare luxury of paper. Nothing would be wasted.

I come across a poem just a few pages later.

In the darkest places of the night
my soul, once so forlorn, is finally free.

For I have found a Love who is the Light;
He gave my stolen virtue back to me.
He walks with me though trials and troubles stay,
And death and demons hover all around,
But greater is the Love that dwells in me
And fiercer is the Friend that I have found.
I shall not fear the waning of the day,
nor bear the shame of an evil father's whim
The Sky-Maker illuminates my way.
There is no guilty stain on me in Him.

I finish reading and look up to the sky. The words float there among the clouds and continue to speak to me. I wish I understood what they were telling me.

Gordon looks over at me. He says nothing.

"Gordon, Adanna's writing is really powerful. I mean, you're the writer. What do you think?"

He smiles. "Writer or not, I think you know when words have power. Yes, her thoughts, and the way she communicates them, are astounding. Well beyond her years."

"What do you think? Could we include some of her words? Is that too strange? I think we should lean on Bill to have it printed tomorrow. Front page."

Gordon laughs out loud for the first time all day. "Oh, Lord have mercy. He's so U.S. politico-centric. Should be working for the *Washington Post*, if you ask me."

I think back to the lunch I had with Bill when I got this assignment. "Yeah, his middle name is 'Party Line,' but what have we got to lose?"

Gordon is slowing down for a turn that brings us toward town. We pull up in front of a store that thankfully does look like an old Safeway. I'm shocked that this thing is actually sitting in the middle of a country that's starving to death. The parking lot is packed.

"This is not good." Gordon's eyes dart back and forth, surveying the scene.

The store is overrun with people running up and down the isles. Women and children are carrying out boxes of water and food. Their arms are stuffed with as much as they can hold.

Gordon runs his fingers through his hair, and flecks of mud float off and settle on his lap and around the car. His eyes are bloodshot.

"This is why it's so tough getting aid to people who are living in the country. Fear drives the middle class to clean the stores out of everything, leaving nothing for the ones who need it most. It's plain selfish hoarding."

"I've seen this disconnect between the haves and have-nots in other countries. Without infrastructure, the poor are out of luck. What do you think we should do?" I know that's the only question for Gordon right now.

"I see only one more option." He's already pulling out of the lot. "If we try any of the other stores around here, I'm afraid the result will be the same. We'll head to Mbabane and pray there is something left. Since Mbabane is above the flood zones, it probably hasn't been affected like the lower areas."

"Then let's hurry. Time is wasting."

We arrive in Mbabane late. Too late to make it back to the village tonight. We'll have to stay here overnight.

"The SPAR is there on the right." Gordon points and the car stops with a lurch.

"The parking lot looks quiet. Hopefully, that doesn't mean the shelves are already empty."

I walk into the store with a twinge of nervousness. I am elated to see that it is well stocked. It's obvious that there has been a small rush, but nothing like in the city of Manzini.

Gordon takes control, clapping his hands together. "Okay, let's try to come as close as we can to $1,600. Stuart, you round up $1,000 worth of water and I'll spend the rest on food."

"Sounds good. See you at the front."

I go straight to the manager. That's a ton of water, likely over two thousand bottles. I walk up to a man I presume is in charge. He's one of the few older men I've seen. This gray-haired Swazi is big, but not fat, and carries his body with a slow, controlled confidence. He is wearing glasses that do little to hide the deep crows feet around his eyes. The glasses look like 1950s army issue. He has a military air.

"Hello, are you the manager?"

"I am, in fact. How may I help you?" I can tell he is sizing me up—scrawny American, worn jeans and T-shirt, dirty matted hair.

"We need to buy $1,000 worth of water, the biggest bottles possible for the best price."

He looks at me like I've just escaped from a Swazi asylum.

"Sorry, I can't help you."

"What do you mean you can't help me? I have money, and I am desperate."

"What do you know about desperate?" He laughs. I don't flinch.

I have learned a lot about desperation lately. He continues the interrogation. "Okay, then. Tell me: Who are you with?"

"With? My friend and I are with the *New York Times*. I'm a photographer. We're doing a series of stories on your people." I emphasize the last two words. "On the plight of Swazi people."

"Nope. I can't help you." He starts to turn away, and I realize this is going to take some careful work on my part. I slow my words, trying to empty them of emotion.

"Sir, we are trying to help a village that has no drinkable water because of the flood. We're involved in a relief effort to help them. Sir, my friend is in your store right now getting food for us to take there in the morning."

He squeezes his lips together and shifts his mouth back and forth. "So, what you're telling me is that this is all going to help the people here in our country?"

"Yes, absolutely."

"Do you mean our people in the villages? Swazis?"

He looks over the black-rimmed glasses, now resting on the tip of his nose. He gives me an "I want to believe you" look but is still unconvinced. Maybe a Helping Hand contingent was already here.

"Sir, I promise. Look at me; I'm filthy from trying to help."

He laughs. "I saw you pull up. You and your friend are the dirtiest people to come in here all day—and the dirtiest white people I've ever seen." He pauses. "Okay. I will choose to believe you. How many bottles did you say you need?"

"A thousand dollars' worth."

Gordon appears from down the aisle with two enormous pushcarts, each stacked high with fifty- and hundred-kilogram bags of rice, beans, and corn. No need to pick up any extras. This is about bare necessities.

Within the hour, the trailer and car are loaded. The sunlight is gone, and without being able to see our way back to the care point, we concede to staying the night in a hotel.

We jump back in the car and start to pull away. I can hear a faint news report coming from the radio. I crank up the volume.

"Swazi Radio AM 1060—the only station in Swaziland. The flooding throughout the region has been extensive. It is believed there are over twenty thousand dead and a hundred thousand displaced and in need of food and clean water. The death toll may rise as further reports surface."

"This is horrendous," I say to myself. To Gordon. And maybe to God.

"I can't help but think of what will happen to all the children."

"It breaks my heart, Gordon."

"I need to tell you something. The thought has crossed my mind a hundred times, and I have to tell somebody."

"Tell me, Gordon."

"I've considered adopting Adanna, Precious, and Abu."

"What? That's incredible! I can't think of a better parent. Can you do that?"

"I can. Because I've been living in Swaziland for over a year, I would meet the criteria of an adoptive parent."

"Gordon, you'd be making such a difference in their lives. You'd give them a family forever, a father, safety, security, a future."

"I'm only one man, but it's something I can do to make a real difference. Remember what I told you about not losing the big picture?"

"Of course."

"Well, what we've got trailing behind us? What we're doing with these articles? That's big-picture stuff. Important stuff. But Adanna ..."

The next words catch in his throat. "Adanna and Precious and Abu, they're my small picture."

As he speaks, I imagine the four of them standing together for a photo. I snap the mental picture, and it brings a smile.

"I just love them all so much," he says. "Adanna has been a mother all her life. I want to take that pressure off, love her, and let her be a child again."

"I told you before, and I'll say it again."

Gordon has a smile on his face from ear to ear, and his eyes are starting to water.

"Okay, go ahead. Say it."

"You're a saint, man."

Chapter Twenty-six

Gordon Clandish—Special to the *Times*

Matsapha, Swaziland, Feb. 16—Three days after intense rainfall led to flooding in southern Manzini, thousands of people are left without food or clean water. Most are children under the age of 12. Nearly 25 percent are heads of households, having lost parents or other caregivers to AIDS.

The government of Swaziland says it has no need of international aid, but the only relief to come from within the country came in the form of wolves in sheep's clothing.

Earlier today, two semis from the Swazi aid organization A Helping Hand made their way down muddy roads to the Thembini Care Point, run by Pastor Walter Malaza. Hundreds from the community had come to take refuge on this higher ground in hopes of finding food and water.

Flood victims jumped and cheered as representatives from A Helping Hand unloaded large containers of food, water, and sanitation supplies. A second and third wave of vehicles pulled up to the care point, and organization officials stepped out and onto a platform where people had been organized into lines to receive aid. The officials, who appeared dressed for a political convention, handed small brown paper bags to villagers while hired photographers took photos.

Each bag contained a small amount of rice, a seasoning packet, a tea bag, a bar of soap, and a religious pamphlet, the food being barely enough for one meal.

Officials from A Helping Hand distributed the paper bags, then drove off in their Mercedes vans, and the rest of the relief crew loaded the rest of the needed supplies, including filtered water, back into the semis and retreated from the scene.

Relief workers would give no comment about their unusual distribution methods or motivation.

A disheartened Malaza said, "We were herded like goats with the promise of help, only to be forsaken by our own people."

A United Nations resident coordinator for Swaziland, Mncobi Msibi, said in a telephone interview from Mbabane that he had never heard of A Helping Hand.

"Refugees are short of clean water, food, and shelter, but the situation remains under control," Msibi said.

For the time being, government officials have declined offers of more extensive aid.

Just one kilometer away, another scene stood in contrast to that at the care point. A twelve-year-old Swazi girl, a resident of Thembini, had more than a dozen local orphaned children seated outside her hut, doling out every bit of food and water she had in her home.

This young girl, Adanna Dlamini, had been given food for herself and her two younger siblings by a U.S. visitor a few days earlier. When asked why she didn't save it to take care of her own family, she answered, "These children are here, and they are hungry. Why would I not feed them?"

Adanna and her siblings, ages five and two, lost their mother recently to complications of AIDS. Her mother had been infected with HIV by her husband, who left the family four years ago and is presumed dead. Adanna is one of thousands of vulnerable orphans in this area, alone, ignored by some relatives and community members, and often suffering egregious abuse at the hands of others.

This is a familiar story throughout Africa. In the absence of a competent medical system and the antiretroviral medicines, thousands of children watch their parents die from AIDS. The AIDS crisis in the United States, by contrast, is more under control. Today, Americans are more likely to commit suicide than die from AIDS.

This frail young girl, looking more like an eight-year-old than a preteen, has every reason to despair, but even after personal tragedy and a natural disaster that has swept her community, killing thousands, she remains open to bestowing good. Open to hope.

Adanna is not only a relief worker but also a writer of uncommon talent and perspective. The pages of a journal, given to her by a Finnish teacher of writing, are filled front and back with her words.

My Country

Today the violet bird came to me
in the half light,
when the sun and moon
nod to one another across the same plane
Then arc!
One to greet day, the other night.

Bird of my country past
You swoop and search the ground.

I believed you my own,
When Momma gave me an offering
From her pot to scatter along the path
I let corn slip through my hands,
Which you found with your regal beak.

Bird of Swaziland,
Your bead black eyes search my soul.

Understand: I no longer draw water
From a river swallowed by earth
I have no maize, from this scorched land.

Bird of Sorrow—
Only crumbs of dry earth fall through my hands

Which ache for the pail of water
The feel of corn
The touch of my mother
Her voice, like a morning bird, saying
Sawubona, my child. Greet a new day!

Chapter Twenty-seven

As we drive out of the hotel complex on the way to Walter's, it's clear that something has shifted. Everyone is moving, working to clean up, but as they look at our passing car, their eyes are empty. They reach outward with their hands when they see what we're carrying in the trailer. As we near the care point, we pass two boys wearing ragged shorts. I look in the passenger mirror to see them running after us.

"Are you seeing this?" I turn toward Gordon.

"Yes. An all-too-familiar sight. You know, if we stopped …"

"We'd be overrun. We'd never make it." I look again, and the boys have stopped, bent and panting. I have a rock in the pit of my stomach.

As we near Walter's care point, the children recognize us, waving enthusiastically as if we were some kind of Swazi rock star, and run alongside the trailer.

"We're like the pied piper." Gordon's eyes are darting back and forth, trying to avoid the crowd. He's tense. I roll down the window and try to wave the people back.

As we arrive at the care point, a baptism occurs. They see food and pass from death to life. The expressions on their faces, their body language, hand movements all change.

The gogos, standing motionless, jump to their feet, clapping their hands and lifting them to the sky. Their joy is contagious, and Gordon and I both laugh out loud.

The noise draws more people, and before the dust has settled in front of us, we are surrounded. The door is jammed shut because we are pressed in from all sides

People clamber and bang on the truck. For a few seconds, I'm afraid. They're grabbing at the packages on the trailer. Never have I seen such a hopeful panic.

"Gordon, what do we do?"

"Try praying."

Slowly and cautiously, I roll down the window.

"Please ... move away from the truck. We're trying to help you."

Hands fly into the cab looking like a hundred worms wiggling through the air, groping and grasping.

"Roll up the window now!"

"I can't, they won't get their hands out."

"Roll it up, and they'll move their hands."

The vehicle is starting to rock ever so slightly back and forth.

"They've gone mad."

"Not mad, just desperate."

"Gordon, look. They're ripping into the bags on the trailer."

"Okay, when I say go, open the door and push as hard as you can. We'll plow our way through and try to get this under control."

"I'm not sure that's such a good ..."

"Just do it. One, two ..."

A high-pitched, ear-piercing crack whistles through the air, then another. The people scatter like ants, taking cover away from the vehicle. Some fall to the ground, others cower under trees with their hands over their ears.

"What was that?"

"No clue."

"Wait … there's the answer. Look."

A man stands with a rifle pointed in the air. He's yelling something in S'swati, and though I don't understand a word of that language, I can tell everyone is doing exactly as he says.

"That's Chief Bhulu. Thank God."

"What is he doing?"

"He's shooting in the air to control the crowd. These people are afraid of guns."

"Yeah, me, too."

He's coming this way, and Walter's right behind him. The chief waves his hand, holding the rifle, and the remaining crowd parts like the Red Sea. We climb out of the Land Cruiser. The chief is speaking rapidly in S'swati.

"The chief says he is deeply sorry for the behavior of his people."

He shouts loudly at them again, and Walter continues to interpret.

"We are not animals! No matter how much we suffer, we bind together as one." Turning back to us, the chief continues.

"They don't know any better. When you are in precarious circumstances, as we have found ourselves in these last few days, people forget themselves in their push to survive."

Gordon speaks. "Chief Bhulu, it is my honor to see you again. We understand. I'm sure we would have acted the same had we been in a similar circumstance. We are here to help with provisions. It's not much, but it will help until more assistance arrives."

Walter's eyes are wet with tears. He lets the chief do the talking, jumping in only to offer interpretation. I nod toward him, and he puts his hands together, as if in a prayer, then waves them forward toward me, a supreme gesture of gratitude.

Chief Bhulu's voice is loud and clear. "My brothers, please accept our gratitude for this sacrifice. You will be safe here. You have my word."

The crowd creeps toward the chief, cautiously, as if he might turn and smite them at a moment's notice.

"We appreciate your hospitality. Gordon, let's get these things to the people."

A giant smile crosses Walter's face, the kind you would give to a close friend you haven't seen in years. Then, he bull-rushes me with his arms wide open and practically suffocates me with an embrace.

"Thank you, thank you, Stuart, for not forgetting us."

"We're just doing what we can. What is right."

He steps back, then puts his hand on my shoulder. He says quietly, "Brother, you are God's vessel. You, my brother, are the hands and feet of Christ, the hope of Christ to the people."

We head back to the trailer, where the chief has begun to assemble villagers to help unload the goods.

The process of serving all these hungry people runs smoothly, thanks to the leadership of Walter and the chief. People line up, as they did for the not-so-helpful Helping Hand caravan; children first, the elderly, women, then the men.

Walter steps onto a rock and calls out to the crowd, "Let us pray." Out of reverence, respect for Walter, or fear of the armed chief at Walter's side, everyone quiets down and turns toward him.

Walter's powerful voice—inflection and intonation perfected by years of preaching—carries across the crowd like a mighty wind.

"Gracious God, thank You for remembering Your people.…"

Voices rise out of the crowd, "Yes, Jesus. Mmm-hmm. Yes, Father."

"Bless the servants who brought this food. And may our government do what is right and continue to provide help for all who need it here in our country. God, remember us, Your people. Amen."

Walter and the chief usher Gordon and me to the front, where the supplies are stationed. Gordon immediately dives in to help, passing out food and a toothy smile as rich as I've ever seen from his face.

"I'll be back in just a minute …" I say, then turn toward the car. Before I have gone two steps, Gordon calls after me.

"Getting your camera?"

"Yes. I thought maybe …"

Gordon holds his hands out in front of him, indicating the crowd. "I don't think this is a news story, Gordon."

"But it's good news. It's the best sort of news. I thought if maybe I got some photos …"

"Stuart, do you hear that voice?"

I look around, puzzled.

"I hear lots of voices, Gordon. What do you mean?"

"Listen closer …"

I strain to hear, then shrug my shoulders.

"Listen, Stuart … *listen* …"

And suddenly I hear it. The voice from so many years ago. The same voice I heard in the church service. And in hearing it, I am finally changed.

Feed My sheep.

I walk back and stand next to Gordon. He sees it too—in my eyes. The people who come to me are the same needy, hungry people they were five minutes ago. They still wear the same torn, worn clothes and carry the same broken bowls. But they are no longer strangers.

I look to my right and see Adanna, trailed by Precious and Abu. Precious jumps up and down again and again, vying for my attention, until I wave. I see Abu's little hand waving at me, and my heart clinches. Adanna gives me a smile, but it is two smiles. One, the smile of a happy child; the other, the smile of someone who is thankful for a good friend.

Gordon bends toward her and puts his hand on her slender shoulder. He is saying something I can't hear. Then he turns toward me.

"Stuart, Adanna's journal is still in the Land Cruiser. Don't let me forget."

I nod.

After the last person has been served, I help carry the remaining supplies into the church building. Then I head to the car to get Adanna's book.

It has already been a long day, but I am not tired.

Adanna sits under the trees with Gordon. Walter and the gogos are busying themselves with preparation for another wave of hungry locals we have been told are just minutes away.

Children are running around, playing tag or chase or some other game only children play, their laughter and yelps dotting the

afternoon with joy as delicious as the meal they have just enjoyed.
Women sit in circles, chatting away. Nearby, a group of men is also
engaged in a lively discussion. I am reminded of a time when Whitney
and I visited her family in South Carolina. Neighbors would stop by
the sprawling front porch "to jaw," as Whitney's dad would say. At
the time, I thought the potluck chatter was silly, a throwback to
a time that no longer existed and served little purpose. Certainly
it was something I had never known. I teased Whitney about the
"small-town small talk" for months afterward. She always smiled and
never once told me I was being inappropriate. But now, as I sit here
and watch the people talk with one another in a language I don't
understand, I realize just how wrong I was.

The smell of fresh wood permeates the air, and our clothes smell
like we've been standing in front of a barbecue all day. This is one of
the good smells of Africa.

Gordon is leaning back on his elbow, mouth wide open, laughing
with the women.

I sit down next to Adanna and hand her the journal.

"You left this in Gordon's car. It's a beautiful book."

"Thank you, Stuart. Frida ... I mean this book ... is precious to
me." Precious looks over at us when she hears her name and smiles.
I wave to her, but she has already turned away and is chasing other
children and giggling. Abu is doing his best to follow her.

Adanna folds her hands in front of her dirty dress, turns her head,
and rests her chin on her shoulder. Her skin and hair are flecked with
light brown spots, her eyes sallow looking. She starts to cough, and it
goes on for so long I wonder if it will ever stop.

"Are you all right?"

She holds up her hand, finishes a cough, then says, "I am fine."

I am not convinced, but her smile does its best at scaring away my worry. It will be so good for her if Gordon can adopt them.

"I have something to tell you," I say, "and I hope you're not upset with Gordon and me."

"What?"

"We read your journal. We read 'Frida.'"

I can't read her expression.

"You are such a beautiful writer. And … well … we should have asked you first … and by not doing so we broke a very important rule in journalism … but we included one of your poems in a newspaper article he wrote. I hope you will forgive us."

"It's okay." She sits with her legs tucked under her dress, her chin on her knees, and closes her eyes. I put my hand on her back and without a second thought, offer a silent prayer, *God, bless this child.*

Precious and Abu run up and tug on Adanna's dress.

"Play with us. Play with us 'Danna!" No wonder Adanna is so tired. I am jarred by the sound of Gordon's satellite phone.

"Hello?" Gordon says. He covers the phone. "It's Bill."

I can hear Bill's sonorous voice as if he were sitting with us.

"Gordon, I got the article and Stuart's photos."

"Great, Bill. We're with the people in the village right now."

"Stuart's there? Let me talk to him."

Gordon hands me the phone.

"Hey, Bill."

"Stuart, I have to tell you: You're back, man. The photos you sent are spectacular, and you know I don't use that word a lot. What's gotten into you? And the photo of the girl?"

"Adanna." She opens her eyes and picks up her head.

"Yes. You got your front page." I can feel my face get hot. Gordon's mouth is agape.

Bill continues, "Great work, Stuart. And the article will be on the front of the International section. Those Helping Hand bastards even got *my* cold blood boiling."

"Thanks, Bill. This is great news."

Gordon slaps me on the back.

"What does this mean?" Adanna asks Gordon.

"It means the world will see your goodness, Adanna."

I turn to her. "Remember the photo I took outside your home, when you were feeding the kids?"

She nods.

"It will be on the front page of the newspaper tomorrow morning, Sunday's edition. Many, many people will read it."

Gordon adds, "And the story about you and your poem will also appear in the newspaper."

"Which poem?" she asks. Gordon and I shoot each other a look of panic. Did we make a mistake?

"'My Country,'" answers Gordon. We look at her, searching her face and seeking approval.

Her shoulders drop. "Oh, good."

I feel like weeping, looking at her.

"Adanna, you are going to be a famous poet."

"And your people will get recognition, maybe even more help, because of you." When Gordon says this, Adanna's head jerks up with a start. A strange look crosses her face.

Walter leans over and kisses her forehead like a proud father.

The gogos follow, hugging her small body. She looks happy. For the moment, we all have reason to be happy.

A few minutes later, Gordon gets up and walks Adanna, Precious, and Abu back to their hut. When he returns, the sun is beginning to disappear behind the hills, and activity has waned in the care point. He looks concerned.

"Adanna is completely exhausted. And she's been coughing a lot. Have you noticed she's been coughing? I'd like to get a doctor out to take a look at her. I tried to get her to come back with us tonight, but she insisted on going back home with Precious and Abu. Who can blame her for wanting to be in her own place."

"Gordon, why don't we stay here tonight? Then we could be close to Adanna and also be ready to help in the morning. Walter said they are going to need more help tomorrow."

Walter walks toward us. He is weary but at peace.

"We want to stay here tonight," Gordon says, "so we can help you in the morning. And to tell you the truth, I wouldn't mind staying close to Adanna."

A shadow passes over Walter's face. "Yes, we will have to keep watch on that child. Have you told Stuart of your plan to become a dad again?" Walter's eyes brighten.

"He has," I say, patting Gordon on the back, "and it's the best thing I've heard in years."

Gordon turns to Walter. "You know, Stuart is going to be a dad too."

"I am!" I'm surprised by my excitement.

"Really? Congratulations. Oh, Stuart, you are going to make a really good father. God bless you and your wife."

"Thank you, Walter."

Walter starts back toward the church and motions for us to follow. The two men in front of me have taught me more about how to care, how to act like a true father, than anyone else.

"If you want to stay tonight, I would be grateful. Why don't you stay here in the church? We don't have much for beds, but it will be more comfortable and might keep you safe from—" He stops. "Well, whatever might be prowling around at night."

Gordon and I lie on mats in a closed-in porch. We can still see outside through the torn screens and open windows. There are dozens of others lining the floor along with us, obviously displaced from the flood. They don't seem to mind a bit that we are here.

Darkness transforms the yellow grassy hillsides into gray layers, the outer edges of a black hole.

"How are you feeling about the front-page photo?" he asks. "You seemed a little less excited than I thought you'd be. Front page is big news, Stuart."

"Yes, I know it is. And of course I think it's great."

"But ..."

"Does it seem exploitative to you?"

"Ah ... I wondered when you'd get to that question. What do you think, Stu?"

"Well, when I think about the photo I took of the people slaughtered in the DRC, the one that won me that stupid award, I wonder if I'm as bad as those phonies from A Helping Hand."

"Maybe we don't always have good motives for what we do...."

"Yeah...."

"But I don't doubt that, ultimately, you are a good man with a good heart. And maybe in the past you weren't—or maybe you just didn't see it. But you are a different man from the Stuart who met me at the hotel when we started this story. Swaziland has changed you. This is what happened to me after I lost my family. Showing our Adanna feeding those children, what could be more good than that?"

"Maybe you're right. It is a difficult line to walk. I want to do the right thing—far more than I want to make a name for myself. That might not always have been the case, but I am sure of it now. It's big-picture stuff, isn't it? That's where the good will come. Right?"

"Yes, big-picture stuff."

In the dimming light, I can just make out tears forming in Gordon's eyes.

"Gordon, thank you."

"Thank me? For what?"

"For everything. For walking through the muck with me. For being a friend. For challenging me. And … maybe most of all … for what you're doing for Adanna and Precious and Abu. They are three very lucky children." And now I'm choked up too.

We are silent together. In a matter of minutes, I can hear Gordon snoring softly. I've never been one to find sleep so easily.

It has been a good day. A life-changing day. And yet, a feeling of despair settles on me. I shiver and lie under my blanket. I watch as the last rays emanating from the sun are extinguished like a multitude of candles.

I miss Whitney.

And my unborn child.

Chapter Twenty-eight

The night passes without incident, though I awake exhausted. I look around the room; Gordon must've slipped out earlier.

The morning brings new anxiety. What do you do in a catastrophe zone? I know what to do when I'm behind my camera, but without it? I feel lost.

Walter walks into the room, far more cheerful than anyone ought to be this early in the morning.

"Stuart, good morning. How did you sleep?"

"Oh, fine, thanks." He can see right through my lie but doesn't offer a challenge.

"Come and have some tea." I follow him out into courtyard. The sun is shining faintly through the clouds.

"I have a very important job for you. It is not a pretty job but a necessary one. You still want to help?"

"Yes, anything, Walter."

"We need help digging graves for the people who lost their lives in the flood. There are already several men working on it, but it is not enough."

I gather up my tired reserves, trying to make certain I don't reveal my real feelings about his request. Did he see me flinch?

"Give me a shovel, and show me where to go."

Even as I agree, my stomach twists into knot.

Walter leads me to the gogos, where I sip tea and eat a small bit of pap. I am miles away—both literally and figuratively—from my morning Starbucks coffee and maple-nut scone.

Walter hands me a shovel and offers a look of sympathy. But he has other concerns. With a flick of his hand, he points me in the right direction. I walk down a muddy bank to where rows of graves have already been dug. Bodies are lined up just beyond the graves.

I would guess there are at least three hundred people awaiting their final resting places. I can't help but wonder if it's wise burying the dead next to a river. But so many are buried here already. My place in line is decided for me. The man next to me looks up and gives me a manly nod. There's no script for this.

The shovel breaks the ground easily, like a knife cutting through soft cheese. The ground is saturated. I shovel and toss, shovel and toss. I'm living in the sharp land of necessity now. I am doing something with my hands to honor the dead and the living. It seems so inadequate. So incomplete. I fall into rhythm with strangers who are burying sons, daughters, mothers, and fathers. The sound of shovels cutting earth forms a strange symphony.

Clouds cover the afternoon sun, a welcome respite from the heat. After a couple of hours, I stop. My back hurts … but I am surprised at how quickly my wound has begun to heal. I would be stuck in my bed, whining for chicken soup, if I'd hurt myself back home.

I decide to make my way back up to the care point, to take a break and check in with Gordon. I look behind me as I make my way up the hill: eight neat graves for eight bodies. As I crest the hill,

I see Gordon talking with a doctor. It's the black American doctor
from the hospital.

"Hey, Gordon. Dr. Smith, how are you?"

"Hello, Stuart. I should ask how that back of yours is."

"Oh, it's fine."

"Let me see it."

I pull my shirt up and it tears slightly against the scab.

"Hey. It's looking surprisingly good. Are you still taking the
antibiotics I gave you?"

"Uh, yeah ... no ..." I really haven't had time to think about it.

"Well, I suggest you do. Just to prevent infection."

"Yes, Doc.

Chapter Twenty-nine

♦◇■ Adanna ■◇♦

The first light of morning streams into the hut, and I push myself up and out of bed. Precious and Abu lie sleeping on their beds. I make my way to the door to walk down the path that leads to everywhere.

I am very tired. Coughing kept me awake, but I want to feel the morning sun on my back. It is a comfort to walk the path my momma did every morning. I miss her today with a deep ache. I walk with slow steps, and the cloud-muted sun falls on my shoulders.

My legs are weak, so I pause to sit on the large rock where I often would sit and write or wait for my daddy to come home when I was very young. My legs look like small brittle sticks. It is suddenly hard to take in a breath, and I am afraid.

A shadow falls on the path. I turn to find a stranger. He walks toward me. Lost in my daydreaming, I didn't even hear him.

"You look like you're in deep thought. Mind if I sit with you?"

Startled but not scared, I tell him it is okay. He sits beside me.

"Where did you come from?" I ask.

His skin is dark but his eyes are a deep ocean blue.

Studying his face, I ask again, "Where is your home?"

He laughs. "My home is another place." He pauses. "As is yours."

His voice is musical and soothing.

"No," I tell him, "my home is not far. Just up the path. I was born by that jacaranda tree, and I have lived here ever since."

"This is not your true home, Adanna."

"How do you know my name?"

"I have known about you a long time."

This man is strange indeed.

"Someone who knows you well sent me."

I wonder if he is a friend of Mr. Gordon or Pastor Walter.

A flock of geese flies high over our heads and honk loudly. They are heading somewhere important. Tagoze told me once that the one leading the flock is cutting the wind for the others so they can rest until it is their turn. How I miss him.

I begin to cough and the man reaches over to place his hand on my shoulder. Immediately the coughing stops.

"I am here to tell you, you were placed here for a time such as this. You have used your gift well, Adanna, to help your people."

His words remind me of someone, but I cannot remember. I am so weary, so tired and weak I can hardly hold up my head. My breaths seem to stop short in my throat and then I suddenly understand.

"The illuminated man ..." I say. He smiles.

"It is time for you to come home, sweet girl."

"Who will take care of Precious and Abu?" My words fall out like the last drips of water from an empty cup.

"The Father has appointed someone to take care of them. They will be treated with kindness and love."

I nod. I close my eyes for a moment.

"Thank you," I say, but when I look up, he is gone.

I stumble home and crawl onto my bed. Precious and Abu are

still asleep. I pick up Frida and lie on my side, facing the wall like always, and find just enough strength to write.

My breath is shallow, and it rattles in rasps and wheezes, but I no longer feel any pain. My body feels light. My eyelids are rocks. I cannot keep them open.

"Adanna?"

I know this voice, like a mighty river.

A familiar smell surrounds me, like the most fragrant flower in the world.

My eyes are closed, but I can see him—the illuminated man. I sit up, lifted by a strength I did not know I had. He extends his hand, and I see my name written on it. The *A* is the exact same kind I make when I sign my name.

"Adanna, you are my daughter. I love you and am well pleased with you."

His words cut to my heart. This has been the desire of my soul, to be loved as a true daughter. I look at him and feel his love. Words I've never spoken come from my mouth. "Holy are you, illuminated man, giver of gifts, and lover of my soul."

He tilts my face up, and I look deeply into his eyes. There I see her face, her body now beautiful in a magnificent flowing robe, glowing with the colors of a thousand suns.

"Welcome home."

I run to her arms, open for me.

"Momma?"

Chapter Thirty

In short order, a line has formed, and Dr. Smith is put to work at the care point. Gordon stands next to him, helping with translation. He looks a little anxious, but I know his heart well now. He will not deny these children care just to rush out to Adanna's side.

I lean against a tree at the edge of the care point and sip some water. Gogos diligently sweep the area with brooms made of twigs. It looks to me like they are merely rearranging the dirt but they are doing so with great purpose and dignity.

Kids are kicking a soccer ball back and forth near the graves. It is a surreal picture, these children at play surrounded by death and destruction. The ball is kicked hard, and it flies into the air, drawing a shallow arc that matches the shape of the dirt mounds beyond. I do not need my camera to remember this image.

I decide to head to Adanna's house--to tell her about Dr. Smith—that he is here to help her.

Along the trail, I am stopped by the surprising discovery of tiny flowers. They are a dazzling dark blue with small white centers. Something long since forgotten floods back to my memory. I know this flower. My grandmother taught me all about flowers. This was one of my favorites: the African blue squill. They are only a few inches high and look like a blue spike of nettles, but I know Adanna will love them. I gather up a few into a small bouquet.

As I continue along the path, I see two figures coming toward me: Precious and Abu.

"Hi, you two!" I yell ahead. They run to me, and I bend down to hug them. "Where's your sister?"

"She's resting," Precious says. "She isn't feeling well, I think."

"Why don't you two head to the care point. There's a nice American doctor there who is giving people checkups. Mr. Gordon will bring him to check on Adanna soon too."

"Okay, Mr. Stuart." I watch the two of them walk slowly down the path, hand in hand.

I approach the house and lightly tap on the door.

"Adanna? Are you awake?"

Nothing. I knock harder.

"Adanna? Hey it's Mr. Stuart. I've brought you something."

Peering inside, I see Adanna lying on her bed. I open the door and walk slowly toward her.

"Adanna."

She doesn't respond. I carefully place my hand on her shoulder and give it a light shake. I break into a cold sweat.

Her skin is like ice.

"God, no! Not her. Please, not her."

"Adanna …" I say again, softly at first. Then louder. Nothing but silence. I kneel down and look around at her face.

Her eyes are closed, and there's a look of tranquility. I kiss her cold forehead, then gather Adanna's small body in my arms, holding her close. I carry her down the path toward the care point. Gordon is walking toward me, followed by Precious and Abu. When he sees me, he breaks into a run. My stomach goes sour, and everything along the path blurs into a haze.

"What's wrong? What's wrong with Adanna …?"

I have no words.

He reaches us, and I gently place her in his arms.

"No … no …" Gordon falls to his knees, his words trailing off into silent sobs.

Gordon buries her in his chest and wails a cry of deep loss.

He suddenly stands and starts running back to the care point, Adanna flopping in his arms. I want to follow, but I can't. I am frozen, numb. Something compels me back to her hut. I walk inside and notice the blue flowers scattered along the floor. Then I see her journal. I pick it up and open it to the last page. Her penmanship is shaky. It looks as if an old woman has written the entry. In the dim light, I read.

> A strange man came to me on the path,
> Kind with a voice like music
> Like a friend. He told me this isn't my home.
> I was not scared.
> I have come to you day and night
> Telling you things deep in my heart.
> My sadness and joy.
>
> The stranger with blue eyes like the sky said I had
> done my work.
> It is okay to go, the Father has appointed someone to
> take care of my Precious and Abu. I will miss them so.

My breathing is slow, my body light, like air.

Today, I will go to the home of my ancestors.

My real home.

I am not scared.

I put the book in my back pocket and step outside. I feel detached from myself, unable to feel. I look over at a tree near her house and see a shovel. It's the shovel I was using to dig graves earlier. I don't even remember carrying it with me to Adanna's house.

It is then that the floodgates finally open. I cry as I have never cried before.

And then I start to dig.

Some time later, a procession comes down the path. Walter is leading the solemn march. He is holding Precious's hand, and his wife is carrying Abu, who is sleeping. Gordon follows with the doctor who looks an actor who has just stepped onto the wrong movie set. They are carrying Adanna's body on a makeshift gurney. Others follow a few steps behind. It is strangely quiet.

Precious walks up and peers into the hole. Walter looks at me, his head nodding, sadness fixed on his face. My eyes meet Gordon's, and I can see that he is grieving not only for the loss of Adanna, but other losses too. There's nothing for either of us to say.

They bring her body next to the grave and set it down. A few of the women start to cry. Precious joins them, and her wails wake Abu. He looks around, confused at first, then joins in the mournful chorus.

The sun is dipping, its last light shooting brilliant colors through the wisps of clouds to the west.

Walter opens his worn black Bible, but he doesn't even look at it. He doesn't need to.

"Then I heard a voice from heaven say, 'Write: Blessed are the dead who die in the Lord from now on.' 'Yes,' says the Spirit, 'they will rest from their labor, for their deeds will follow them.'"

After her body is lowered, the people each throw in a handful of dirt. With great sadness, I take the shovel and finish the job, covering up a most beautiful soul with the soil upon which she walked.

As the night falls, I am the last to leave. But before I go, I walk back into the hut and collect the scattered flowers. I lay them gently on the grave and offer a whispered prayer.

"Take good care of her, God. She was one of Your best."

Chapter Thirty-one

We spend another night at Walter's place, but unlike yesterday, we've been sitting under a tree since morning tea, not speaking. Gordon is at the end of himself. I don't know if it will help or hurt, but I finally decide to give Gordon Adanna's journal.

I reach into my back pocket and hand it to him.

He slowly opens the book and reads, and as he does, his countenance changes. A veil of grief is lifted. He reaches over and grabs my arm, squeezes it.

"Thank you."

Walter is standing with the gogos. Somehow, there's still enough food for everyone to make it through another day, perhaps even two or three. It doesn't make any sense. We were certain the food was nearly gone by the end of the day yesterday.

A group of children yell in S'swati and point down the hill.

"Gordon, what is that?"

"What?"

"Look down the road."

Gordon and I follow a group of boys, who are moving like a swarm. A motorcade is heading this way, and a crowd is forming along the road.

Walter has joined the group, craning to see.

"What's this about, Pastor?"

"I have no idea."

"Are those flags on the cars?"

"Those are the king's vehicles! He must have sent an emissary to help. Praise be to God."

A shout like an old gunpowder cannon erupts from the people. They begin dancing in the streets, in the mud. Tears stream down the gogos' faces as they hug one another and twirl like agile ballerinas. The men are stomping their feet into the ground and hopping up and down like grasshoppers, like an ancient tribal dance.

Black limousines and Mercedes roll to a stop in front of us, and two huge men get out of a car and take their places by the doors of a limo. Two more come from behind and join them.

One of the men opens the limousine door, then bows as a man wearing an elegant, vibrant red and black royal robe steps out. People immediately fall to the ground on their knees, bowing their faces low to the ground. This is not a royal emissary; this is royalty itself, the king of Swaziland.

"Greetings, brothers and sisters. I bring the warmest good wishes of her majesty the queen, the *indlovukazi*, and the whole Swazi nation. I am here to bring news to you, my people."

People slowly stand to their feet.

"You have suffered through this flood. All that you have worked for has been washed away. But I, your king, am here to comfort you and to care for the needs of those who mourn."

Quiet sets in like an anchor. Some people begin to sob, others seem hypnotized by the presence of royalty.

"A tremendous outpouring of kindness has come from the

international community." He pauses for effect. "They have heard about your plight." Another pause. "And they have seen your pictures, read about your struggles ... grieved for your dead. You will no longer hunger and thirst. As I speak, vehicles are moving in this direction, packed with food, water, medicine, and clothing. All of your needs will be met. I give you my word."

A loud cheer breaks the silence. It seems loud enough to reach all of Africa.

"I am also here to honor someone who has become a hero of Swaziland. We all owe her a great debt. It is because of this one that the international community has come to our aid during this great time of crisis. Where is the little one who lives in this village named Adanna?"

The cheering ends abruptly. People look from one to another.

"Adanna, where are you?" the king asks again. "Today, she is the most famous person in Swaziland, perhaps in the whole world." He holds up a newspaper, and a collective gasp escapes from the crowd as they recognize Adanna's face in the picture. Some of the women begin to cry.

"Excuse me, your majesty?" I say.

He looks at me with unmasked curiosity.

"Yes, my friend. Come forward. Do you know where she is?"

"I am the photographer who took her picture."

The king's countenance changes, warms toward me.

"Your majesty, Adanna isn't here, but I will show you where she is resting." I motion for Gordon to come alongside me. The king motions for two bodyguards to follow him.

"Do you mind a short walk?" He shakes his head and follows. Gordon and I begin to tell him her story, walking toward the mound he's not prepared to see.

Chapter Thirty-two

New York, 2008

The trees of Central Park look like they're on fire, vibrating with color as the sun takes the chill out of this clear autumn day. The rent for this new apartment is outrageous, but the view from this balcony is worth it. Now that I've added speaking to my job description along with freelance photography, I can manage it. I'm still traveling, but mostly in the States these days, speaking about my photos and work and the HIV crisis around the world. Wangari has booked me on her docket as she makes the rounds in the diplomatic circuit. I think we make a good team.

I'm holding a card in my hands that has left me completely undone. It's homemade, the work of a creative five-year-old girl in a faraway land. A huge pink "Congratulations" is written neatly across it. It is careful, precise work. Probably Gordon's—but clearly with direction from his beautiful daughter.

An already familiar cry peals from the next room. I wouldn't be surprised if people in the apartment below hear it. I am certain I could hear it from across the park, in the deepest sleep, or surrounded by a noisy crowd.

I dash down the tiny hallway, the scent of autumn now mingling with the smell of fresh paint. I walk over to the crib and reach down to pick up my daughter. My hands look like a giant's hands next to her tiny body, just five pounds four ounces at birth. But she's the biggest gift I've ever received.

"Come to Daddy, sweet girl. It's okay."

Whitney walks into the nursery.

"You're supposed to be resting," I say.

"It's okay. I think she's hungry." Whitney's long hair is pulled up in a mess on top of her head, and she's wearing the same light blue warm-up suit she's worn for two days, but she has never looked more beautiful.

I hand the baby to her.

"I guess it's lunchtime, sweet 'Danna."

Whitney walks over to the rocking char and sits down.

"I want to show you something, Whit." I collect the card and the gift that came with it, still unwrapped. Whitney reads the card:

God bless your Adanna and may He give her the gift of words that will someday honor Him and her namesake. With love, Gordon, Precious, and Abu.

I open the gift. It is a beautiful journal, empty, awaiting words.

There's also a photo of the gift-givers. Precious has on a bright yellow dress, and Abu is wearing dress pants and a red button-down shirt. Gordon is … well … Gordon. They are eating ice cream and grinning.

Whitney opens the small book and reads the inscription:

Those tears will run
Soon in long rivers down the lifted face,
And leave the vision clear for stars and sun.

"Those words are beautiful."

"That's the inscription that was in Adanna's journal. It's from a poem called 'Tears' by some famous poet who lived a long time ago. Adanna wrote about this poem in her journal. She said that it tells us sorrow is a part of life, but our tears can leave us with clearer sight, if we look to God."

I realize at this moment, the life and death of one little girl has turned my face toward the sky, toward heaven. The object of my vision is clear. There is still much mystery, much that I don't understand. But one thing I do know: God is life and the giver of life.

Whitney has tears in her eyes. I kneel down and look at my baby girl. She has my mouth and Whitney's eyes and nose.

"We chose the right name, Stuart."

"I think it was chosen for us."

Adanna.

Father's daughter.

... a little more ...

When a delightful concert comes to an end,

the orchestra might offer an encore.

When a fine meal comes to an end,

it's always nice to savor a bit of dessert.

When a great story comes to an end,

we think you may want to linger.

And so, we offer ...

AfterWords—just a little something more after you

have finished a David C. Cook novel.

We invite you to stay awhile in the story.

Thanks for reading!

Turn the page for ...

- **Discussion Questions**
- **An Interview with the Author**

Discussion Questions

Use these questions to discuss *Scared* in a reading group or simply to explore the story from a new perspective.

1. What was your emotional reaction to the opening of this story? Was it easy for you to read? Why or why not?

2. In what ways did you identify with Stuart? Adanna?

3. How did the story inspire you? Challenge you?

4. What about the characters or story made you angry or upset?

5. Although this is fiction, it's based on real-life experiences. How does knowing that Adanna's story isn't far from fact impact what you take away from it?

6. What is the significance of the role Tagoze plays in this novel? Why does he get a chapter of his own?

7. How do the various characters grow and change throughout the story?

8. What was your reaction to the ending of the story?

9. How did Stuart ultimately use the gifts he had been given to make a difference?

10. In what ways (if any) has this story changed you? What are some practical ways you can make a difference in the lives of the Adannas in our world?

Author Interview

Let's get right to the big question: What was your inspiration for this story?

Adanna's story is based on a real story. The first time I went to Africa, I was constantly confronted with tragic real-life stories of beautiful children. It was unbearable. There was one little girl I met outside of the capital city of Swaziland; she had the most precious, innocent face I'd ever seen. She was happy and filled with joy. Then the director of the orphanage told me her story. He said she was rescued from an abusive situation, although at first they didn't know how badly.

They took her in and loved her as their own. She had the typical signs of neglect: filthy from head to toe; ratty, shredded clothes hanging from her body; and bruises and cuts from being hit with sticks and hands. The first day she was there, all the kids met together in a group to play a game. When the game started, this little girl was unable to hold her bladder and had an "episode" in front of everyone. At first the teachers believed that she had never been potty trained. Day after day, the same thing occurred. They took her to a doctor and realized that the abuse was much more severe than they assumed.

Both of her parents died from AIDS, then a distant uncle took her in. Her life was reduced to the life of a slave. She was forced to work fifteen hours a day, and her uncle sold her body to men in the community so he could have money for alcohol. Then he began violently raping her on a daily basis. Thus the reason for her incontinence.

Her story became the story of many little girls I met throughout Africa. It was more than I could handle. It still is.

I was compelled to act and had to tell their story. I have to believe that as people read *Scared*, they will be moved with compassion and also compelled to act.

What other characters or circumstances are based on real life? Without revealing specifics (unless you want to), where did they all come from?

SPOILER ALERT

Almost every character in the book is taken from a real relationship I have with someone in Africa. For example, Pastor Walter is one of the people I admire most in Swaziland. He is a church planter who cares for hundreds of orphans in his community.

I know that in times past, Walter has fed the many orphaned children he cares for while his own children have gone hungry. He's an amazing man. The faith he has for God's provision in his life surpasses mine in so many ways.

He gives out of the very little he has, when it's difficult for me at times to give out of my abundance. I remember when he told me about how he was called to care for all of these orphans in his village. He said that the Bible verse that kept ringing in his ear was James 1:27, "Pure and undefiled religion is taking care of orphans and widows in their distress." So he said to God, "Hey, God, You know I am a poor man. Send me some wealthy people to help me." God's response was immediate: "Listen, boy, put your hand in your own pocket, and give to them as I have given to you."

That's what Walter did. Today, he cares for one thousand orphans in eight different care points. He's truly an inspiration to me. In fact, if you visit www.ScaredtheBook.com, you can view a documentary on the life of the real Pastor Walter.

Some of the events are real. The story about the organization pretending to help people after the flood is true. African people have been used and taken advantage of in terrible ways—another reason why it's so important that people who genuinely care get involved, keep their word, and show them what love really looks like.

Clearly the themes in **Scared** *are things you're passionate about. What drives that passion?*

I believe everyone needs to know about the suffering the children in Africa endure. It's the definition of injustice and shouldn't be allowed to exist in the twenty-first century. I know this is difficult for people to hear. After all, nobody likes to feel helpless or guilty regarding situations such as this. I assure you that's not my intention. But reality is reality.

What I want people to know is how easy it is for them to make a tremendous difference in the life of a child suffering in poverty. A mere five dollars can be the difference between life and death. That amount of money can provide life-saving malaria medicine, one hundred meals, or a mosquito net.

My passion is driven from the core belief that not only can

everyone in the West do something to help children trapped in poverty, they must. God's kingdom comes when God's people tackle issues like these and change the circumstances because of their love. We are the answer, that's why we must act.

This is your first novel. Describe the process you went through. What did you learn along the way?

Grueling—that describes the process. I've written three nonfiction books to this point, and writing them came more naturally. Nonfiction tends to be more linear, which is how I'm wired to think. I'm so left-brained! Writing a novel was a completely different process. I paid the price for the years I didn't pay attention in English literature and grammar classes in college and high school! I had to go back and relearn those English lessons in a very short period of time.

A novel is more like a tapestry. Every scene, every chapter, every word has to be woven together. And everything, and I do mean *everything*, has to be described. In nonfiction that's not necessary, but in fiction it's a must.

What did I learn? I learned that anything is possible if you put all your heart, mind, and soul into it. Believe me, there were times when I wasn't sure I'd make it to the finish line. There were days when nothing I was writing made sense, nights when nothing would come out right, and weeks when I couldn't write because of my crazy schedule. I probably wrote over one thousand typed pages just to get three hundred.

Of course, I had the help of some brilliant people throughout the process, like Lisa Samson, Claudia Mair Burney, Moira Allaby, and Steve Parolini, who helped me chisel off the rough edges and shape it brilliantly.

In the end, I'm very pleased with how the novel turned out. It's a difficult story, but one that focuses on the true meaning of life and where we all need to place our hopes no matter what country we live in.

How did the story change from your first draft to the published version?

SPOILER ALERT

There were several major changes that took place.

One was Stuart's character. At first, he was much more self-centered and egotistical; he wasn't likeable at all. Don't get me wrong; he of course still has many issues to work through in the first half of the finished book.

His character was inspired by a man named Kevin Carter. You may not recognize his name, but you would know a picture he took. It was a photo of a little Sudanese toddler on the way to a food center who had fallen in the dirt. She was completely emaciated and obviously on the brink of starvation. In the background sat a well-fed, quite plump vulture waiting for her to die. It's horrific. Well, Mr. Carter became famous for that shot and later won the Pulitzer Prize for feature photography. Becoming famous for a photo like this, along with the evil and suffering he viewed through the lens of his camera was more than he could bear. He committed suicide about sixteen months after taking that photo. Here's a portion of what he left in his suicide note:

"I am depressed ... without phone ... money for rent ... money for child support ... money for debt ... money!!! ... I am haunted by the

vivid memories of killings and corpses and anger and pain ... of starving or wounded children, of trigger-happy madmen, often police, of killer executioners...."

Stuart was headed along the same path as Kevin, but the encounter he has with Adanna changes him. He undergoes a transformation that re-creates his values and his view on life, which turns him into a new man.

I also changed the number of tragedies that happened to Adanna. Sadly, what happens to her in the book happens to millions of children in our world today. It's injustice of the worst kind. But I couldn't do one more terrible thing to her; I couldn't bear it. There was a scene were she had to sell her body for a loaf of bread to feed her brother and sister, but I took it out.

The ending is completely different than I wrote it the first time. It was changed about three times. Previously, Adanna didn't die. She became a bit famous for her poem and went throughout Africa speaking on AIDS and abuse. That was heartwarming, but it wasn't reality. This ending is the right one. It fits. It hurts, but it fits.

You include a rather sly (and subtle) reference to Children's HopeChest in Scared. *Tell us more about that organization and your role in it.*

Ha, ha, yes, very sneaky of me! Without a doubt, Children's HopeChest is my passion. It represents what I will do for the rest of my life. I've seen this organization save the lives of so many widows and orphans around the world. The key for HopeChest is relationships. We want to empower people to actively engage in the lives of the poor.

The heart of HopeChest is to be the living reality of that James

1:27 passage I mentioned earlier: "Pure and undefiled religion is taking care of widows and orphans in their distress." We do that by providing for their needs in five areas: physical needs, education, medical/dental, emotional, and spiritual. It's a holistic, redemptive, long-term approach to care for orphans in a way that is practical. Our goal is to provide the necessary love and care to widows and orphans so they become leaders in their communities. They will be the generation that leads their countries out of poverty, death, and despair. That's what we believe.

My goal is to connect everyone who has a heart for this kind of ministry to HopeChest in a way that transforms their life, and the life of the widow or orphan they touch. If you're interested in engaging at that level, check out www.HopeChest.org or call or e-mail me!

What do you hope readers will walk away with after spending time in Adanna's world?

I hope through Adanna's voice and life, readers are moved on such a deep level about the plight of orphans like her that they are compelled to act. There's one startling truth I've discovered in helping the poor in our world, and it's this: The difference between life and death for widows and orphans in our world is me and you. Seriously! As I've said, five dollars can be the difference between life-saving malaria medicine and death; it's the cost to provide clean water to someone for a year; and it also can provide one hundred meals to orphans in Africa. Every single person reading this can do that.

I think it's also healthy to walk in other people's shoes. *Scared* provides the opportunity to do that. To see the world through the life of an orphan growing up in Africa, in the midst of complete destruction is alarming. I can't help but to ask the question, what if it was me or my kids? What if we were the ones born in a different place? This is more than just being thankful to live in America. It's about identifying with someone else's pain and being moved with compassion.

It's my firm belief that God has already sent the answers to solve the world's most difficult issues, and the answer is people like us getting involved. So take a step to help, just one, and it will change your life forever!

What are some practical ways readers can help the situation in Africa?

One, go to www.ScaredtheBook.com. There's a contest going on right now that will help three incredible African orphans win the dream of a lifetime! An all-expense-paid education—primary school, secondary school, even college and university. Whenever I talk to kids in Africa, they always tell me their number one need is an education. Not food, not water. Why? Because they say that without an education, they'll die anyway. On the Web site, you can be a part of fulfilling this dream and vote for the winner. This is a writing contest, and whoever receives the most votes will be declared the winner in each category: short story, memoir, and poetry. We are also raising a million dollars that will go in an education fund to help pay for thousands of orphans' education. Check that out at www.OrphanEducationFund.org.

Two, you can help provide one hundred meals to needy orphans in Africa. How? Go to www.5for50.com. There are five practical steps listed that will help you really make a difference in the lives of the poor. We'll even send you a free bracelet just for signing up.

You can get my nonfiction book *Red Letters: Living a Faith That Bleeds*, and get educated about the problem so you can position yourself to make a difference.

My blog is another good resource, www.CThomasDavis.com. It has tons of links, stories, and resources to help you on your justice journey.

Last but not least, check out the Children's HopeChest Web site, www.HopeChest.org. There you can sponsor a child, sign up for a trip, or find out how to be more involved.

Are there plans for more novels? Nonfiction works? What's on the drawing board for the future?

Scared is actually the first book of a series I'm writing. The next book finds Stuart Daniels in Russia exposing one of the most villainous and evil industries on the face of the earth, the child sex-slave trade. This book is a thriller, keeping you on the edge of your seat from the very first chapter. It is a headfirst dive into the culture and history of Russia and includes a dangerous confrontation with the mafia in an attempt to free girls who are sex slaves. Stuart will be stretched more than ever. He goes underground in hiding at an orphanage and meets a little boy who is an artist and changes his life.

I'm also working on a nonfiction book that focuses on merging ancient Christian practices into our lives in a way that reveals the kingdom of God through everything we do. I'm very excited about both of these projects. Stay tuned to my blog to find out more about when these will release along with special contests I'll be running and information about videos of Africa and Russia that helped inspire these books.

I shall live in hope of getting what i seek – another day.
— Swazi proverb

Make a
life-changing
difference
for an orphaned
child today.

See how at
www.scaredthebook.com

⟹ Step behind the scenes with author Tom Davis.
See posts, blogs and meet the real Adanna

⟹ Learn about the Scared $1 Million Education Fund
and writing contest for Orphans in Africa.

★ Full scholarships for top entrants in Poetry. Memoir and Short
Story. Play a part in changing the future for an orphan when you
give and vote!

For Swazi orphans like Adanna, you are the difference.

Read More from Tom Davis

Author Tom Davis encourages us to move beyond words and become Christ to those in need. Filled with remarkable stories of hope and mercy *Red Letters* and *Fields of the Fatherless* will inspire you to love "the least of these" and discover the joy found in becoming the hands and feet of Christ.

Red Letters: Living a Faith That Bleeds
ISBN: 978-0-7814-4535-1

Fields of the Fatherless: Discover the Joy of Compassionate Living
ISBN: 978-0-7814-4847-5

To learn more visit our Web site or
a Christian bookstore near you.

800.323.7543 • DavidCCook.com

David C Cook
transforming lives together

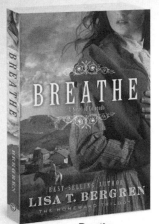

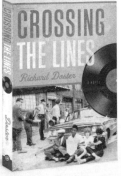